Born in the Northwest of England, and currently living in Bolton with his partner, Daniel has always had a passion for history and for those individual stories of people who lived through great moments in time. After studying history at University, his career moved away from academia, but he has now returned to his passion of sharing the stories of ordinary people as they struggled and fought to find their place within the great story of human history.

To Evie, Oliver and the rest of the Duckworth clan, your support means everything!

Special thanks to Dad for passing on your love of history and bringing Gereon to life.

Finally, I will be eternally grateful to Ryan for helping every step of the way.

Daniel Duckworth

THE FIELDS OF BRITANNIA: THE DARKNESS BEFORE THE DAWN

AUSTIN MACAULEY PUBLISHERS™

LONDON • CAMBRIDGE • NEW YORK • SHARJAH

A CIP catalogue record for this title is available from the British Library.

ISBN 9781035870608 (Paperback)
ISBN 9781035870615 (ePub e-book)

www.austinmacauley.com

First Published 2024
Austin Macauley Publishers Ltd®
1 Canada Square
Canary Wharf
London
E14 5AA

Chapter 1

The last embers of the fiery sunset danced across the surface of the Solway Firth, with the tips of its fingers illuminating the great stone fort at its edge. For a fleeting moment, the light flickered off the polished iron breastplate of a solitary figure standing atop the wall before dusk enveloped the land as the sun disappeared below the horizon. Dominicus sighed as he straightened up from leaning on the ramparts, stretched his back, and was met with a satisfying crack. Sunset was his favourite time of day and often brought his father to mind. "Views like this are good for the soul," his father would say. It also brought an end to his shift, and that meant hot food, a warm bed, and maybe even a drop of wine if the prefect was in a generous mood.

Three summers had passed since Dom first came to the fort at the western end of Hadrian's Wall, and a more peaceful station was not to be found anywhere else in the empire. Nor one more dull. Certainly, they had the ever-troublesome Picts to deal with, but most of those peoples lay further east and would rarely cause trouble around a major Roman fort, filled to the brim with trained legionaries.

Life in the legions was not what Dom had expected when he had followed his family to Britannia, with dreams of glory and conquest in his heart. The career of a legionary did not mean fame, riches, and writing your name in the history books as the next Achilles; it meant one thing only: routine. Rise early, train hard, watch for hours, and repeat. He often heard stories around the mess table from the veterans of the Rhine legions of great campaigns and battles with armies so large that their footsteps shook the earth. But here in quiet Britannia, it was hard to believe that any of those stories were true.

Not that Dom had been given a choice in his career, of course. One of the many divine emperors that had ruled in years gone by decreed that all sons must follow the trade of their fathers. Therefore, he had been lined up for a military life before birth, as had his father before him. Even so, growing up listening to the epic stories of great warriors and generals and famous battles, who would not want to be a legionary? "Anyone with a brain," according to his father.

So far, there had only been one raid from the wild northern tribes over the wall in the years since Dom arrived. And there had been nothing glorious or epic about it, as a hundred men wading knee-deep in blood and filth hacked wildly at each other. Dom had acquitted himself well in that skirmish, bloodied his sword, received a pat on the back from his centurion, and then proceeded to vomit uncontrollably. He had learned then the lesson his father had tried to teach him: battle was not glorious but terrifying, confusing, and deafening as men screamed in anger and pain. And yet, as soon as it was over, Dom could not help but feel a twinge of excitement about the next fight and spent his days hoping to hear the call to arms once again.

Unfortunately, that had been two years earlier, and the memory of that muddy afternoon fight now cold and forgotten. As would be his supper if old Gereon did not hurry up. As if responding to the rumbling of his stomach, a trumpet blared out twice from within the courtyard. Looking down the wall to his right, Dom could see the figures of other soldiers stirring and collecting their shields, as the rest of the day watch prepared themselves to be relieved, ready to enjoy the simple comforts of the fort.

Dom took the opportunity to turn his back on the northern coastline and look down on the courtyard below. There was ordered chaos in the yard as men moved from the barracks and the mess hall to the armoury, preparing themselves for a frosty night's watch atop the wall. After a few seconds, Dom made to turn back to face the empty countryside, knowing he was pushing his luck by looking the wrong way if he was caught by one of the eagle-eyed centurions.

As he was turning, however, something odd in the busy courtyard caught his eye. Down by the stables were two filthy, wild-looking ponies that looked entirely out of place next to the purebred stallions of the legion's officers. Next to these ponies stood two men who made their steeds look well-groomed in comparison. Broad-shouldered and wrapped in thick furs, the men stood three or four inches taller than the nearest legionaries, with full beards and long matted hair. They looked as if they had risen straight from Roman nightmares. Dom could feel his blood boiling as he looked down upon the Picts. They had spent the last three hundred years trying to keep these savages out, and now two of them were standing right there in the Roman fort, bold as brass and looking entirely unimpressed.

Dom was certainly risking ten lashes from his Optio now if he was caught still staring the wrong way, so he hastily turned back to face the north and gripped the top of his shield in frustration. A few moments later, he heard the familiar clink and thud of his fellow soldiers as the replacement guards climbed the steps up to the wall, with all but the last soldier marching past him on their way along the battlements. A battle-scarred veteran of the Rhine legions, Gereon was a barrel-chested ox of a man, with cropped grey hair, brown eyes, and a broad, kindly face. Despite his 50 years, he always exuded vigour and health, in the opinion of young Dominicus, who deeply admired the old warrior.

"Evenin' son, anything to report?" asked Gereon.

"Who the fuck let them in? Aren't we supposed to be keeping those bastards out?" Dominicus exploded furiously, pointing down towards the savages in the yard. "Has the Prefect lost his damn mind?"

Gereon's face hardened at once. "Get a hold of yourself, boy! I think it's you that's lost his mind, shouting about the prefect in the earshot of the officers!" Dom clamped his mouth shut with immense effort, but there was no hiding the fury in his face.

"Better," said Gereon, nodding. "I've seen lads spend three nights in the infirmary for less, and I've told you before to keep an eye on what you say and to whom you say it!"

"Now, I'm going to assume by 'them' you mean our esteemed guests in the courtyard?" continued Gereon. "They're here to see Lucian, and I'm sure our honourable prefect has a perfectly good reason for allowing them in."

Dom snorted at this. He spoke again, now in a more hushed tone: "You must be going senile if you're starting to think Lucian is honourable. I know for a fact you told old Val you reckon he's fudging his numbers in the reports back to Rome and taking a bit off the top. And now he's fraternising with the enemy!"

Gereon shook his head, amused by the young man's short fuse and naivety. "You're showing your age again, lad; every prefect takes his bit off the top; it just comes with the job. But I will admit, I don't like the thought of even one of those Pict bastards on this side of the wall."

The veteran's face hardened for a brief moment before he smiled and continued, "But it's not our job to ask questions now, is it? It is best to ignore them and crack on, I say. Go on and get yourself down to the mess hall; I'm sure the rumour mill will be in full spin with their arrival." Gereon patted Dom on the shoulder as he finished speaking and gently pushed him in the direction of the steps.

Still raging, Dom made his way slowly down the steps, sweeping his eyes over the darkening yard for any sign of the barbarians. They were nowhere to be seen, and the light coming from the windows of the officer's lodge suggested they were already inside with the prefect. As his anger began to ebb away, it was replaced with anxiety. Dom could not push away the thought that there was something not right about this.

He knew the line had become somewhat blurred along the border of the Rhine between barbarians and Roman citizens, with friendly tribes occupying Roman territory with the blessing of the Emperor and German warriors filling the ranks of the legions. After all, old Gereon himself was of Germanic descent, but here the line was much clearer. On our side of the wall, there was civilisation and peace; on their side of the wall, there was nothing but chaos and savagery.

Making his way into the armoury, Dom placed his shield in the rack and began to untie his breastplate. Once his kit was neatly stored away, he made his way over to a large barrel of fresh water by the door for a quick wash before supper. As Dom stood over the tub, he caught his reflection on its surface. Looking back at him, he saw a tall, lean man in his early twenties, with thick brown hair cut short and hazel eyes peering out from under heavy eyebrows. Splashing water over his face, he felt the stubble on his chin as he ran his hands over his checks and made a mental note to shave the following morning. He made his way back outside and crossed the yard to the long building that made up the south side of the fort.

As Dom entered the mess hall, he was met by a blaze of light and noise as a large fire crackled happily in the centre of the room and a few dozen men were chatting noisily at the wooden tables either side. A savoury smell was in the air, and his stomach growled. Heading to the fire in the middle, he grabbed a wooden bowl from a pile on the floor and filled it with hot stew from a large metal pot that hung above the flames. Dom dropped into the nearest space on the benches and attacked his bowl in earnest.

"Hungry, are we, lad?" grinned old Val as he climbed into the seat opposite. Another of the Rhine veterans enjoying the quiet life at the end of his career, he was a squat man with long, hairy arms and a heavily scarred face.

"Starved. But never mind that! What's going on? Am I the only one who seems to have noticed the enemy has walked right into the fort?" Dom replied, his anger returning at once.

Val waved his hand through the air as he replied, "Oh, calm down, son, what can two blokes do against three hundred of the legions finest?"

"It's the principle! We're supposed to be keeping them out, not letting them in! What can possibly be gained from talking to savages like that?" answered Dom.

"Oh, it will be yet another attempt at peace, I'm sure, swearing of oaths and exchange of gifts as we head towards the winter, so both sides can be sure of a nice long rest before it's all forgotten and back to business in the spring," said Val airily as he took a swig from his wooden cup.

"I'm telling you, there's something not right about this. Have you ever known any Roman prefect to invite them over to our side of the wall for peace talks? And how or when did they even get through? I've been standing on that wall all day, and nobody came through the gate!" argued Dom.

"They came from the east, so there must be two prefects at least who have let them in, unless they've climbed it unnoticed—and I'm not sure which thought is worse..." Val said, his voice trailing off. Dom thought he saw a glimmer of worry flash across the hard features before the grin returned as Val continued, "Anyway, however they got here doesn't matter; two men are not a threat, and that's that lad. There's no point worrying about it; they'll be gone tomorrow, no doubt, and it will be back to a quiet life for us."

Despite himself, Dom felt his anger and anxiety start to ebb away at Val's wise words. "I guess you're right," he sighed, "as always."

"Correct, young Dominicus, and don't you forget it," Val said, wagging a finger at him as he chuckled.

The rest of the evening passed pleasantly enough; the emotion brought on at the sight of the barbarians did not return to Dom, and he happily joined in with his comrades' favourite pastime—Tali, or knucklebones as the locals called it. Having already lost most of his wages this month playing that fickle game of dice, Dom joined in with the heckling and encouragement of tonight's players. With the fire now burning low and the long day taking its toll, Dom called it a night and headed to the barracks.

As he collapsed onto his cot and listened to the snores of the men around him, the feeling of anxiety crept back into his stomach. Now he was no longer being reassured by old Val or distracted by games; the threat of the enemies within the fort loomed large. He understood why battle-hardened veterans, so confident in their own ability and the might of Rome, were undeterred by the arrival of the Picts, but few of the men in this fort had seen what Dom had.

He knew what they were capable of, and even one of those bastards on this side of the wall was too many for his liking. Eventually, he fell into a broken sleep, seeming to wake at every noise and expecting to feel the sharp bite of a dagger at any moment. The night marched on, and dawn was soon breaking through the windows once more. For now, all remained quiet at this lonely end of Hadrian's Wall.

Chapter 2

Alberic leant over the side of the wooden ship, looking down along the long boat to the shores ahead as the choppy waves sent a spray of ocean mist up into his face. The tall white cliffs in the distance were coming ever closer, and the cries of gulls were loud in the air. He felt, rather than saw, his father approach from behind.

"Enjoying your first sight of Britannia?" asked Alawar. A short man and broad in the chest, with blue eyes twinkling out from underneath wild eyebrows. The afternoon sun glinted from his shaven head and golden beard.

"It's certainly a sight to behold," replied Al. Standing a few inches taller than his father, he had inherited the bright blue eyes and golden hair, which he wore long and braided.

"Remember this moment. Our children's children will tell tales of this day and the rise of our kingdom." His father's eyes shone as he spoke. Al could not help grinning at his father's words, despite the worry in his heart. The Saxon king had an aura of inevitability about him; it drew men towards him like moths to a flame and made him easy to follow.

Despite the personality of the great man, the alliance he had formed amongst the ever-warring tribes of The Jutland had not come easily. Over the last decade, he has conquered smaller tribes whilst bringing others in with honeyed words, relentlessly dragging his people together under one banner. For a while, rumours had spread through the camps as to where this great army would be pointed, but for King Alawar, their destination had always been the same: the Isle of Britannia.

"For as long as the oldest and wisest amongst our people can remember, our people have been at war. If not with the Romans, then the Franks. If not the Franks, then with the Germanic tribes. If not with the Germanic tribes, then with each other. How long can we continue down this path before the Saxons become another tribe lost to the annals of time?" Alawar sighed and leant on the wooden rail.

"If we stay in our homeland, this cycle will continue. The land is too poor; good soil is prized above gold and gemstones—our ancestors have always known this, and for decades we have fought to claim new land and take our people south. Time and time again, the Romans have stopped us; they defend their borders relentlessly. The future of our people does not lie in the south, and it never will."

Al had heard this speech a hundred times at least; as soon as he had learned to talk, his father had been drilling this message into him. But here, on the precipice of the venture Al had spent his entire life waiting for, the words felt fresh, and he felt his heart stir as Alawar continued.

"Our destiny lies on the Isle of Britannia. Richer soil is not to be found anywhere. Protected by the sea and Saxon swords, it will be a kingdom that can last a thousand years. It is said that great Woden and the rest of our gods have not yet abandoned that wild place, and it is here that we will protect our culture from the poison of Christian priests."

Despite himself, Al could not help but voice the one nagging concern that refused to budge from the pit of his stomach, even with his heart soaring alongside his father's ambitions.

"But Father, how can you be certain this time will be different?" I Asked Alberic quietly. "Every time our people have marched against Rome, we have failed."

The king turned to look at his son, smiling at the young man's courage to challenge him. "The Roman presence on the island is the weakest it has been for a century. With the Alemanni preparing for another invasion across the Rhine, the Romans will have to make a choice: reinforce the border in Gaul or send legions to Britannia. By the time they turn their attention north, we will be secure and in place to defend against anything they can throw at us."

"But we still have to dislodge the legions already stationed there," Al pressed.

"Our nation has never been brought together as one before; we will show Rome the true might of the Saxon people. An army filled with green recruits and tired veterans will stand no chance against us!" his father replied confidently.

"How do you know so much about the Roman position?" asked the young man.

The king smiled at his son's naivety. "Spies, lad. We have been sending traders and merchants to the Isle for months now, passing through every Roman settlement and taking note of their strength."

Al took a moment to think over his father's words. Finally, he replied, "It will still be a hard fight. Carolus is especially worried."

Alawar scoffed and straightened up. "'Course he's worried. I didn't hire him for his bravery but for his brains. Your tutor need not fret, however, as there is one more piece to our plan that will all but guarantee victory." The king walked along the centre of the ship towards the prow, with Al following behind.

"As we speak, the northern tribes beyond the Roman wall are marching south. It took a lot of promises and an eye-watering amount of gold, but this alliance will be crucial; facing invasion on two fronts, the legions will be crushed between us." The king's blue eyes glinted with malicious pleasure as he spoke.

Al's original concerns were replaced instead by a new fear upon hearing this. "How on earth did you manage to form an alliance with the Picts?" He asked, deciding against his urge to repeat the stories of the wild tribes and their practices that now raced through his mind. Dark rituals in ancient forests, consorting with demons, and the sacrifice of children to honour evil gods.

His father saw right through him, of course. "Despite what you've heard around the fires at night, the Picts are not mindless savages. They're people like you and me who have long desired to retake their homelands from the Romans. They're naturally untrustworthy of anyone not from their island, but we have convinced them that this is our only hope of driving the Romans off for good."

Al was in awe of what his father had achieved. Bringing the Saxons together was one thing, but forming an alliance with the Picts was astonishing.

"We've also sent envoys to the Scotti pirates in Hibernia, letting them know the western shores of the island will be ripe for plunder in the coming months. With any luck, the Roman defence will be stretched across three fronts! But our envoys haven't returned yet." The king frowned for a moment before continuing, "We can't hold off the attack any longer. We won't be able to count on the support of the Scotti, but it shouldn't matter in the end."

As father and son spoke, the white cliffs had continued their steady march closer, and the pair could now make out the small beach at their feet and the outline of stout wooden buildings high above. The coastline looked deserted, with only a couple of fishing boats pulled up high on the shore and away from the tide. A large, weather-stained hut stood a little further back from the boats, its door swinging slowly in the breeze.

Alawar left his son at the prow, stalking back between the rowers to the stern, before signalling to the nearest ships following in their wake to continue straight on. Behind the lead ship, the rough waves were full as far as the eye could see, evidence of the huge force Alawar was bringing down upon Britannia. The tall wooden frames of the warships resembled a forest that moved ever closer to the cliffs. There were dozens of banners flying high from the tips of the masts, depicting ravens, boars, trees, and swords, amongst countless other symbols, each one flying full and stretched tight in the breeze.

The sun was low in the sky as Al felt the keel of the ship scrape along the shingle, coming to a staggered stop. Immediately, Al joined the men pouring from the sides, throwing ropes down, and wading through the surf. It did not take long for the crew of the first ship to pull it up and high out of the water, keeping the beach as clear as they could for the next vessels to arrive. Al stood panting as he let the guide rope fall, and his countrymen around him continued with their tasks. A handful called for their weapons to be passed overboard and headed in the direction of the fishing hut. They were not inside for long before they emerged, shaking their heads to indicate the place was empty.

As evening drew on, the beach became a hive of activity as the first arrivals departed to erect camps in the low hills that bordered the beach, and the remainder of the armada continued to pull up on the shore. There was still no sign of any Roman presence, stoking the confidence of the Saxons. King Alawar sent a handpicked group of men up into the hills and east, along the cliffs to scout the nearby Roman fort and to see if a defensive force was preparing to march out to challenge them.

Al stood on the shoreline, watching the continuous flow of men and goods being offloaded from the ships. He could hear songs coming from the camps in the hills, and the smell of roasting meat was tantalising, making his mouth water. He took a deep breath and closed his eyes. It had been a good day, and he felt pride once more at everything his father had achieved. As he looked over the scene and the sheer size of the Saxon force hit him, he wondered how any army could stop them. His father's dream would come true, and Britannia would provide a bright future for their people.

A tall, thin man was winding his way through the chaos towards him. His grey hair thinning on top and stooping from age, Carolus, the Greek scholar, came to a stop beside the young prince.

"Your tent has been prepared, and we must take every opportunity to continue your studies. For sure, there will be fewer moments in the coming months." Carolus said, speaking the Saxon dialect with barely an accent, a rarity amongst the Greek and Latin speakers of the empire.

"How could I possibly concentrate in the centre of all this?" asked Al.

"A prince must be able to concentrate in the most hectic of places, or he won't remain a prince for long. Especially here, surrounded by enemies," replied Carolus.

Al looked at his tutor in surprise. "Enemies? The Romans are nowhere to be seen."

Carolus sighed and looked despairingly at his pupil as he spoke. "The alliance your father has created is unprecedented in both size and ambition. Naturally, it hangs by a thread. Your father's tribe may be the largest, but it is filled with men who were sworn to other kings only a few years ago. How many men gathered here genuinely believe in his vision?"

"But they have sworn an oath to follow him!" said Al, outraged at this suggestion of potential betrayal.

"They swore to come *with* him. Every decision that has been made so far has been made during the king's council. The force of nature that your father is, he has been able to bend the council to his will. However, most of the other kings here only want one thing: to plunder and take advantage whilst Rome is weak. I fear what will happen when the ambitions of those men clash with those of King Alawar. Or worse, what will happen to us all if King Alawar were to fall in battle?"

Horrified by his tutor's words, Al was left speechless. The idea of anyone betraying his father was one thing, but his father falling in battle was incomprehensible. He knew it was his destiny to succeed the king and lead his people, but he did not feel ready for this task in any way.

Although Carolus was well paid for his role as Alberic's tutor, he had come to care deeply for his students. As a young man, Carolus had learned philosophy at the feet of the Greek masters before heading to Rome to listen to the legendary rhetoric of the politicians and lawyers. With a bright future ahead of him, he found himself swept up in the debauchery of the capital city. Instead of becoming a famous and established scholar, he had been forced to flee under the cover of night to escape the moneylenders who were after him.

Heading to Gaul, hoping to lose his creditors in the wild, he had settled in Mainz, where he had quickly picked up the dialect of the Germanic and Saxon tribes and landed a comfortable position as a translator for local governors. It was at this time that he had met Alawar, and as with most men who met the Saxon king, he had taken to him at once. When the offer to tutor the young prince came along, it was an easy decision for the Greek scholar.

"Come along now, young master; don't take heed of the worries of old men. The king is a wise man and fearless in battle. Perhaps you're right; with everything going on around us, we can skip your lessons this evening. Let us head for your father's tent; the bards will be in full voice tonight, I'm sure."

Al gratefully accepted the change in conversation and forced his fears to the back of his mind. Escorting his tutor back through the activity on the beach, they climbed the low hills towards the forward camp, listening to the Saxon songs of war grow louder.

Chapter 3

The early morning air was cold in Dom's lungs as he climbed the last hill, and the Roman fort came into view. As the company reached the crest, the centurion called double time, and he instinctively matched the increased pace of the man in front. Most of the garrison grumbled about the daily eight-mile march, but Dom enjoyed the feeling of strength in his legs and knew the importance of keeping fit. The men came clanking into the yard and were called to a halt, coming smartly to a stop whilst still keeping in rank.

One of the summer recruits near the back of the column had misjudged by a fraction of an inch and stumbled into the man in front. The Optio, the centurion's second in command, was onto him in a flash. Dragging the unfortunate sod out of the line, he rapped him briskly on the helmet with his cane. After berating the young man until he was blue in the face, the Optio commanded him to run the circuit again at double pace, giving him another whack with the cane to set him on his way.

As the soldier jogged back out of the yard with his head bowed, Centurion Maximillian stepped forward to address the assembled troops.

"Right then, gentlemen, we're going to have a little competition to see just how much the new lads have learned. The last man standing will receive double rations tonight."

The soldiers in the yard shuffled around, creating a wide circle, grinning at each other as the Optio came out of the armoury carrying shields and wooden training swords.

"Val, you can start. Let's see how little Brittanicus fares against a Rhine veteran." He first handed a shield and sword to the experienced soldier and then to Brittanicus, and the young man scowled at his nickname but knew better than to respond. The fight was over in a flash. The British recruit came charging forward with his sword held high, swinging it down overhead as Val neatly sidestepped and whipped his sword round. He caught his opponent neatly on the helmet with a thud.

"Disgraceful!" Barked the Optio. "You're on half rations until you learn how to swing that sword properly! Dominicus, take it from him before he hurts himself."

The Optio scratched his chin as he surveyed the circle before pointing to another young recruit. "Julian, your turn. Let's see if you can do any better."

Dom stepped forward and took the weapons from Brittanicus, who stalked off red-faced and humiliated back to the circle. His opponent, an Italian from the gutters of Milan, marched confidently to the centre as he swapped with Val. Enjoying the familiar weight of the shield on his left arm, Dom moved forward slowly with his sword held at his waist, watching Julian closely. Dom feinted low before suddenly whipping his sword high, and the young Italian managed to bring up his shield at the last moment as he circled left.

Dom pressed the attack, this time bringing his sword up high before smashing his shield towards Julian's chest and catching his opponent off guard. Julian stumbled back, dazed from the hit, as Dom continued forward and thrust his sword under his opponent's shield, with its iron tip punching into the Italian's stomach, who doubled over gasping. Dom stood back as the Optio began yet another tirade and handed over his weapons to the next pair making their way into the ring.

The competition lasted most of the morning, with Dom winning his next two fights before coming up against a talented Pannonian legionary who caught him with a neat counter to knock the sword from his hand. Knowing he would be sporting a colourful bruise on his wrist in the morning, Dom took some small comfort in the fact that the same Pannonian went on to win. The morning march and the sword tournament had wiped the events of the previous night from Dom's mind, and he happily joined in with the banter and jostling of the men once the fights were over.

After a hasty lunch, the trumpets called out the changing of the guard, and Dom joined the rest of the soldiers heading to the armoury to gather their kit and head to the wall. Replacing a sour-faced legionary who had covered the morning shift after Gereon, he settled into his usual spot and leant his shield against the ramparts. It was a cloudless day, with the sun high and bright in the sky. Looking north, he could see the River Esk flowing into the Solway Firth and the rugged hills rolling off into the east.

Now alone once more, the anxiety from the previous day started to creep back, with Dom having little distraction to keep his mind away from the arrival of the mysterious savages the previous evening. He felt a wave of frustration sweep over him and replace the anxiety, and he pounded his fist onto the hard stone wall. He had sworn to himself he would kill every single barbarian he could lay his hands on, and the thought of even two of the bastards walking out of the fort unharmed was galling.

Eventually, the wise words of his veteran comrades came back to mind, and he felt his anxiety and frustration lessen. Val and Gereon had fought all over the empire, and if half their stories were true, they had been in some really difficult situations. If they were not worried, then it was good enough for the young soldier. He forced the topic to the back of his mind, and after a while Dom felt his thoughts wandering off into the familiar daydreams of fighting in glorious battles as he idled the hours away.

Another uneventful day was nearing its end when Dom was stirred out of his daydreaming by familiar trumpet calls. Frowning, he looked west and saw that evening was still an hour off, before noticing the calls were not coming from behind but along the wall to the east. Picking up his shield, he strained his eyes to see what the cause of the alarm was. His heart skipped a beat as his gaze landed on the unmistakable shape of a large host of people making their way slowly through the hills towards him. At this distance, he struggled to discern any colours or banners.

"Men approaching! Call to arms!" Dom shouted down into the courtyard. Rather unnecessarily, as the garrison had already begun to muster in the centre of the fort facing the heavy wooden gates, fully armoured with weapons drawn, forming neat ranks behind their officers.

"Open the gates! By order of the Prefect!" came another call, this time from the entrance to the prefect's lodge.

Dom whirled back around to face the north puzzled and again peered out, trying to distinguish whether the approaching host was friend or foe. He could not see any legionary eagle or banner, nor did they appear to be marching in orderly ranks. It was clear they were not Roman legionaries, so why would the prefect give the order to open the gates? His thoughts swirled in his mind as he tried to make sense of the situation unravelling in front of him.

The dark mass marched steadily forward, and still there was no clear indication of who they were. He heard someone climbing the steps behind him and turned to see Gereon approaching.

"What's the word, Dom? Any idea who it is?" asked the veteran, a look of concern on his face.

"I'm not sure yet, but I can tell they're not ours. And if it's not Romans, then who else could it be but the fucking Picts?" replied Dom.

Gereon frowned as he replied, "It can't be. Otherwise, the prefect would be ordering us to the wall, wouldn't he? He must be expecting them, whoever they are; maybe some poor sods are seeking asylum—there's still a few settlements between here and the Antonine Wall after all."

Dom did not reply to this. He could not shake the feeling of impending danger and continued to stare intently as the group approached. It was hard to tell in the gathering gloom how many there were, but it looked like a thousand at least. The prospect of a force that outnumbered their garrison arriving without a challenge was making Dom's stomach churn.

"Fucking hell… you were right, Dom; there's no mistaking them at this distance," muttered Gereon. "Barbarians approaching! Close the gates, sharpish!" he called down to the men below.

"Stay where you are!" came a harsh voice. "I have given the order to open those gates, and until I give the order to close them, they shall remain so." Strolling into the yard in a brilliant white toga, the Roman Prefect Lucian Pulvis made his way towards the soldiers holding the gate.

"But sir, if it's barbarians approaching, why are we keeping them open?" asked the guard holding the left side, a note of panic in his voice.

"Centurion Maximillian, twenty lashes for this legionary for insubordination. See to it at once," barked Lucian, watching coldly as the soldier who had dared challenge him was dragged away by two others, followed by the grim-looking centurion.

The soldiers stood like statues in their ranks, grim faced to a man. The air was thick with tension as the Romans waited for the first of the Picts to reach the gate. Their prefect stood with his arms clasped behind his back, looking calm and smug. After a few minutes, they could now hear the rough speech of the wild tribesmen as they came within a hundred yards of the wall.

"I don't like this one bit, Gereon. There can't be any good reason for letting enemies through in such large numbers." Dom said, struggling to hide the anxiety in his voice as he continued, "Even if Lucian believes whatever promises they have made, what is to stop them from wreaking havoc once they're through and out of sight?"

"Not sure… I've never seen anything like this before," replied Gereon. "I don't fancy chasing this lot all over the country if they're let loose. Maybe they've offered their services to the Emperor? They could be heading to the Rhine; it's common to hire tribes to fight for Rome down there." The older man's face was filled with a look of worry that Dom had never seen before.

The first unruly ranks of the barbarian force had now reached the gate, and without breaking a step, they marched straight in. On and on they came until the first half of the host was fully inside the fort. Dom noticed with dismay that his early estimation was short, and the true number of Picts was closer to fifteen hundred, outnumbering the Romans by at least five to one. At the head of the barbarian column was a tall man, wearing rich furs that barely concealed the gleam of armour below. With long wild hair contrasting the neat and well-oiled hair of the prefect, Dom watched as he drew the Roman leader into an embrace. He could see the smug look of satisfaction in the prefect's face as he greeted the man like an old friend.

As the two leaders chatted amicably, Dom watched the enemy warriors closely, but he was unable to hear what was being said between the two men. He noted with another pang of anxiety that they too seemed tense, staring at the opposing legionaries with hands close to their weapons. Looking back towards the prefect, he caught the swiftest flash of silver, and Dom cried aloud. He watched in horror as the Roman stumbled back, hands clasped to his chest and a fountain of blood pouring over his fingers, staining the spotless white toga a deep red. With a sudden scream of rage, the Pict warriors surged forward, hurling spears towards the stunned legionaries.

The Roman soldiers tried to close ranks quickly, but the swiftness of the attack and the chaos caused by the spears thrown at such short range prevented them from locking shields before the enemy was amongst them. The Roman line buckled at once, and the barbarians were swarming into the gaps, hacking wildly. Dom roared in anger and frustration and started towards the steps, fury in his eyes and desperate to help his comrades. Before he had taken more than two steps, however, he felt an iron grip on his shoulder, which held him fast and pulled him in the other direction.

"Don't be fucking stupid, boy! There's nothing we can do from here—we need to send out the alarm!" shouted Gereon furiously.

"We can't just leave them to die!" Dom roared as he struggled to break free.

The stench of blood reached their nostrils as the unmistakable cries of dying men rent the air above the deafening sounds of swords on shields. The battle had quickly turned into a slaughter. Hearing the argument above them, the Picts closest to the steps turned and started hurrying forward to climb the wall with a shout.

"If we don't warn the legions, the whole country could be fucked! We've got to run for it!" Gereon shouted.

With a last fleeting look at the carnage below and noticing the barbarians surging towards the steps, Dom turned and began to follow Gereon along the wall to the east. Behind them, they could hear the cries and shouts of the Picts taking up the chase. Thinking quickly, Dom paused and kicked a barrel filled with spare javelins towards the steps. He was met by cries of surprise and pain as the heavy barrel tumbled down towards their pursuers.

The wall in front of them was deserted, with the guards having made their way back to the fort at the sight of the host approaching, and the two legionaries made good ground. The sounds of fighting behind them started to wane, and before long, Dom could hear nothing but the pounding of his iron-shod sandals on the smooth stone below him and the blood pumping in his ears as he raced along the wall into the darkness.

Chapter 4

"This is *humiliating*," muttered Alberic in frustration. The day was nearing its end, and the Saxon assault on the Roman fort was in full swing. From his vantage point atop the nearby hills, he could see the ladders had reached the walls, and pockets of men were fighting on the battlements.

"It is only prudent for a king to protect his heir; if you were to fall in battle in the first assault, who would continue your father's vision of a Saxon Britannia?" replied Carolus, attempting to calm the young prince.

"If I don't prove myself in battle, then who will follow me? They will think I'm a coward who hides with the baggage train, whilst braver men cover themselves in glory," Al retorted, making no attempt to hide the bitterness in his voice.

"You already have proven your bravery in the battle against the Franks last summer. To fight now would be a needless risk," Carolus replied soothingly.

Al scoffed. "That wasn't a battle; it was a slaughter. I arrived when the fight was already won; the only blood on my sword at the end of that day was from men running away. And the tribe knows it. This isn't Rome, Carolus; there is no hoodwinking or grand rhetoric that will fool the men of my tribe. They follow strength first and foremost, and if I don't fight with them and for them, they will cast me out the day my father dies."

"Which won't be for many years, if the gods allow. And by that time, you will have had your opportunity to fight and win glory for your family."

Al did not respond to this. He had spent his formative years training daily, knowing his life would be spent on the battlefield. He was as talented with sword and spear as anyone around him, and he yearned to feel the battle lust and frenzy the men sang about at night. Al knew his father kept him sidelined as he wanted to ensure his line continued; perhaps keeping him out of the action was also out of love and concern for his son, but he could not keep Al safe behind the front lines for much longer. As his eighteenth birthday approached, the boys he had grown up with were already seasoned fighters, and Al was not deaf to the murmuring of his people that their prince was yet to take to the field.

The Greek tutor cleared his throat, breaking the silence. "Although I have no taste for battle, I do find being this far removed from events frustrating and unsettling. Your eyes are better than mine; have we taken the wall yet?"

"It looks like it, but it's hard to tell—wait, I think I can see the gate opening," replied Al.

Sure enough, the tall wooden gates of the Roman fort were being pulled slowly inward, and a surge of dark shapes was making their way towards the entrance. It was clear now that the Saxon forces had taken the walls and opened the gate for the main force. The battle was all but finished, and there would be no mercy for the Romans still alive inside. Al observed as sections of the main force peeled away from the left flank. With torches in hand, they headed towards the clusters of buildings that stood a few kilometres from the fort.

"And so, it begins." Carolus said, speaking softly. "I feel for those who dwell nearby, I only hope they had the sense to flee and not linger to protect their property."

Al turned to look at him in surprise. "You feel for them? Why? This is the way of war, 'vade ad victor spolia,' as the Romans would say."

"I am glad I have managed to teach you *something*," Carolus replied with a small smile. "Unfortunately, the spoils of war often take form in the murder and rape of innocent people, not just taking possession of their wealth. Think for a moment how those people must feel. Seeing thousands of men rush towards them, knowing to stay and defend what they have worked to provide for their families, means nothing but death and torture. A cruel decision is to be made: to stay and die or to flee and starve."

Again, Al did not respond to this. He had been raised to understand that anyone not strong enough to fight for themselves risked these things happening to them. The gods only favour the strong; however, upon listening to the old man's words, he was surprised to find himself feeling slightly uneasy, as he thought about what fate had in store for the peaceful citizens of this island, who would soon find their lives torn apart for the sake of his father's ambitions.

"It's us or them," Al finally replied, defiantly. "If we hadn't come here to find a peaceful and plentiful place to provide for our people, it would be Saxon women and children running from Franks, Germans, and Romans."

"I agree, my prince, but that does not mean we should be blind to the horrors of war. I know your father will not be pleased with this. How can we come to settle and rule these lands and co-exist peacefully with the residents of the island if we pillage every house we come across as we march north?"

As Al pondered over these words in silence, his feeling of uneasiness lingered as he watched the first of the flickering torches reach the closest hamlet, disappearing as the men holding them entered inside. Turning back to the fort, they could now see the banner of King Alawar flying above the gate, a red bull's head on a white field.

"Come, let us make our way towards the fort and to your father. I'm sure he will want to share this moment with you." Carolus made his way forward and down the hill towards the mass of people still milling around the gates, with Alberic in tow.

As they forced their way through the crowd, the smell of blood and death hit Al, causing his afternoon meal to threaten its way back up. Al clenched his mouth shut, willing his stomach to settle. Vomiting here and now at the smell of battle, without having fought, would be the end for him in the eyes of the warriors. Inside the large courtyard, there was a mound of corpses starting to rise as Roman bodies were dragged and thrown unceremoniously onto it. The Saxon warriors who had fallen were being lined up in a quiet corner and could be mistaken for a row of sleeping men, lying peacefully in the shadow of the wall.

Al and his tutor made their way for the large building on the left side of the courtyard, with the door hanging off its hinges and light blazing out. Inside, there were dozens of men lounging on wooden benches, nursing wounds, and congratulating each other on their victory. Tall tales were already being spun of great feats as men boasted of their bravery during the fight. To the right, a smaller group of men sat in a semi-circle, heads bowed, in discussion. Al made his way along the side of the room towards this group, where his father sat in the middle of the king's council.

King Alawar sat leaning back, his left hand holding his hip, a steady trickle of blood falling through his fingers. The other kings and tribe leaders stopped their conversation as Alberic approached.

"Congratulations, Father, and to you all, for a resounding first blow against the Romans," Al said formally, bowing first to his father and then to the men on either side. "Are you wounded?" He added, with worry in his voice.

"Barely." Alawar responded, smiling at his son. "It is nothing to worry about. If each victory comes at the cost of a small scratch like this, it's an easy price to pay."

Alawar's pleasure at his son's arrival was not shared by the others. To a man, they glared at the young prince and did not hide their feelings for him, having sat out the battle.

"I will pray to the gods for your swift recovery, Father. And I ask you for the honour of letting me lead the charge at our next battle." Al said as he looked directly into his father's eyes, hoping his father would sense his son's burning desire to prove himself.

"All in good time, my son. Join us; we are discussing our next move," Alawar pointed at an empty seat at the end of the row.

Although his father had bid him join the group, Al knew it was not an invitation to contribute but to listen and learn from the council. As if there had been no interruption, the men launched directly back into their conversation. Al watched the men around him as they talked, noting that each of them carried signs of having fought in the battle. It shamed him to sit in his clean clothes amongst such warriors. Old King Caelan nodded at him as their eyes met, but the rest either ignored him or wore expressions of open hostility. Each man here was a leader, a king who commanded the respect of hundreds of loyal warriors, and Al was amazed once again at his father's ability to control such a group.

There was clearly an ongoing disagreement regarding the direction they should take next, with one half led by a ferocious-looking man with a heavily scarred face and his left eye missing, wanting to split the army into traditional war bands, setting fire to the south of the country in the hope of splitting up the Roman forces. The remainder, primarily the oldest men amongst the group, wanted to march east along the coast to the next major fort, providing a long stretch of friendly coastline for the arrival of the families, still waiting to cross the channel.

King Alawar remained silent for much of the discussion, listening to each person in turn and not yet providing an opinion. A short man wearing a tattered cloak and dented helm came panting into the room, quickly making his way behind Alawar and began whispering a report into his ear. The king frowned as he listened, but the conversation between the others continued. Once the messenger had finished, Alawar raised his hand, and silence fell almost at once.

"Our priority must be bringing our people over before the weather turns. We need as many safe landing spots as possible, and to achieve that, we must take Rutupiae. Holding the land between there and Dubris, we should be able to start the migration at once. All those in favour?" Alawar swept his eyes over the council, his eyes lingering on the one-eyed king, who was clearly irked by his choice, before finally nodding with satisfaction. Although not unanimous, enough of the other kings had fallen in line with his decision.

"It is settled; we will leave a token force here to hold the fort and the landing point. In the morning, we shall send out war bands east along the coast, with orders only to secure the beaches. They are not to start pillaging the surrounding area. Meanwhile, the bulk of our force will march on towards Rutupiae Fort." Alawar now straightened up properly and turned to look at the towering man sitting to his right.

"King Broga, I have received reports that some of your men have already started to attack the nearby settlements. Pull them back at once." Alawar's bright blue eyes flashed as he spoke.

Broga was a huge man, his bare arms scarred and heavily muscled, and his hair and beard so wild it looked as if his eyes and nose were looking out of a bush. A bronze circlet shone atop his head, and his armour gleamed in patches from beneath the blood and grime of the day's battle.

He had not said much so far and now looked away from Alawar, clearly bored by the council's proceedings. "My men have fought bravely and are enjoying the rewards of their labours. Who are we to deny them this? No, I will not call them back," he replied lazily.

The tension in the air grew heavier with every word. Broga's tribe was not one who had been beaten into joining the alliance, but one that had been bargained with and had been the last to join the expedition. Unlike most of the men gathered here, he was Alawar's equal, not his subordinate. Al was holding his breath as he looked from his father to the towering King Broga, mesmerised by the battle of wills.

"The purpose of our journey here has been made very clear, King Broga," started Alawar, his eyes boring into the other man. "We are here to form a Saxon kingdom that will last a thousand years. We will never know peace if we rape and destroy every settlement we find! I will not allow the men to run wild and unchecked, threatening everything we are aiming to do here. Call them back *now.*" The emphasis placed on his final word threatened consequences for further defiance.

King Broga turned back to look at him, measuring his opponent. Finally, he said, "Very well, I will order them to return."

King Alawar nodded with satisfaction and leant back once more with a soft grunt.

"But I will not pull them back again. You speak of "our" vision, but this is yours, not mine. My men are here for glory and wealth, and we will have it, with or without your leave." Broga said, his voice as hard as iron.

"There will be glory and wealth for all, Broga, but it does not need to come at the expense of the people living here. We will take it from Roman soldiers, not peaceful farmers," Alawar replied calmly, and this time he had not looked at the other king, thus missing the open hostility King Broga wore at being brushed off by what he considered an equal.

"It is time now for food, drink, and rest. Break out the Roman wine!" King Alawar shouted, to great cheers and applause from the men in the centre of the room. Standing up and swaying slightly, he made his way back out into the courtyard, with Al and Carolus rising and following quickly behind.

"I need this cut seeing to, it's driving me mad. Send for a slave, Carolus. I will take the Prefect's quarters as my own. Also, have wine and food brought to me as well," grunted Alawar, before trudging off across the blood-spattered yard.

Al watched his father closely as the older man walked away, noting the slight limp and steady drips of blood that followed in his wake. He felt as if his heart would burst with admiration for the stout man, watching how he dealt with the council and the strong personalities of his fellow kings. Al sent a silent, familiar prayer to the gods. If he turned out to be even half the man his father was, it would be a life he could be proud of.

"I see now what you were saying last night, Carolus. Already, the fragile strings of our alliance are fraying. King Broga will be a problem for Father." Al said, speaking quietly so as not to be overheard by the men bustling around them.

"Men like your father are exceedingly rare, Al. Most of those following him will cheer at his words of conquest and peace, but for them they cannot look further than the next meal, the next fight, and the next opportunity to enrich themselves," Carolus said, before frowning as he continued, "If King Broga were in charge, the whole island would be in flames by now, and we would find ourselves surrounded by enemies on all sides. There is no limit to what people will do if they are pushed to their breaking point, and the entire population could well be up in arms to oppose us if we don't approach this carefully."

Carolus turned, smiled at the young man, and patted his shoulder. "For now, there's nothing for us to worry about; let us enjoy this evening and our first victory. Go back and join the men and listen to their songs of battle. I will see to your father's wishes."

The tutor marched off and out of the yard, into the gloom. Al stood for a moment in the chilly night air and looked again at the pile of dead Romans by the gate. It was an odd feeling to think that any of those men could have stood in this very same spot the evening before, not knowing their lives would be cut short the following day. Al sighed heavily before he turned on his heel and walked back into the warm building behind him, determined that when they reached the next Roman fort, it would be others listening to his tales of bravery and not the other way around.

Chapter 5

The muscles in his thighs were cramping painfully as Dom crouched low to the ground, watching the light from a nearby torch flicker through the criss-cross of branches behind which he was hiding. During the day, the tangle of bush growing along the base of Hadrian's Wall would have provided minimal cover, but in the pitch dark, the two Romans were praying it would be enough to keep them out of sight until their pursuers had passed. His ankle throbbed painfully, and he bit his lip as he tried to stay silent.

Initially, Dom and Gereon had kept up a fast pace and managed to put some distance between themselves and the Picts, but the heavy armour of the legionaries had eventually slowed them down to a steady trot, and the lightly armoured barbarians were closing the gap. Knowing they could not continue along the open top of the wall without being caught, Gereon had proposed they drop down and vanish into the darkness beneath them. Knowing it was a risk falling from this height in the pitch dark, but having no ideas of his own, Dom agreed and found himself following the old veteran as he quickly lowered himself over the wall, dangled for a moment, and then dropped.

Dom had let out a cry as he landed and felt his ankle turn under him, slipping on a smooth rock. The noise of their fall alerted the Picts immediately to their change of course, and they had struggled on for only a short distance before the sound of soft thuds behind them told them their followers had followed suit and were bearing down upon them. Knowing he had no chance to outrun the barbarians, exhausted and now carrying an injury, Dom had made the decision to crawl headfirst into the thick, wiry bushes that grew for miles along the unoccupied stretches of wall. Gereon had hesitated for a moment before following.

Unable to stand for fear of giving themselves away and with too small a space to sit or lay down, they were forced to stay crouched as their tired bodies protested. The closest torch was now within touching distance of the brambles, and Dom could hear the rough speech of the northern tribes again as they spoke to each other in hushed, angry voices. He felt Gereon tense next to him and placed his own clammy hand on the hilt of his sword. Surely the game was up, and they would be discovered at any moment.

The man carrying the torch had come to a stop, its light flickering above them as it illuminated the silhouette of the figure on the other side of the tangle. Dom recited a silent prayer in his head and prepared his aching legs to jump forward. But at that moment, a rough voice barked out what sounded like a command to Dom, and the torch swung in the other direction. They saw the light quickly receding as the man holding it moved away. Gereon breathed a barely audible sigh of relief, and after waiting for at least ten more minutes, he began to struggle back through the bushes, with his young colleague close behind.

"Fucking hell, lad, I thought that was it. I've no idea how they didn't spot us!" panted Gereon as he placed his hands on his knees.

Dom was leaning heavily against a gnarled and ancient tree, gingerly assessing his ankle. He found it ached terribly, but he was able to put enough weight on it to get moving.

"Well, I won't be winning any races with this, but I should be able to keep up with you as long as we go slow," said Dom. "Do you reckon we continue east along the wall? At some point, we'll run into those pricks again if we do."

"We'll have to head south for now. Try and loop around and make our way back to the wall once we've put some distance between us," replied Gereon as he straightened up and stretched his back.

Following this moment of respite, they trudged off once more into the darkness. It was a cloudy night, and the moon was hidden, but there was just enough light for them to pick their way through the small cluster of trees. It was silent in the woods, with the only noise coming from the soft scrape of their sandals as they disturbed piles of dead leaves. After a short while, the trees thinned, and they found themselves looking out across wide open country, with rolling hills and farmsteads dotted around.

The terrain before them was too exposed to continue directly south. The moment the sun rose, they would be spotted if their pursuers were still in the area. They took a moment to catch their breath and shared a little water from what remained of Dom's ration; he had already drunk most of it during his watch. Pausing a moment, they looked back west, the thought of their comrades, who had surely all perished during the sudden assault, weighing heavy on their minds.

Anger flared in Dom as he thought of Lucian's betrayal. Gereon seemed to have come to a decision, and without another word, he led on, skirting along the edge of the wood and heading east before coming to a sudden stop before Dom.

The dense patch of trees had come to an abrupt stop and in the distance, directly north-east of their position, a great fire was blazing. Although it was too far for them to make out much detail, it was clear the fire raged in the spot they had expected to find a solid Roman fort. Instead of finding some much-needed rest and comfort in the knowledge that swift Roman retribution would be brought down upon the Picts, it dawned on the two soldiers that this was not the work of an overly ambitious clan leader but an organised attack upon the entire province. Dom dropped onto the stump of a nearby tree cut down long before and put his head in his hands.

"Out of the frying pan, eh, Dom!" Gereon said, with a forced note of cheeriness in his voice. "The whole of the north has emptied and been thrown at us by the looks of it… We've got no choice but to head south then, for Eburacum. We'll have to risk the open country, but if we've any luck left, the Picts will be enjoying their victory and planning their next moves for the moment. We might yet make it without being spotted in the open."

Gereon was not a man for quiet despair or contemplation; he was a man of action, and Dom was grateful that he could rely on the old soldier even now. His world had flipped upside down and was burning, but the grizzled veteran stood tall and would continue an unstoppable force.

"We'd best get going then. I won't be able to walk all day tomorrow without a little rest; we need to find somewhere to hole up for a short while," said Dom, groaning softly as he stood up.

Together, they made their way down the gentle slope and cut straight across the land. It was well-maintained and predominately farmland, providing food and materials for the soldiers stationed at the wall. They would be able to maintain a good pace for the moment, but soon this stretch of occupied land would be followed by wild moors with dark forests and steep hills. The first signs of dawn were approaching as the two men came across a desolate stone building, standing alone by a trickling stream, the early morning light playing on its surface.

Gereon forced open a rotted wooden door, and they entered inside to find the roof had long collapsed, but the stone walls seemed solid enough. Placing shields in a corner but keeping their swords close to hand, they headed back outside and knelt by the stream, drinking deep.

"Go on now, lad. Get your head down for a bit. I'll take the first watch," Gereon said, gesturing for Dom to head inside the hut.

"Make sure to wake me in a few hours for my turn," Dom insisted.

Limping back inside, he lowered himself down onto his backside, his back resting against the hard stone wall, and almost immediately fell into a deep sleep, his exhausted muscles finally able to relax.

No sooner had Dom's weary eyes closed when he found himself being gently rocked awake by Gereon.

"It's been about four hours, I reckon, lad. I tried to give you as long as possible, but I'll be asleep myself any moment now. I'll only need a couple of hours, and we can swap again."

Trading places with Gereon, Dom moved towards the doorway and stood leaning against it, his ankle aching as he looked north-east for any sign of movement. A column of smoke still rose in the distance, but all else around seemed quiet. After a quick wash in the stream and another drink of the icy water, he propped himself up against the doorframe, staring out into the fields. As his watch drew on, he ran the events of the previous night over and over in his mind.

Why had Prefect Lucian let them through the gates? He could not think of any scenario in which doing so would not result in the same disaster for the soldiers of Rome. A fresh wave of despair flowed over him as he thought about the flames in the distance, which indicated it was not only their fort that had fallen. Whether it was the result of bribes or just honeyed words, this was a level of sophistication otherwise not associated with the barbarians of the wild north, and it filled Dom with a deep fear.

As he continued to scan the landscape, his gaze settled on a farmhouse on the crest of a hill to the east. His despair changed to sorrow as he thought about the fate the Picts would have in store for the peaceful citizens of Britannia. Unbidden, memories from his past came rushing to the forefront of his mind. His eyes filled with tears as he recalled a burnt and broken hamlet, a place of peace that had met a violent end. Coming home on leave with expectations of impressing his father, wearing his new legionary attire, he instead found the broken bodies of his parents lying in the muddy street. Victims of a Pict raiding party, the entire village had been destroyed and its people tortured and killed; their blood was used to form crude barbaric messages of triumph on the walls.

To this day, Dom did not know how long he had knelt beside his mother's body; it could have been minutes, hours, or even days. It was only the arrival of a legion patrol attracted by the smoke that stirred him from this catatonic state. After burying his family, he had sworn revenge against those from beyond the wall who had shattered his world. Yet here he was again; the new family he had formed with his comrades at the fort had met the same fate as his parents, and again, Dom had been unable to prevent the disaster or protect them. The frustration at his helplessness felt like a lead weight in his chest.

The late autumn sun was making its steady decent into the west when Gereon stirred and came to join the young soldier in the doorway.

"You've let me sleep too long, Dom! Bloody hell, I'm starving... Are you ok, lad?" Gereon's eyes had landed on the young man's face, and he noticed the despair and sorrow that lay upon it.

"No, I can't say that I am... But it's irrelevant; we need to get moving. It's too quiet out there; I've not seen a soul." Dom said, making his way to his feet as his stomach gave a timely rumble, wincing slightly as he put weight on his injured ankle.

"That's the spirit, lad; we've got a duty to fulfil. Despair can wait until it's over," Gereon said, patting Dom on the back. "It sounds like you're as hungry as me. I suggest we head over to that farm on the hill; we'll have to chance it and see if someone friendly is around; we won't make it far on empty stomachs otherwise."

The two soldiers made their way cautiously through the hills and towards the lone building in the distance. It was almost evening by the time they arrived, but no candles or torches could be seen from inside. Gereon approached the front door warily and knocked once. He waited for a few moments with his ear close to the wood. Signalling to Dom to stand ready just behind him, he put his weight against the door and pushed it open. The room inside was deserted, but several passages led off the main room, their interiors dark and threatening.

Creeping inside, they drew their swords and hefted their shields as they waited, their ears straining for any sound of movement anywhere in the building. The seconds ticked by, and still nothing could be heard. Dom signalled that he would head left, and Gereon took the right passage. He moved cautiously, his sword held out in front of him, gritting his teeth as he ignored his aching ankle. Dom made his way through the corridor slowly as his eyes grew accustomed to the gloom. He checked the two rooms on the left side of the passage, finding a well-stocked pantry and a storage room filled with broken barrels.

Continuing along the passage as it turned right, he could see Gereon at the other end making his way along towards him. The corridors linked up, and they could see a path to Dom's right that led back to the main room, and on the left, it went off to a sleeping area. Gereon led the way inside the large bedroom, finding a couple of small beds that had been pushed up against the far wall, but a quick glance inside showed it was also deserted. They straightened up and sheathed their swords, relief washing over Dom.

"It seems like the people here had the sense to flee once they saw the fire in the north. I've found the pantry back there; it looks well-stocked too," said Dom.

He led the way to the small room, and they quickly rifled through the shelves and sacks, filling a cloth bag with dried meats, cheese, and a dozen withered apples. They devoured a couple of old loaves that must have been baked a few days before and quickly left the farmhouse before the owners returned or the Picts arrived. Strengthened by their meal and feeling confident with a good supply that would see them through at least a week, they left the building and headed directly south-east, aiming to join up with the main road that led from Eburacum to Hadrian's Wall.

Dom's ankle ached as they moved forward, but he knew to slow down or stop would mean death if the barbarians overtook them on their march south. Heads bowed and remaining silent, the Romans marched on into the darkness. If they had paused to look behind them, they would have seen a long trickle of lights in the distance. The Picts were on the move.

Chapter 6

Tears flowed silently down Prince Alberic's cheeks and into his beard as he looked down upon the cold, expressionless face of King Alawar. He felt numb and disassociated from the world around him. He could hear the cries and prayers of the druids outside the tent, but their voices seemed muffled. A trickle of tribal elders came and went, some patting him on the shoulder as they passed and offering words of comfort, but the young man heard and felt nothing. The world had ended abruptly, and Al waited for oblivion to take him.

King Alawar had slowly deteriorated in the days since the assault at Dubris. Although his wound had only been minor, it had since become infected. He had spent the last two days bedridden whilst fighting a fever, and a foul odour had clung to the man in his final hours. The priests had said their prayers and made sacrifices to the gods, but it had all been in vain. The enigmatic and powerful Saxon king had died only eight days after arriving on the island he had spent his entire life planning to conquer.

News of the king's illness had spread through the army quickly, and with it came a wave of anxiety amongst common soldiers and leaders alike. The strong personality of Alawar had first brought them together; his brilliant mind had already provided them with an easy victory; they had come to rely on him even if they did not respect him. Even those like Broga, who believed they had their own claim to lead the great army, knew the worth of the great man. Whilst Alawar had travelled by waggon, attended by his son and slaves, the army had continued its course as decided during the council in Dubris. As to what would happen now that his authority was lost and his life was ended, it was anybody's guess.

Unfortunately for Al, oblivion did not take him. The numbness he had felt at the immediate news of his father's death was now fading. A feeling of sorrow crashed into him, so sharp that his chest grew tight as if an icy grip had closed on his ribcage, and he struggled for breath. He finally tore his eyes away from the body of his father and stumbled out of the stuffy tent into the open air. He still could not breathe, and panic was coursing through him. He fell to his knees, and he could feel his body trembling. Not caring that those around him could see his weakness, he gasped as he knelt on the cold ground.

After a few minutes that felt like a lifetime, the iron grip on Al's chest started to lessen, and his breathing gradually returned to normal. Al struggled back to his feet, his head feeling light, and a dull ache pulsed from behind his eyes. The reality had finally sunk in: his father was dead and gone from this world. He was alone in a foreign land, surrounded by enemies inside and outside the tribe he had known all his life. He would be forced ahead of his time to step up and lead his people if he could.

Carolus approached slowly, his head bowed. "Al... Words cannot express my grief at the loss of King Alawar. A giant of the Saxon peoples, he will live long in the memory of your tribe. May he rest in peace, drinking and hunting forevermore in the company of his forefathers."

The sight of his old tutor was like a balm to the young man. He would not have to face his future without support, and the advice and knowledge of Carolus would be crucial for him in the coming months and years.

"Thank you for the kind words, Carolus; he was a great man and a better father. I only pray I can live up to the legacy he has left me," Al replied.

"You're stronger than you know," said Carolus quietly. "You will lead your people to glory; I am sure of it."

Al looked away towards the east, troubled. "I fear I may never get the chance. Another battle rages, and again, I am not involved. I know most of the original families will support me out of respect for my father, but the new men? I'm not sure."

"I'm sure it will be fine; they can hardly hold this against you. You have not sat out the battle out of choice or by order of your king; you have been grieving the loss of your father," Carolus reasoned.

Al did not look convinced. "We shall see this evening. Once the battle has convened, the tribe will be gathered, and I will be crowned or exiled." Silence followed the prince's words as both men contemplated the struggle ahead. After a while, Carolus placed a gentle hand on the young man's shoulder and gestured for Al to follow him.

They set off through the camp and in the direction of Rutupiae Fort to see how the Saxon assault was faring against the main Roman garrison in the southeast of Britannia. The Saxons were expecting a tougher fight, and upon clearing the mess of tents and having a clear view of the battle in the distance, both students and teachers could see that this was the case. The ladders had again reached the Roman walls, but this time there was a lack of any substantial cluster of warriors up on the battlements.

The Romans were holding their own for the time being. Al saw again that sections of the main Saxon army still in the fields outside of the fort were starting to peel off and head in the direction of buildings in the distance. A wave of fury swept through him as he saw this.

"How dare they disregard my father's orders! He told Broga at the council to keep his men on a leash!" Al fumed.

"I feared this would happen. Your father has not even been laid to rest, and his vision for a Saxon Britannia is crumbling," said Carolus sadly.

"Not if I have any say about it," said Al furiously. "As soon as I am made king, I will force Broga back in line!"

Carolus looked worried at his young ward's outburst. "Careful, Al, you must not act rashly. King Broga commands a force that is equal to that you are set to inherit. Furthermore, those men are utterly loyal to him. You must tread carefully here for the sake of your people."

Al rounded on his tutor angrily, "My father wouldn't have stood for this! I have a duty to him and to his dream… My dream."

"I know, Al," said Carolus patiently. "But you mustn't throw your life away! Secure your position first; challenging Broga now is a battle you cannot win."

Alberic turned away and did not reply. He understood the value of Carolus' words, but the idea of his father's orders being ignored within hours of his passing burned inside him as though his stomach was full of hot lead, filling him with fury. He watched as the battering ram at the gates of the fort finally broke through, the noise of the splintering wood carrying over the din of battle. The warriors that were clustered around began pouring inside. The fight was all but over, and the great Saxon army had struck another blow to the Roman defence of Britannia.

A slave had brought food and ale to them as they stood watching, and Al chewed the bread slowly without tasting or taking much notice of what he was eating. The day was nearing its end, and the distant noise of battle had finally dwindled. Tutor and pupil set off towards the fort, with Al casting a final look over his shoulder at the tent where his father's body lay.

As the pair approached their victorious countrymen, they were once again assaulted by the smell of battle; however, this time Al seemed indifferent to the foul smells. In fact, he barely even registered them. Inside the fort, they were met with a similar scene to what they saw at Dubris. There was another pile of Roman dead climbing slowly higher, but the line of Saxon bodies was longer, and there were many still lying where they had fallen. There was no raucous singing for now; the battle had been hard-fought, and the warriors were still catching their breath. The fort at Rutupiae was larger than its Dubris counterpart, with several stand-alone stone buildings within its walls. The pair headed towards the largest of these, which stood on the opposite side of the courtyard.

It looked more like a villa, or a governor's house, than a traditional legionary building. Its white façade was splashed with blood, and the bodies of fallen legionaries lay sprawled upon its steps, waiting to be dragged to the pile. Al and Carolus made their way up towards the door, picking their way through the carnage strewn before them and through a small entrance room before emerging into an inner courtyard. Here, the mood was livelier than out in the yard. There had to be a hundred men gathered here at least, with some lounging on soft couches and others leaning against stone columns.

Doors ran off at intervals along the walls at either side, and to Al's disgust, he could hear the screams and crying of women from deep within the building. An important Roman official must have been stationed here, and his wives and female slaves were now suffering an awful fate at the hands of the Saxon invaders. King Broga was sitting on a wooden bench in the middle of the gardens, covered in blood and holding an amphora of rich wine.

As Al entered the yard and the men closest to the gate noticed him, a handful of men came over to greet him. As they bowed their heads and offered condolences, the young prince noticed that each man was of his father's household guard, men who had known him his entire life. He noted that the other kings and tribal leaders did not rise to greet him or offer their sympathies. Instead, they looked at him with a mixture of indifference, hostility, and mild interest.

As the last of the men who had come to speak with Al finally stepped aside, King Broga stood up, and a silence fell over the courtyard. Unfortunately, this only made the pitiful sounds coming from the rest of the building clearer as the king smiled.

"A toast to the great King Alawar." Broga said, raising the amphora in the air. "He was a good man, and we have a lot to thank him for. His wisdom will be missed in the coming days, but the Saxon people will continue his vision." He drank deep, blood-red wine running down his wild beard before lowing the clay jug and continuing, "Britannia will be ours. It is regretful that he did not live to see the fruits of his labours."

Al heard the men gathered around murmur his father's name as they raised their own drinks, and he cast his eyes around to see who else was present, desperate to see friendly faces in the crowd. He spotted King Caelan, but the old man didn't acknowledge him this time; he was staring determinedly at his cup. The one-eyed king whose name escaped Al stood beside Broga, and he did not raise his cup to toast the fallen king.

Although King Broga had spoken well, his eyes were cold and remained fixed on Alberic as he gave his speech, the hint of a smile playing at the edge of his mouth. His biggest rival had been removed, and he was clearly joyous at the news, even if he tried for now to hide it.

"I thank King Broga for his kind words," Al replied stiffly. He was struggling to suppress the anger that was smouldering inside of him at the sight of the smug king and the sounds of horror echoing around.

"My father was indeed a great king and a wise man. The wisest amongst us, wouldn't you agree?" Alberic continued, speaking to the room at large and hearing a murmuring of assent.

"It leaves me wondering, then, why the last order he gave has been disregarded within hours of his death!" Al's voice was raised now as his anger finally spilled over. "You speak of continuing his vision, but that vision never included the rape of innocent people! You shame the memory of the man!" Al heard Carolus whimper behind him, whispering something that he could not hear over the sound of blood rushing in his ears.

A few of the men around had the decency to look uneasy at these words, but most looked impassively back at him. Broga smiled lazily back at Al as he spoke, "Even a wise man misjudges. Our warriors have given their blood to take this land, and they deserve the spoils of victory. We will take both the island and everything it has to offer."

The men around him cheered as he spoke, their minds racing with dreams of every battle ending with the same outcome: a Saxon victory that brought with it riches and a woman for every man. Their eyes were wild with greed and lust.

Broga raised a hand requesting in silence and then pointed it directly at Alberic. "And you, a cowardly boy who hides in the back, has the audacity to tell our warriors what they can and can't do!"

A fresh wave of prickly anger rushed over Al at these words. "I am no coward! And I am no boy—I am a king, and I *will* protect the legacy of my father!" He shouted back.

"You're a king now, are you?" Asked Broga mockingly before speaking to the room at large, "Men of the Heruli tribe! Do you take this coward to be your king?"

The warriors of Alawar's household guard moved closer together, shielding Alberic, as jeers and insults were fired towards the prince from the rest of his tribe. Al saw old King Caelan grimace, but he did not come to the aid of the young prince.

"I didn't think so… Great warriors need a great king, and who better than I?" Broga's eyes were bright as he spoke, and his words were met with a deafening roar from men who would have died for Alawar only hours before. Broga had just cemented his place as the new leader of the Saxon army, with over half of the gathered forces now sworn directly to his banner.

The men in front of Al faltered; they could see the way the wind was blowing, and their loyalty to the old king was withering as the prospect of death loomed over them. Al's mind was racing, and he could not think of anything to say. In the blink of an eye, his future was being ripped from him, and he was powerless to stop it. He had known it would be a difficult transition, but he had never accounted for a usurper to sweep the crown from under him.

"Out of respect for your father, I will not spill more of his blood on the day of his death." Broga said as the cheers died down. "Alberic, you are hereby banished from the Heruli. Your claim to the throne is forfeit, and you will leave at once. You are not welcome in any land ruled by my people, and you will receive no mercy if you ever return." Broga said, waving his hand lazily through the air.

A handful of his most loyal men pushed their way through the crowd, roughly grabbing Al and Carolus, dragging them outside. Al could feel hot tears on his face for the second time that day as he was jostled along, the frustration almost unbearable. He had lost his father and his tribe on the same day. Carolus was silent as he was dragged alongside him. The eyes of hundreds of men in the courtyard were cold as they stopped their tasks to watch. Here and there, Al spotted a familiar face, but nobody called out to stop or question Broga's men.

They were unceremoniously thrown to the ground outside the fort. They scrambled to their feet and stumbled away quickly. Al made to stop and turn back, but Carolus held his upper arm and forced him along. The Greek tutor knew Broga could change his mind at any moment and send men out to finish the job before Al could put some distance between them. The former prince allowed himself to be led across the fields by his tutor, towards a belt of trees in the distance. The feeling of numbness began settling in again as his world ended for the second time in a matter of hours.

Chapter 7

It was the fourth day since the Pict assault, and in the early morning light, the two Romans crested a small hillock, watching the fast-flowing River Ouse to their right make its way down to the city of Eburacum. From their vantage point, they could see the Roman fort standing tall in the centre, and the two tired soldiers were joyous at the sight. Even more so with the notable absence of flames and smoke pouring from atop the fort and with no enemy force in sight. Dom patted the old veteran on the shoulder with a grin. The end of their road was in sight.

Their journey had been an arduous one, as their path had taken them straight into the mountains and dales that ran straight through the centre of the northern half of the province. Twice they had found themselves blocked, first by a bog that stretched for miles and then by a deep ravine that they had no chance of jumping over. Each time they had been forced to turn around in order to find an alternative path, the fear of seeing men approaching on the horizon filled their hearts, and they fought with a despair forever lingering, ready to drag them down to its depths.

However, their luck had held. Each detour had not taken them too far from their intended direction, and they soon found themselves back on the right track. The only people they had seen in the days since fleeing south had been the odd lone figure watching them pass from atop high hills. They knew that some of the ancient Celtic tribes still dwelt in the empty moors, neither accepting nor challenging Roman hegemony, and continuing to live the same simple lives they had before the conquerors had first arrived on the island. Whilst they offered no threat, they had been left alone, but the Romans had felt the constant presence of unfriendly eyes on the backs of their necks.

Although only a few days had passed, the two legionaries were barely recognisable. Their armour and clothing were dirty and ragged from the rough trek; they stank of sweat, and their stubble was turning into short beards in the absence of a razor. For most people living in the province, this would not have been a major problem, but for the obsessively clean Romans, the lack of bathing and clean clothes left them feeling like wild animals.

Gereon slapped Dom on the back and returned a grin. "Let's not waste any time; chances are we'll have only a matter of hours to get the place ready before the bastards are on us."

Leading the way, he set off on a light trot down the hill and along the river, eager to get inside the safety of the fort. Dom took another moment to cast his eyes over the picturesque scene before following his companion down the slope.

"It seems a bit quiet, don't you think? Last time I passed through here, there were people heading in and out from every direction. Hunters, traders, fishermen, legionary patrols—it's odd to see only a few people around, even at this distance. Do you reckon word has reached them already?" Dom was keeping pace with his comrade as he spoke, ignoring the dull ache persisting in his ankle.

"Hopefully, Dom, if someone managed to flee on horseback, they would have made much quicker time than we did. It will make our lives easier if they're already aware of the menace on our heels," Gereon replied.

They stopped for a short rest after an hour or so, drinking and washing as best they could in the river beside them. The midday sun was bright, and the temperature was pleasant. Now, they were within sight of safety, the terror of their ordeal was starting to ebb away. Dom and Gereon stretched out on the soft grass, listening to birdsong from a nearby thicket. It was at this point that they heard a small group of people hurrying up the track towards them. These were the first people they had encountered properly, and they were glad at the sight as they approached.

"Ho there!" called Gereon cheerfully as he stood up to greet the travellers.

It became clear that before Gereon had moved or spoken, the approaching people had not noticed the Romans lounging by the river. At sight and sound of the old veteran, they flinched and cowered immediately, throwing arms up in the air and looking back over their shoulders, clearly deciding whether it was best to turn and run in the direction they had come.

Dom frowned as he stood up next to Gereon. "Be at ease, we're legionaries. We mean you no harm."

The man at the front of the small group, stooped with age, barked a harsh laugh at this as he replied, "Is that right? You mean us no harm if we give you

46

the clothes off our backs and hand over our daughters for your pleasure, eh? We haven't got any more to give, so if you're going to kill us, then get on with it!"

The two soldiers took a step back at the man's outburst. They were shocked by the words and the venom in the man's voice.

"We're soldiers, not bloody bandits! We don't want anything from you!" Gereon replied, his shock replaced by righteous indignity.

The old man laughed again. "Well, the line is a bit fucking blurry now, isn't it? Your friends back there," he jabbed his finger back in the direction of Eburacum, "certainly don't see any difference between the two!"

Dom raised his hand up and said, "Slow down, old man; we've just come through four days of hell to get here, and we have no idea what you're talking about! Tell us your story and your grievances, and we swear we will take them to the governor."

The old man stood a little straighter as Dom spoke and visibly started to relax, though he still eyed the pair of them suspiciously. "Well, you've chosen a poor time to visit Eburacum, and the governor won't listen to what you've got to say. Won't be listening to much of anything anymore, actually, since his head has been removed from his shoulders."

Gereon paled as he heard this, but neither Roman interrupted the old man, who shook his head and spat on the ground before he continued.

"The chaos started two nights ago. I don't know the whole story—only bits and pieces that we've heard from others before we managed to get out. A rider arrived in the night via the North Gate, apparently, shouting bloody murder about fire and terror along ol' Hadrian's Wall. He was taken straight through to the fort, and the old governor was roused from his bed. The next morning started like any other… until we heard an almighty commotion from inside the fort." The old man started to pace up and down as he spoke, his hands moving as he spoke.

"Before long, there were soldiers streaming out in every direction, telling everyone to gather in the forum for an announcement. Once most of those who live near the centre had gathered, the senior centurion stepped forward and dropped the governor's head onto the floor at his feet. He told us he was a traitor, and he would be in charge for the time being… He also said that there would be some changes. He warned us that defying his soldiers would result in immediate execution."

Dom's head was spinning; he could barely make sense of what was being said. Legionaries had killed a provincial governor? *The man is surely crazy,* Dom thought. There had to be another explanation.

"He told us all to return home, but we had barely been there five minutes before soldiers were arriving and demanding new taxes. Most people resisted, and that's when the slaughter began. Some of us paid up, but that made no difference; the next day they were back again. They've gone mad with power! We had no choice but to flee; most of the city has. We're heading north for now to wait it out."

"Has the entire world lost its fucking mind?!" Shouted Gereon furiously. "The entire Pict nation has come forth to burn the country to the ground, and now you're telling me the legionary garrisons have revolted?"

It was the old man's turn now to be shocked at the other's words. "The Picts have come south? It's true that they're over the wall." His pacing came to a stop, the colour draining from his face as he spoke.

"Over it? They've bloody smashed straight through it! They'll be swarming over these hills by nightfall, and now you're telling us that there isn't a sizeable, organised force anywhere north of Camulodunum to stop them!" replied Gereon, as he turned away with his hand on his head.

Dom felt nauseous at everything he had heard. Not only had he seen their prefect betray his own men, but he was now hearing that a full garrison of his comrades had overthrown a governor and declared themselves dictators. Instead of a warm bed, a bath, and the comfort of being surrounded by allies, they found themselves stuck between dangerous enemies. There was no question of Dom and Gereon joining up with the rebels, even if they were inclined to; the garrison in Eburacum would not take kindly to any legionary presence arriving in the city now, however small. They would not want to risk news of their treachery leaving the city if they could help it.

The old man had been having a frantic, whispered discussion with his fellow citizens, but now he turned back to the two Romans he had distrusted just moments ago, with fear in his face.

"What do we do now? We can't go back, and we can't move on—you must help us!" He pleaded.

Gereon turned back to him, sadness in his eyes as he looked at the pitiful figure. "What would you have us do, friend? If we were a match for thousands of barbarians, we would have stayed to fight. There's a ford just a few miles upriver; I suggest you cross and strike west until you hit the mountains. You'll have a chance in the valleys there to hide."

The old man nodded but was clearly dismayed at Gereon's response. He gestured to the group behind him, and they started moving again, hurrying along with heads bowed. The Romans could hear them crying softly as they passed, devastated by the news.

Gereon turned to his comrade; his moment of shock had now passed, and his old, resolute attitude was back. "Come on, Dom, we need to keep moving south. There's nothing here for us now; we're as likely to be killed by those treacherous bastards as the savages still following us."

Dom was stuck in a fixed stare, looking at the distant city of Eburacum without taking in any details.

"Go where, Gereon? Head south again to find yet another Roman fort overrun, by friend or foe?" Dom said quietly. He could feel the fingers of despair creeping around him once more, and he fought to remain calm.

"Well, we have a simple choice, Dom. We can either continue south or we can strike west, the same as that lot, and hide in the hills. But if we do survive, do you know what they do to deserters? It isn't pretty. No, we have no choice but to keep on moving," Gereon said.

Dom stirred himself out of his reverie. The old veteran was right—it was their only option. Neither man was of a criminal disposition; if they somehow avoided the Picts moving south, that would be their only option for the future. He shouldered the cloth bag of rations, now half empty.

"You're right, Gereon. Let's get going. If my memory serves, there is another crossing point further downriver. We can cross there and head into the forest. I propose we head southwest towards the fort at Lunt; it should only take us a few days of hard marching," Dom said.

Gereon nodded and turned promptly, leading the way downriver. The pair moved a little more cautiously than before, their eyes now peeled ahead of them rather than glancing forever backwards. Luck may not have been with the Roman province, but it was with the two legionaries. The bright midday sun danced and sparkled off the river, but their dull, dirty armour prevented it from giving their position away to anyone looking out northeast from within the fort.

Approaching a small ford, they rushed over and increased their pace to reach the forest ahead of them. As they ran across the stretch of open ground between water and wood, they heard a familiar trumpet call blare out in the distance. The sentries of the rebellious legionaries in Eburacum had sent up the warning call. Panic swept through Dom's body like a shockwave; if they had been spotted, the rebels in the fort would no doubt send out riders to hunt them down. They sprinted the last hundred yards and charged into the forest, breaking through the low hanging foliage at its edge, and turned back, panting to see if they could spot any pursuit.

There was no movement between the densely packed buildings around the fort or in the open miles of land from the city to the forest edge. Dom found himself holding his breath as he peered through the twigs and leaves, his head spinning. But nothing stirred in the open land between themselves and the city as trumpets continued to blare out. *But if it wasn't for them then who was it for?* Dom thought as he looked back towards the northeast, and he finally fell into despair's cold embrace at what he saw.

On the very edge of their vision, they could see a swarm of small black shapes moving across the ridge of a hill, the midday sun glinting here and there off what could only be polished metal. The Picts had reached Eburacum, and from what the pair could see, the separate forces that had attacked the wall had clearly regrouped. Neither Dom nor Gereon wanted to wait to see what would happen next, and in unison, they turned and sprinted as fast as their blistered feet could carry them deep into the dense, gloomy forest.

Chapter 8

The leather ropes cut into Al's wrists as he knelt in the mud, his hair plastered to his face in the heavy rain. To his right lay Carolus, face down and unconscious, after receiving a deft blow to the back of his head to silence his protests at their capture. The downpour made it difficult for him to see, but Al could still make out dozens of figures moving around them. He should have been able to understand their language well enough after Carolus' drawn-out classes in Latin, but the men around him were speaking in low, hushed tones so that he could not overhear.

It had been only two days since their forced banishment, in which they had wandered blindly through the British countryside with no real direction. Carolus had tried to speak words of comfort to his ward, encouraging him with plans of making their way to Londinium to find refuge with the Roman leader, using their status as royalty. The Romans would delight in the prospect of having a friendly Saxon king in their debt and would no doubt support Alberic in regaining control of his tribe—or so Carolus had believed.

Al had not yet spoken a word since that night at Rutupiae. He listened to Carolus rattling off various schemes, but words would not come to him. What he wanted to say was that he did not care. He did not care about regaining his position, he did not care about revenge against Broga, and he didn't care about seeking help from anyone. If he were left alone, he would have simply sat down and let his life fade away. Broga had taken everything Al had ever known, and those he had grown up with had abandoned him without hesitation. His only friend left in this world was an old man who had been paid to teach him, and he could not understand why the Greek scholar had not yet fled.

What Alberic had missed in his stupor was the fact that Carolus had long stopped seeing his relationship with the young prince as that of tutor and student; he cared for Al as if he were his own blood. The thought of just leaving him to his fate had never crossed the old man's mind, and he ached at seeing the look of emptiness in the exiled prince's eyes. If he could have taken the young man's pain, he would have done so in a heartbeat. He knew that only time and distraction would heal such a heavy loss, so he had instead busied himself in trying to get Al to focus on their immediate future.

Although the seed of a plan had taken root in Carolus' mind, finding relief in the support of the Romans as befitting their rank of exiled royalty, he had no idea where Londinium was. He knew it was roughly west of Rutupiae, but the terrain was rough, and they had struggled to maintain a consistent bearing in that direction. It was on one of these detours through a narrow valley that they had walked straight into a legionary patrol, which had appeared like ghosts from either side to encircle them.

It was clear that the element of surprise for the Saxons was now lost, and the Roman defence of Britannia was preparing to counter the invaders advance into the heart of the province. The soldiers had not hesitated in roughly binding Al and Carolus, deaf to the tutors pleading that they were not enemies of Rome. If Carolus had been alone, he would have been untouched and probably questioned what he knew about the forces in the east. But there was no mistaking Al for anything other than what he was: a Saxon. His long blonde hair and beard were enough to tell the legionaries where they had come from.

Al had remained silent as he was bound, offering no resistance. The Romans then jostled and prodded them along the valley as Carolus continued to try and reason with them. The Romans pressed their prisoners on fast enough that the Greeks had no breath left to speak, and the small group did not stop as the day drew on. It felt like hours had gone by, and the prisoners were exhausted after the long run with empty stomachs. The two prisoners were stumbling and faltering in the darkness, jostled by the men on either side who had melted into dark shapes, when they finally saw torches in the distance.

They arrived in a small camp, made of a handful of tents lined up neatly in two rows and ringed with torches thrust into the ground. As the ambushers arrived at the camp, Carolus saw that there were more men already there, making them forty in total by his count. The heavy rain had started then, causing the torches to sputter and quickly turning the ground into a churned mess of mud and sludge as rough hands forced the captives to their knees. Again, Carolus tried to reason with their captors, and this time he was met with a whack from the flat side of a legionary's sword, resulting in him swiftly falling unconscious and face down on the ground.

Al felt as if he were being awoken from a long slumber as he stirred and looked around him, the pain in his wrists from the rough bindings suddenly coming to the fore. He could barely remember the events of the previous two days; he felt like a mist had fallen on his mind. Now the fog was clearing, and the numbness that had plagued him was replaced by a dull ache of hunger in his stomach to accompany the sharp pain in his wrists. The threat of immediate danger had finally shaken him from his depressed stupor. He caught sight of Carolus lying slumped in the mud, blood trickling down his cheek. He felt a twinge of panic at the sight; the thought of losing the old man was more than he could bear. It did not matter now whether he wanted to live; the old man needed him, and a desire to protect Carolus burned like fire.

The shapes in the rain around him seemed agitated, which confused Al as he felt his knees sink an inch lower into the mud. Capturing a pair of Saxons surely could not be the reason for their concern, but the closest solders stood stock still, and their hushed tones sounded worried and angry. Al was bemused by this; the Saxon army could not have reached this part of the island already; it would have taken them at least a day to break camp, which he thought unlikely without his father there to rouse them. He doubted they would end their feasting early, and it would be several days before they considered what they would do next and a few days more before they started to move.

With no immediate threat of attack from the Saxons, he had assumed the legionaries would be calm and begin to question their captives, but their actions gave the impression they were expecting an attack at any moment. He strained his ears to try and catch anything the Romans were saying or to hear anything from outside the camp, but the rain was not letting up and it continued to hammer down. Without warning, pandemonium broke out all around them.

Al heard a wild cry from behind, followed by the distinct twang of bowstrings, and saw black shapes crumple to the ground around him. The soldiers roared and started to charge past the kneeling men into the darkness beyond. Now he could hear the screams of fighting and dying men, and the sounds of a sword on a shield rang out into the night. For the moment, the two captives were forgotten as the legionaries fought the mysterious force.

Looking around wildly, Al caught sight of a body that had fallen close to him, with an arrow protruding from his back. He started shuffling over to the corpse as quickly as he could without losing his balance. His hands still tied behind him, he clumsily turned around and used his right leg to roll the body over. It took a few attempts with the heavy armour weighing the body down. After an immense effort, he succeeded in rolling it over, revealing the legionary's gladius on the ground. Al almost laughed in relief that the soldier had drawn the weapon before being struck dead by the arrow. He shuffled backwards now, his back and neck aching from the awkward angle he was keeping as he looked over his shoulder and moved through the mud.

Lining up his body so that he would fall with the blade underneath him, he fell onto his back. Scrambling with his fingers, he managed to grip the metal blade and turn it at an angle, wedging it into the mud so it would remain still. He then started to saw frantically at the bonds, and the sharp sword made light work of the tight leather cords. His arms suddenly became free, and he felt the blade cut into his shoulder as he fell onto the blade, the bonds snapping loose.

Biting back a cry, he scrambled to his feet and wrenched the sword out of the mud. He felt the wound and found it wasn't deep; it had only nicked him through his tunic. He crouched, moved over to Carolus, and quickly cut away at the Greeks' bonds. The sound of battle continued, but the shouts and cries were fewer, and he realised with a pang of fear that the fighting was nearing its end. He managed to rouse his tutor with a few sharp slaps to the face and hissed in his ear.

"By the gods, Carolus, wake up! It's now or never; we need to run!" Al said.

Whether responding to his words or the slapping, the Greek groggily came around and started to sit up. It only took him a moment to remember their predicament before he started to stumble to his feet. Al placed his arm around Carolus to steady him as the tutor began to sway.

"I'm sorry, Carolus, but we need to run," Al whispered, casting a look around him to see if anyone was approaching. "Can you manage it, or should I carry you?"

"I'll be fine," Carolus mumbled, his voice barely audible. "Let's go."

Al nodded and gestured for Carlous to follow him, and they set off on a crouched run into the heavy rain, towards a gap between two flickering torches. The space in front of them was mercifully deserted, and they rushed forward. Al kept close to his mentor, ready to catch the old man if he stumbled or fell, whilst listening desperately for any signs of pursuit behind. They were still exhausted and starving, but the adrenaline coursing through their veins kept them on their feet.

Almost an hour had passed since their escape when the rain eased to a drizzle. Al and Carolus came to a panting halt, with the old man collapsing onto a fallen tree to catch his breath.

"What happened back there? How did you get free? Who was attacking the Romans?" Carolus asked between panting breaths.

"I don't know who attacked, but it wasn't the Saxons. They were shouting in Latin, I'm sure of it. They attacked with arrows first, killing those closest to us. Once the rest of the soldiers moved off to respond, I was able to shuffle over to the nearest body and use this gladius to cut my bonds free." Al showed the sword he still gripped in his hand to his mentor. "After that, I cut your bonds and managed to bring you around. You know the rest after that."

Carolus looked at Al with a sense of wonder and pride. "Incredible, my young prince! That couldn't have been easy to achieve; you must be blessed by your gods."

"I'm not a prince anymore, Carolus, and the gods must have a fickle sense of humour to desert me at Rutupiae and support me now," Al replied.

"Well, let's not talk about that just now. We need a plan," Carolus said, gingerly feeling the cut on his face. "If the Romans survived their assault, they would know by now that we have escaped and will be on the hunt. The downpour will have hidden our tracks for the most part, but they know this country better than we do. What we need is a place to rest and something to eat."

Al looked around him. The storm had passed, and a bright moon had emerged from behind the heavy clouds, allowing him to see more of the area they had run into. They stood in the middle of a wide, flat plain with dense trees to the north and hills to the east. Looking west, he could see lights flickering from buildings still hidden in the dark.

"We must have come from those hills to the east; I don't recall us leaving the valleys during the march with the Romans. I can see some lights to the west, probably a settlement of some sort," Al said, as he pointed. "I suggest we head in that direction and see if we can steal any food, then make a break for the forest in the north; we should be able to hide well enough in there."

Carolus nodded and slowly climbed back to his feet, stretching his aching back. The two men set off again, this time at a brisk pace, as the adrenaline now faded away and their aches and pains returned. The rain had washed much of the blood from the old Greek's face, and Al could see the gash on his cheek was not too deep. Their rain drenched clothes weighed heavily upon them, and their feet throbbed painfully. The night was quiet, but they kept their ears strained for the sound of clinking armour, and the fear of the Romans catching up with them never left their minds.

As they approached the lights that Al had seen, they could smell the acrid scent of smoke on the breeze and the now-familiar scent of blood. Al motioned to Carolus to crouch, and he now led the way with the sword held out in front of him. What Al had presumed where torches turned out to be the last embers of a great fire that had ravaged what must have once been a handsome estate. The stone building in the centre still stood tall but was now black from soot. The wooden outer buildings had collapsed in on themselves and still smoked in the soft rain.

Carolus gasped and came to a halt, gripping Al's arm as he pointed to the right of the building. Crudely strapped to a wooden post was the ruined body of an elderly man, his entrails spilling out of his abdomen and falling to the ground in spirals. Two small bodies lay at the foot of the post, their tunics covered in red marks. Al tore his eyes away from the horrific scene and scanned the estate once more. There was no sign of anyone alive in the yard, and he moved towards the entrance of the villa.

He had not taken more than three steps when he saw a shadow flicker across the doorway. His heart in his throat, he gripped the sword in his hand and called out, "Come out! We know you are in there!"

Perhaps intrigued by the strong accent of Al's Latin, he saw somebody move to the edge of the door frame. After a few tense seconds, a young woman slid into view. Her stola was ragged and torn, and her hair hung lank and matted over her face. She shifted the hair out of her face and stared at Al, not saying a word.

"Are you alone? We don't mean you any harm. We were only looking for help and perhaps some food before going on our way." Al spoke gently and lowered the sword with relief.

The young woman did not reply at first; her bright green eyes fixed him with a piercing stare, and the look of suspicion and hatred was clear on her face. She was almost as tall as him, and her hair ran down to her waist. Although she was covered in black soot and filth and there was a clear cut on her right cheek, Al was startled at her beauty.

"If you try and touch me, I will kill you." Her voice was like steel, and a fire burned in her eyes. Al noticed for the first time a sharp knife in her hands, its blade covered in dried blood.

"I have no intention of coming any closer, I swear," Al replied, staring at her.

The look of hatred did not leave her fine features, but the suspicion began to fade slightly.

"You won't find much food here. They took almost everything. There were some winter stores in that hut over there, but I doubt you'll find anything," she pointed over to a partially destroyed building standing to one side.

Carolus shuffled on in that direction, whilst Al remained looking at the young woman, transfixed.

"Thank you," he said quietly. "My name is Alberic, prince of the Heruli— well, not a prince anymore…" His voice faded, and he looked down at his feet. Old habits die hard, and the memory of his banishment returned painfully.

Her expression had not changed, and she said nothing in response. Carolus came back over, cradling bundles of cloth.

"There is barely anything left but some old, cured meat that managed to avoid the blaze. It's tough and tastes of nothing more than fire smoke, but it will do." He said this before he cautiously approached the woman and laid most of the bundles a few steps away from her. "I have taken only enough to last us a couple of days; we do not plan to rob you of everything."

The woman just stared at him, again without speaking, but Al had noticed her hand tighten around the daggers hilt as Carolus drew nearer.

Al cleared his throat and spoke once more: "I thank you for this; it is clear you have lost much, and the gods will bless you for your generosity. Are you sure we cannot help you in return? What has happened here?"

The woman opened her mouth to speak but shut it almost at once. Tears sparkled in her green eyes. Carolus, however, nudged Al and pointed at a message written in blood over the doorframe. Al had not noticed it before, having been so transfixed by the young woman. He looked at it for a moment, deciphering the words. Reality dawned on him as he translated, "***Death to the Masters***."

Chapter 9

"I don't think we have much of a choice, lad," said Gereon. "We won't get much further on empty bellies."

The two men were lying on their stomachs down in the tall grass at the base of the hill that stood tall on the river bank as it curled around a small village. The day was dull and gloomy, even though it was only just past midday, and the grey clouds above threatened a heavy downpour. In front of them, they could see Roman legionaries standing guard in a ring around the village, each man twenty metres apart. Their trek through the British countryside had taken them through forests, over fields, and across rivers, and their clothes were stained and in dire need of cleaning. The idea of a warm fire was extremely enticing to the tired soldiers.

During their journey, they had come across groups of people travelling in all directions, but they had made sure to avoid each and every one. They had all been made up of families who hurried along with their belongings, oblivious to what was around them, and every face they saw was terrified. However, this was the first time they had encountered any Roman presence since their disastrous discovery at the fort in Eburacum, and Dom was worried about what they might find. He had battled with his fears in the days since fleeing further south, and he felt as if despair would overwhelm him once again at any moment.

"It's been over a week since Eburacum; the chances this lot is from the same group are slim. We desperately need food and a good rest; we've got to go for it." Gereon continued in a hushed tone.

Dom could not shake the feeling of anxiety that was now ever present in the pit of his stomach. To be this close to fellow legionaries whilst having doubts about whether they were friends or foes was deeply frustrating to the young Roman. The world had been so simple only two weeks ago, and now even the most natural of choices had to be carefully thought over. The desire to be surrounded by friendly faces burned deep within him, and he made up his mind.

Dom sighed as he replied, "OK, let's go."

He slowly brought himself up to his feet, Gereon rising to his right. His ankle was still aching dully, and his back was sore from nights spent sleeping on rough ground. Their food had run out two days earlier, even with careful rationing, and their situation was dire. He was still nervous at the thought of approaching the village, but he could not think of any alternative plans. They would have to double back a long way to avoid the village, and it was likely they would starve if they took another lengthy detour.

As soon as they had stood up and started making their way forward, they heard a call go up, followed by two short blasts from a legionary horn. They slowly made their way forward towards the nearest guard and saw a group of soldiers come trotting into view from within the village. As they approached, Dom studied the legionaries. He could see dented armour on some and a battered shield here and there. They had clearly seen action recently, but who they had fought remained a mystery.

"Ho there!" cried Gereon. "Gereon and Dominicus of Legion Victrix, third cohort stationed at Bowness, approaching."

"You're far from home, Gereon; last time I checked, the wall was two hundred miles north!" A tall legionary called back; he was one of the soldiers whose armour showed dents and old blood was crusted on his helmet, bright red hair showing underneath. "What brings you here? It looks like you've been through hell."

"You've got no idea, mate. Me and the lad are in desperate need of food and a bit of rest. Permission to approach?" Gereon replied, raising his voice slightly as the wind began to pick up.

"Permission granted. Name's Callixtus. Victrix, sixth cohort stationed at Cornoviorum." The tall legionary called back.

The soldiers around visibly relaxed at the exchange, and Dom and Gereon joined the main party as they headed back to the centre of the village.

"Who's the officer on duty?" Gereon asked, confused that it wasn't an officer who had greeted them on approach.

"Dead!" Callixtus grunted. "It's a long story, and one told better with a strong drink. We've set up in the village tavern; the locals aren't too happy about it."

After a short walk between low huts, with unfriendly eyes watching them pass, they turned a corner and found the tavern in front of them, a large and sturdy wooden building. The soldiers filed inside, and Dom enjoyed the warmth that hit him after many nights of sleeping rough in the cold. A large fire blazed in a pit in the centre, and the smell of food cooking made their stomachs rumble painfully.

"Magnus!" Callixtus called out, "Come here, lad." A noticeably young legionary, who must have been barely sixteen years old, came jogging into view.

He saluted rather sloppily as he came to a halt. Callixtus clicked his tongue but did not comment on the young man's poor attempt.

"I've told you before; I'm not an officer. No need to salute or call me sir. Now be a good lad and go and draw a few buckets from the well and bring clean tunics from the carts for our comrades."

Magnus looked with wide eyes at the filthy, wild-looking men standing next to Callixtus, then nodded and ran out of view again. Dom and Gereon were shown to a parlour room just off the main hall, with a rough wooden table and a bench inside. Steaming bowls of stew were brought to them, which did not last long in front of the starved soldiers. Shortly after, Magnus returned carrying two large buckets with water slopping over the sides and fresh tunics over his shoulder. He handed over a pair of scissors to Gereon as well, before hurrying back out.

Once they were as neat and clean as they could be with only a bucket of clean water and a pair of old scissors, which felt to them like they had just spent three hours in a bathhouse, the two men made their way back into the main room. Dom ran a hand over his jaw. It was not the clean shave he was used to, but he was happy to be rid of the filthy beard he had grown in the last couple of weeks. They spotted Callixtus sitting by the central fire and walked over to join him, accepting a cup of strong dark beer as they approached. Dom cast his eyes over the soldiers seated around him and noted that more than a few had dents in the armour or scraps of cloth wrapped tight around recent wounds. Anxiety began to bubble in his gut as he took a seat opposite the tall, red-haired legionnaire.

"To the Emperor, gentlemen," Callixtus said as he raised his own cup. "Now then, care to share your story?"

"Well, long story short, mate, we're fucked," said Gereon cheerfully as he took a big swig from his cup. "The Picts have launched a full-scale invasion; Hadrian's Wall has fallen, and there's nothing stopping them from marching all the way to Londinium and sacking Camulodunum on their way."

There was an outbreak of muttering and curses from the men gathered around. It was clearly not the news they had expected, and they did not hide their shock and dismay that the seemingly impregnable wall had been breached.

"Fucking hell, how the hell has that happened? There's the best part of a thousand men up there!" Calixtus responded.

"It doesn't matter if there's ten thousand if your prefect opens the gate and lets the horde through," replied Dom darkly.

Callixtus gaped at him. "Have you hit your head, lad? You can't be saying that about officers, even amongst us."

"It's true, Callixtus; the bastard opened the gate and let them in. Then they killed him and launched a surprise attack," Gereon said with a grunt. "We can only assume they must have killed everyone stationed there, as it was four against one at least. We only survived because we were on the wall, and we ran for it to send out the warning. We headed for the next fort along, ready to rally the soldiers there, but it was already up in flames."

There was a further outbreak of muttering at this; hearing that a cohort of men had been wiped out due to an act of treachery or gross negligence from an officer, without being able to fight a fair fight, was galling to them.

"We were chased by the Picts all the way to Eburacum. It took us a couple of days, but we eventually made it, expecting to find four hundred Roman swords ready to strike back."

"Wait—expected to find? The Picts haven't taken Eburacum, have they?" A man in his thirties with a crooked nose interrupted Gereon's story.

Gereon laughed humourlessly. "Oh, Eburacum has fallen all right, but not to the Picts. The fucking garrison has revolted, killed the governor, and put themselves in charge."

There was silence in the room. The men had heard stories of garrisons and armies that had revolted in Roman history. The result very rarely ended in a positive outcome for the revolutionaries, and the response from the Imperial Court was usually swift and brutal.

"So, the Picts have overrun the wall, and Eburacum has revolted... So that's three enemy forces in the province, and the legion has probably lost a third of its forces!" Callixtus exclaimed, slamming his fist onto the table.

"What do you mean?" Dom asked at once. "A third enemy force?"

"Aye, why do you think we're out in the arse end of nowhere and not playing dice in Cornoviorum? Bands of Scotti pirates have come over from Hibernia;

they've made common cause with rebels in the Welsh hills and launched an assault on the western forts and towns."

It was Gereon's turn to swear at hearing this, and he drained his cup.

"The first we heard of them was a merchant who came into town shouting bloody murder. By the time we calmed him down and got the full story, they were on the horizon. There are hundreds of the bastards, and they are no pushovers in the field. They attacked the following day; we held them off for a while, but they kept coming. Ol' Prefect Vitellius gave the order to evacuate, make for Londinium or Lunt, and send out the warning." Callixtus spoke darkly as he retold his story and refilled their cups.

"We fought our way through a weak gap in the Scotti lines and made a run for it, but the centurion fell in the chaos. We then ran pretty much nonstop for a day and a half before we arrived here and stopped to catch our breath. Only fifty of us made it." Callixtus finished with a pained expression as he thought of the comrades he had lost in the last couple of days.

"Bloody hell, you did well to get out of that one," said Gereon, impressed. "So, we've got Picts invading from the north, Scotti invading from the west, and the main fort north of Lunt out of the fight. It's a good thing most of the legion is stationed south or we'd have no chance of taking the fight to any one of them."

"It's a royal mess, that's for sure," Callixtus replied with a grunt. "We were planning to stay here for another night, then make for the fort at Lunt. We toyed with the idea of heading for Camulodunum, but that nest of merchants will be a prime target now. If the Praetor is aware of the chaos in his province and has any sense, he will have already retreated to Londinium."

Callixtus refilled his cup for the third time and drained it in one. "I'm assuming you'll be joining us as we march for Lunt." He asked Dom and Gereon.

"We were heading for Lunt ourselves! It will be good to travel with proper company again," replied Gereon with a grin.

"Excellent. Any extra swords we can pick up on the way will suit us all well... I wouldn't be surprised if we find a bit of trouble between here and there," Callixtus replied as he stifled a yawn whilst stretching his back.

"Well, that's enough talk for me tonight; I'll check on the watch and call it a night. We've not got any beds spare, I'm afraid, but there's space enough by the walls, and it's dry enough," Callixtus said as he stood up and made his way back outside into the howling wind.

Dom and Gereon spent the rest of the evening chatting with the legionaries and getting to know the men from Cornoviorum. They went over the events from both sides for hours before every detail and possibility seemed to have been talked through. The beer continued to flow, and Dom could feel himself relaxing for the first time since the night the barbarians had attacked. The men gathered around the fire and started to sing songs of famous battles, and Dom listened without joining in, continuing to drink the strong beer, knowing his head would be heavy in the morning.

Eventually, they bid goodnight to the men around them and found a quiet spot on the other side of the tavern. They dropped down onto the dry, straw-covered floor, hearing the soft scuttling of mice they had disturbed.

"Well, we lucked out once again, Dom. They seem a good bunch, and I reckon this should be the moment things finally turn around for us," Gereon said as he wrapped up his cloak to form a pillow.

"I hope so. At least we'll be marching with fifty swords instead of two. I'll finally be able to sleep a bit easier," Dom replied with a sigh.

They lapsed into silence, and within moments, as usual, Gereon's heavy snores could be heard. Dom envied the veteran's ability to sleep easily in almost any location and spent quite a while listening to the heavy rain thudding on the roof as he tried to fall asleep. Although the news they had heard was deeply troubling, Dom felt a comfort he could barely express at sleeping once again indoors, safely surrounded by his comrades.

Chapter 10

Alberic lay on the cold, damp bed of fallen leaves beneath a gnarled and twisted oak, trying to force himself to fall asleep to no avail. He continued to toss and turn for a few more minutes before accepting defeat and sitting up with his back to the tree and his knees drawn up to his chest. He gazed into the heart of the small fire he had built, lost in thoughts of how his life had changed since arriving on the island. Staring intently into the flames, it took a while for him to realise he was being watched.

Pulling his gaze away from the flickering light, he looked to his left and saw the young woman with green eyes looking at him. She had accepted Carolus' offer of journeying together to Londinium, but she had said little in the hours since leaving the estate. Her face was expressionless, giving no hint to her thoughts or feelings. Al found it unnerving and looked away quickly to his right, seeing his old mentor fast asleep and curled up under his cloak. He felt a wave of affection break over him as he looked at Carolus. Without him, Al knew he would have been dead after the events at Rutupiae.

"Is he your father?"

The sudden question made Al jump, and he looked back towards the woman, who still had not taken her eyes off him.

"No… my father is dead." Al felt his throat tighten as he said those words. "Carolus is my tutor and has been for many years now."

"Your tutor?" The woman's eyes had widened slightly at Al's response. "Who are you?"

"I don't know who I am anymore. But I can tell you who I was. My father was King Alawar of the Heruli tribe, the greatest of the Saxon kings. I was a prince and set to rule my people after him… when he died, my birth right was taken from me, and I was exiled." Al looked back into the fire once more as he spoke, drawing his knees up closer to his chin.

"That was around five days ago, as best I can tell. I have lost my family and my future. I am alone in a foreign land with no idea what the future holds for me." He felt tears rise unbidden and rubbed his eyes quickly.

Clearing his throat, he looked back into those mesmerising green eyes. "Now you know my name and my story, but I still don't know yours."

"My name is Lucia." The young woman replied after a long pause. "I am sorry to hear about your father," she continued rather stiffly, and Al received the impression she was just being polite.

"Well, it's nice to meet you, Lucia. And thank you." Al replied, feeling slightly awkward. "You should try and get some rest; I can keep watch."

Lucia finally took her eyes off the young man to look down at the damp floor, but he remained still. "I don't think I will ever sleep again. I fear the nightmares that sleep may bring." She spoke softly, and Al could only just make out what she had said.

He felt a surge of sympathy for the young woman. Although she had not shared the full story of what had happened at the estate, Al knew she must have suffered terribly at the hands of the rampaging slaves. He was not sure why she had agreed to come with them, but he was glad they had not left her alone amongst the ruins of her home. Before they had set off, she had departed back inside and emerged in a clean tunic with her hair tied back, and the bruises from the assault stood out darkly on her pale skin.

"You can't stay awake forever, Lucia, and who knows what we may face in the coming days? I know it must be tough, but you need to rest now whilst you're safe with us," said Al, speaking gently.

She looked up at him once more, her eyes flashing in the firelight. "Safe?" She repeated, with anger in her voice. "Are you going to keep me safe, Prince Alberic?"

Al blushed at this and started to stutter a reply, but Lucia continued before he could answer.

"No, my safety will no longer be guaranteed by *any* man. My father could not promise it, and neither could you. I can and will look after myself."

"I don't doubt it," said Al, remembering the bloody knife she had held when they first met. "I'm sorry if I upset you; I just meant-."

"I know what you meant, Alberic." Lucia turned her face away from his again.

They had lapsed into silence, which lasted for the remainder of the night. Al fell into an uneasy doze whilst leaning back against the tree, and Lucia barely closed her eyes, even for a moment.

Dawn was breaking through the foliage ahead when Carolus stirred, propping himself up into a sitting position and reaching for the cloth bag which contained their meagre rations of dried meat. Chewing thoughtfully, the silence was finally broken as the old tutor spoke.

"Alberic, are you awake?"

His voice brought Al back to the present with a jerk, and he rubbed his eyes before looking over at Carolus.

"I am. Did you sleep well?" Al replied.

"I would have preferred a bed of warm furs and a breakfast of roast bacon, but I'm feeling rested enough, thank you." Carolus threw the cloth bag towards Al, who reached in, withdrew a piece, and began to eat. As he chewed through the tough meat, he passed the bag along to Lucia, who ignored it.

"You need to eat to keep up your strength, my dear," said Carolus kindly.

She simply shrugged and looked away.

Carolus frowned slightly and turned back to Al. "We need to decide what our plan is. The Romans could still be looking for us if they survived, and with bands of escaped slaves roaming the countryside, we will need to be extremely cautious."

"I know… But where do we go, Carolus? Do you still believe we will find asylum in Londinium after our encounter with those legionaries?" Al replied.

"Perhaps… Our hope lies with the governor, not his soldiers, to provide us with security and support. But I will admit I am not too keen to keep heading in that direction now…" Carolus' voice trailed off, and his brow furrowed as he continued to ponder the best course of action.

Al sighed and looked up at the sky. It looked as if it would be a fine day. After a few minutes, he looked back at Carolus. "I don't think we have any other choice. We may be able to buy passage off the island and head back to Gaul, or you could consult with the governor on my behalf if you still think it's worth it."

Carolus nodded as his face relaxed. "It is difficult to know what the right decision is, but I feel better knowing we have a plan. Now, the next item on the agenda: where is Londinium? I have lost my sense of direction completely since our capture; I don't know how far inland we have come."

"I can take you to Londinium." Lucia interjected, and both men looked at her in surprise. Al had not known she had been listening at all to their conversation.

"My dear, we would be forever in your debt if you could. Perhaps in the city you could find support or compensation for what has happened to your family." Carolus smiled at her as he spoke, but Lucia did not return it.

Instead, she looked at Al and said, "I will take you, but on one condition."

"Of course, we will do whatever we can to help you," Al replied at once, and he cursed internally at how eager he sounded to help the young woman, remembering their conversation during the night.

"I know where the men who…" Lucia's voice trailed off for a moment, and tears were sparkling in her eyes once more. "I know where the men who killed my family are hiding. I won't rest until I have had my revenge, and I need you to help me."

"What can a woman, an untested youth, and an old scholar do against a gang of angry slaves?" Carolus said sadly. "I believe what you want isn't in our power to give, but the governor will surely support you."

Lucia continued to look at Al as she replied, "It's not a "gang," it's four men. I know where they are, and we can take them by surprise."

Al looked back at her, puzzled. "Four men? How can four men destroy an entire estate?"

She looked down at the ground as she replied, "When they first arrived, there were hundreds of them… Father had barricaded the door, and when they couldn't get in easily, they stole everything they could from the storehouses and set fires everywhere."

Although they could not see her face, they could see her shoulders shaking with repressed sobs.

"We heard the mob leave, and after a while, when we couldn't hear anything outside, Father opened the doors. But they weren't all gone; five men had waited behind and ambushed him as soon as he stepped outside." Lucia was now crying freely, and her voice had been reduced to a croak.

"After they had… killed Father, they came rushing in, and my brothers tried to fight them, but they were so small and young. They cut them down without a second thought. Then they saw me and my mother. We tried to fight them, but…" Her voice trailed away again and was replaced with the sound of wrenching sobs.

Al and Carolus were transfixed with horror. "I'm so sorry this happened to you, Lucia," Alberic said quietly.

They sat in an awkward silence until Lucia managed to regain some composure. She began to speak again, her voice barely a whisper.

"After they were done, they ignored us and started to pillage through the house, breaking and stealing everything they could find. As we lay there, we listened to them talk about an old mine that one of them used to work in; they said they planned to use it as a base. Eventually, they decided to leave, but one of them remained behind. He told his friends that he 'wanted another go.'" As she spoke those last four words, her voice turned to hard steel.

"They had left us where we lay, ignoring us as they tore our house apart. Mother had crawled to a cupboard where she knew Father's skinning knife was kept. She had crawled back and kept it concealed under her. When the rest of them had left and only the last one remained, she pulled out the knife and stabbed him with it as he was on top of her."

Al felt as if his heart was physically breaking as he listened to Lucia's story. Carolus was unashamedly crying silently.

"They struggled, and in the confusion, he managed to get the knife and stab Mother in the chest. I jumped on his back, not knowing what else to do, but he must have been weak from the first wound. He collapsed to the ground and dropped the knife; I took it and stuck it in his throat." There was a ringing silence left in the clearing as Lucia finally finished her story.

"My dear…" Carolus said softly, "What a terrible ordeal for a young lady to go through. You have my deepest sympathies."

Lucia sniffed and wiped her eyes on her sleeve. She looked up again, this time turning from one to the other. "Four men. I know where the mine is; it was originally on our land before Father sold it. We can sneak in tonight and cut their throats whilst they sleep. I won't take you to Londinium until this is done."

Carolus shuddered at her words and looked away, unable to hold her fierce gaze. Al, however, looked straight back into those bright green eyes, seeing a furious fire deep within. He knew what it was like to have everything taken from him. If he had the chance to kill Broga, he would take it.

"We will help you, Lucia," Al replied finally. "But we will need to be extremely careful about this. If we alert them, we're as good as dead. Carolus will remain here; he has no weapon and has never been much of a fighter."

"But my prince, I cannot wait here whilst you risk death!" Carolus protested.

"Carolus, you need to trust me. I will not throw my life away needlessly. Me and Lucia can do this, and I will return." The old Greek felt a surge of pride overpower his fears; for a moment, the son had become the image of his father, and power seemed to resonate from him.

"It's too risky, Alberic," Carolus protested feebly.

"I have made my decision, and I need you to do as I say, Carolus, please." Al replied.

The old tutor mouthed something wordlessly but knew he was facing a losing battle and chose not to continue arguing. He bowed his head and resigned.

"Thank you, Carolus. I need you to believe in me, as you once believed in my father," Al said quietly.

Carolus nodded but did not reply. Lucia had watched the exchange with her face expressionless once again, but she too had noticed the change in the young man.

"We should set off now; it's a few hours away, and we need to scout out the area before we can decide on a final plan," Lucia said as she stood up.

Al stood up and stretched before picking up the gladius from where it lay resting against the oak tree. He patted Carolus on the shoulder and turned to face Lucia. She promptly turned on her heel without another word and headed off into the forest, with Alberic following in her wake. The tutor watched until they had faded into gloom between the trees. He pulled his cloak tightly around him, miserable and alone, wracked with anxious thoughts of whether he would ever see young Prince Alberic again.

Chapter 11

Dom was up early and busy cleaning his breastplate and helmet, removing the grime and muck they had gathered during their trek south. He felt a sense of pride as the familiar gleam and shine returned, and once he had finished, he strapped his breastplate on and pulled his helmet over his head. It was good to be wearing clean clothes again, and with his kit returned to legionary standard, he felt like a new man. He was cleaning Gereon's armour when the veteran finally roused himself from sleep and came over to join him on the bench.

"Morning son," Gereon said, stifling a yawn. "You're a good lad; you didn't have to do that." He pointed at the cloth in Dom's hand.

"I don't mind; I've been awake for a while, so I'm just passing the time. Here, I'm pretty much finished now," Dom handed over the breastplate to Gereon, who put it on with experienced efficiency.

"Any idea where Callixtus is?" Gereon asked as he finished tightening the last strap.

"Aye, he's outside calling the outer guards back, so we're ready to leave," Dom replied.

"Excellent. Pass us that bread there, Dom; I'm starving." Munching on the loaf handed to him, Gereon jerked his head in the direction of the door before moving towards it, Dom following in his wake.

It was a bright morning, and the clear blue sky above was clear of any clouds. The ground, however, was still a churned mess after the movement of many men during the rains over the last couple of days. They found Callixtus standing by an ancient donkey, fitting a harness to it.

"Morning Callixtus!" Gereon called out cheerfully. "How soon until we're off?"

"Not long now; most of the men have mustered in the village square now. We just need to do a count of the remaining provisions, and we'll be on our way."

Callixtus said as he finished strapping the cart to the donkey's harness and started rifling through packages and barrels.

"Hmm. Looks like we've got enough to last a few days; we still have some spare clothes and weapons. Could be worse," he said quietly to himself.

He took the donkey by the reins and led it between two decrepit houses and out into a square with a stone well in the centre. Dom and Gereon followed, and as they passed by the houses and into the open area, they saw fifty men standing neatly in ranks, ready to march. They jogged to the back of the column and joined the last row. Callixtus handed the reins to Magnus, the youth from the previous evening who looked as if he were a boy wearing his father's armour and playing at being a soldier.

"Time to go, lads! We're heading for the fort at Lunt to regroup with the cohort stationed there. We have no idea what we'll meet on the road, so we'll be marching in battle formation—you all know the drill. Magnus, you bring up the rear with the supplies." Callixtus promptly turned on his heel and started marching off with the column, following suit.

The legionaries kept a slow pace as they did not want to leave Magnus or the supplies too far behind, and their tight formation prevented them from breaking into the legionary trot that could carry them for miles. They spoke little to each other as they marched, and each man's eyes constantly darted across the countryside to either side of the column, looking for any sign of a threat. They had only gone five or six miles by the time the sun had risen to its highest point, and Callixtus called a halt.

Water was passed along the lines to the men, and word was sent from the front for Dom and Gereon to join Callixtus at the head of the column.

"Everything OK?" Dom asked as he joined the tall legionary, who stood a few paces ahead of the rest.

"I'm not sure," replied Callixtus, frowning. "I don't like the snail's pace that we're moving at, but we can't risk moving any quicker when we're marching blind."

"Should we send out scouts?" Dom proposed. "We're in a good position here; the main column can hold whilst we check if the road is clear."

"I was thinking the same thing," replied Callixtus. "But we've got no officers. I'm just a legionary like the rest, even if I do have a few more years under my belt than most. But it's not my place to command anyone, so we're going to need volunteers."

The men nearest them had heard the exchange and looked uneasily at each other. None of them were cowards, but scouting ahead in unfriendly territory on foot was not an enticing prospect.

"We'll go," said Gereon. "Me and Dom have already spent days keeping out of sight and moving like ghosts in the grass. We'll set off now and report back in a few hours."

Dom nodded, and Callixtus looked grateful that he had not been forced to make someone go. Gereon and Dom set off at a trot, following the road heading south. They had crested a small hill only a few miles further on when they saw that the path headed directly into a thick belt of trees. They moved forward more cautiously now, moving off the road and into the tall grass beside it, crouching low and scanning the gaps between the trees for any sign of movement.

The silence in the woods was stifling as they entered, and they noted the absence of bird calls and scuffling in the undergrowth. It was a sure sign that something had recently moved through this area and caused the inhabitants to flee. They creeped forward, keeping the road on their right and picking their way carefully through the densely packed trees. Dom suddenly threw out an arm and caught Gereon in the chest, forcing him to a halt.

"Stop!" Dom hissed. "Can you see that over there? I think I can see a fire." He pointed to his left, deeper into the trees and away from the main road, where the darkness of the wood was broken by a small flickering light.

Gereon squinted in the direction Dom was pointing, and after a moment, he gestured for Dom to follow. They moved towards the fire, now moving extremely slowly and with great caution not to rustle the leaves underfoot or break twigs. Dom could feel his body tensing, and he loosened the sword in his scabbard. This time, Gereon halted Dom with an arm to the chest and pointed to his ear, indicating for Dom to listen. They could hear voices ahead of them, but they could not understand the language they were speaking.

"You go left; I'll go right. Get as close as you can and try to get a head count of how many there are. Meet me back in here in five minutes," Gereon whispered.

Nodding, Dom set off, maintaining the slow speed and cautious steps through the trees. The voices were getting louder and seemed to be coming from many men. The language was harsh and reminded him of the Pict dialect, yet it was noticeably distinct from it. He reached a tall birch tree that was roughly twenty metres from the clearing with the fire in it. Leaning against it, he slowly peered around the trunk, being careful not to reveal any of his body.

He saw a wide clearing, with sunlight pouring in through the break in the foliage. In the centre was a fire with slabs of meat stuck on the ends of sticks, hanging over the flames. Sat or lay around the clearing was a large host of men, mostly wearing thick furs, but here and there he noticed the shine of armour. With a wave of anger, he also noticed more than a few of them were wearing legionary helmets. They must be from the same group of Scotti that had defeated Callixtus' cohort at Cornoviorum.

He took a quick headcount as best he could and cautiously made his way back to the spot he had split with Gereon. A few tense moments later, he was reunited with the old veteran, and no warning call had gone up. They set off back in the direction of the road, and the men who were waiting for their report, not yet speaking to each other for fear of being heard. As they came back out of the trees into the warm sunshine, Gereon whistled quietly to himself.

"Well, it's a bloody good thing we scouted ahead. They would have heard us coming and ambushed us on the road, no doubt about it. How many did you count?" He asked Dom as they started to jog back through the grass towards Callixtus and his men.

"About eighty, but there could be more. You?" Dom replied.

"Same," Gereon grunted. "Enough to cause a headache, that's for sure."

Callixtus raised a hand in greeting and smiled at the two men as they came trotting back into view.

"How did you get on, lads? You're back earlier than I expected," he said, passing Gereon a water skin.

"About four miles down the road, it enters and passes through a small wood of dense trees." Dom said, as he took a swig from the water skin passed to him before he continued, "We scouted inside and found a camp of around eighty men. They were clearly barbarians, but some were wearing bits of legionary gear, Callixtus, I think they must be Scotti."

"We either go around the woods or we fight them. No other choice," said Gereon as Callixtus swore loudly.

"We can't detour… We need to get to Lunt as soon as possible. We'll have to fight, but the lads won't complain about getting a chance for revenge." Callixtus grinned as he spoke, excited at the prospect of paying the Scotti back for Cornoviorum.

"I thought you'd say that," said Gereon happily, ready himself to finally be on the offensive.

"We could draw them out to us and fight them in the open—what's the terrain like on this side of the woods?" Callixtus asked.

Before Gereon could reply, Dom interjected quickly, "I propose that we split the men into two companies; Gereon can guide one, and I will take the other. If we can sneak through the woods and attack from both sides, the fight will be over before they know it."

Callixtus blinked and looked at Dom with surprise. "Not the strategic insight I was expecting from a man only a few years into the job!"

"The lad's smarter than he looks," Gereon said with a grin, slapping Dom on the back. "I trust his judgement, Callixtus, but me and Dom will follow your lead."

Callixtus stroked his chin thoughtfully for a moment before saying, "It's a sound plan. Gallus, come over here!" He pointed at a brute of a man, who towered over everyone around him with arms the size of tree trunks.

"Gallus, there's a bunch of Scotti bastards in the woods ahead, and we're going to give them a nice little surprise. I need you to split the lads into two companies. You take half and follow Dom to the woods; I will take the others with Gereon." For a moment, Gallus looked puzzled at the idea of following the unknown young legionary from the north into battle, then he shrugged and nodded at Callixtus and strode off, shouting and shoving the column into two groups.

Only Magnus was to remain behind; he would follow with the baggage cart to the edge of the woods and wait for news. The column trotted on again, following Dom and Gereon along the road. As they came over the hill, the two leading men gestured to their groups to crouch and go cautiously as they approached the trees. The legionaries moved like fog through the woods, each man as tense as a drawn bowstring, and all were careful to make no noise. They arrived at the spot close to the clearing, and with a nod, Gereon took his group right, and Dom headed left, followed by Gallus.

Now moving like cats on the hunt, almost double to the ground, the soldiers crept ever closer to the clearing. Dom waited behind the same birch tree as last time and looked left and right to watch the men around him get into position. In front of them, the Scotti were completely unaware of the impending danger; most of them were lying down, with a handful sitting facing the fire and passing drinks around. Dom was amazed at the lack of professionalism from the tribesmen; there wasn't a single man keeping a lookout; they were clearly overconfident after their success at Cornoviorum.

To his right, he saw Gallus watching him, and his brutish features formed into an evil grin. Gripping the handle of his sword tight, Dom took a deep breath and jumped around the tree, crashing through the foliage and screaming incoherently. Not stopping to check if the men around him had followed, he was blinded by a rage building inside of him as the frustration and desperation of the days since the assault at Bowness were finally released. The clearing exploded into pandemonium, as the rest of the legionaries had indeed followed Dom, and Gereon's party had attacked only seconds later.

The first man Dom reached simply gaped at him open-mouthed as if he were seeing a ghost, and the sharp steel in Dom's hand sliced through his throat in a flash. Another of the tribesmen had reacted slightly quicker than his counterpart but had barely drawn his rusty knife before Dom punched his gladius deep into the man's stomach. He felt the blade catch, and it almost slipped from his grasp as the man fell backwards, with Dom ripping it back with savage strength.

He turned just in time to raise his shield and catch a vicious blow aimed at his head. He lunged forward with his shield, using his weight to knock his opponent off balance, and immediately stepped forward, bringing his sword up and into the barbarian's bare chest. The dying man fell to the ground with Dom's sword still quivering in his heaving breast. Taking the opportunity to look around the clearing, Dom could see the battle was already over. His plan had worked to perfection, and the Romans had swept through the camp with brutal efficiency. The last of the tribesmen were being finished off by blood-spattered legionaries without mercy.

Looking down, he could see his armour was spattered with mud and blood, his vigorous cleaning from the morning erased in the skirmish. He could now feel warm droplets of blood on his face, and after sheathing his gladius, he rubbed his cheeks vigorously. They had not lost a single man in the surprise attack, and he grinned from ear to ear as Gereon picked his way through the scattered corpses towards him.

"That's more like it, eh Dom!" Gereon said exuberantly. "Finally, the world makes sense again!"

"Too right! About bloody time, we gave a bit back," Dom said, still smiling as his chest rose and fell with excitement.

They saw Callixtus on the other side gesturing at them to join him, but his expression was not one of joy or fading battle lust, but a frown of concern. They stalked through the dead towards him and saw he was holding a centurion's helmet in its hands; its horsehair plume had been shaved in half, and a long gash ran down the side of it.

"I know this helmet, and I know the man it belongs to. Centurion Publius, stationed at Lunt. This fucker," he kicked the body crumpled at his feet to emphasise his point, "was wearing it. I've known Publius for ten years; do you see the dent just above the cheek plate there?"

Dom and Gereon leant in to see where Callixtus was pointing and saw a small indent on the metal.

"I was with him when he took that blow; he never got it repaired, as he loved to use it as a story for new recruits. He would rather die than give up this helmet. The fact that it's here amongst this lot can only mean one thing… Lunt has fallen to the Scotti."

Chapter 12

Night had fallen, bringing with it a cloudless, starry sky as Lucia and Alberic lay perched on the edge of a stone cliff, looking down into the pit below them. They had been lying there for nearly three hours without moving or speaking. Al's body was aching, and he was desperate for a drink of water but refused to show any weakness. If Lucia was prepared to lie as if she were made from stone until the time was right, then so would he.

Below them, wooden beams marked the entrance to the mine. Having been cut into the side of the trench ahead, the beams held up the tunnel leading down into the earth, and the tell-tale signs of a campfire could be seen from within, although they could make out little of what was happening. On arrival, there had been a man on the lookout, but he had since wandered inside and was yet to return.

Al was deeply worried about their plan. It had been a very brief discussion, and without knowing of any other entrance, they were unable to sneak inside and scout out the interior. It had become clear that, although Lucia knew the location, she had never been inside or spent much time in the area. Al felt more than a little foolish for having raced off to help her when it was now apparent that they were about to take a serious risk. Their plan was simply to wait until it was the middle of the night and kill the men in their sleep.

It sounded so simple, but Al knew there were a dozen different things that could go wrong. They could not know for certain that they would all be asleep or even that all four men were inside. Halfway through the grisly job, they could be interrupted by someone returning or waking up for a piss in the night. They could stumble in the dark and give their presence away, or there could now be more men inside if their numbers had increased or if they were part of a larger group to begin with.

Lucia had refused to listen to his concerns; she had simply asked him if he had any other plan. When he could not propose anything, she shut the conversation down and said she would do it herself if he wasn't willing to help. Al had relented and joined her in the long afternoon watch, stubbornly refusing to break the silence first. Another hour passed, and Al could not wait any longer without drinking something; his tongue felt swollen and rough in his mouth. He muttered to Lucia, saying that he was heading back to the stream they had crossed on their way to drink. To his surprise, she shuffled back from the edge and followed him.

It was only a short walk to the stream, and Al cupped his hands into the icy water and drank deeply, feeling reinvigorated with every mouthful. Lucia had drunk sparingly but was now staring down at her shaky reflection on the smooth surface of the stream, lit by moonlight. Al wanted to say something but found he could not form the words. Lucia finally moved away from the stream back towards the mine, and Al followed. Returning to their perch, they resumed their vigil, although there was still no sign of any movement down in the pit.

The moon had climbed high into the night sky when Lucia finally stirred and nudged Al.

"It's time. I will lead the way." She said, speaking quietly but firmly.

"Wait, are you sure you want to do this? If we make one mistake…" Al's voice trailed off as he tried one more time to make her see how risky their venture was.

"I know what will happen if we fail, but I do not fear death, Alberic. It's now or never, so make your decision." Her face was cold as she looked at him.

Al sighed and said, "All right, I'm coming. Let's go."

They stalked off and around the edge of the pit to an old ladder that was propped against the side. They climbed down it, with Lucia in the lead, taking each step slowly and with their breath held, waiting for the creak of wood to betray their approach. Their luck held, and they dropped softly into the pit without making much noise. Al put his hand gently on Lucia's shoulder and indicated that he would lead, but she shrugged it off angrily and shook her head.

They crept closer to the entrance and peered into the darkness. The bright light of the fire was blinding and made it nearly impossible to see anything in the area around it. They crouched on the threshold for a while, allowing their eyes to adjust. Finally, after blinking and rubbing his eyes furiously, Al could start to make out dim shadows lie on the ground around the fire and felt a wave of relief start to flow through him. He counted four shapes, and all were still. He touched Lucia's shoulder again, and she turned to look at him furiously.

He slowly and deliberately pointed at himself and then at two of the shapes to their right, indicating he would take them and she would handle the others. She nodded and started stalking forward, her long, sharp knife held tightly in her hand, the light from the fire flickering off the polished steel. Al held his sword close to his side and started moving towards his first target, his heart thumping painfully. He crouched over the sleeping figure and heard the man grunt suddenly in his sleep. Al almost fell over in shock but controlled himself; he felt light-headed and realised he was holding his breath.

He looked over at Lucia and saw she was stood over her first target and was looking back at him. She raised her left hand with three fingers outstretched, then slowly counted down. When her left hand tightened into a fist, she suddenly threw it down, clamped it over the man's mouth, and drew the blade swiftly across his neck. Blood spurted into the air, covering her face and arms, but she kept her hand held tight over the man's face as he struggled feebly for a few moments.

Al watched this, transfixed, but finally tore his eyes away from Lucia and looked down at his victim. He took a deep breath, clamped his hand over the man's mouth, and thrust his gladius deep into the neck. Warm blood flowed over his hands, and he felt bile rise in his throat but managed to keep the vomit down with immense effort. The man below him was also struggling feebly, but his life was quickly draining out of him. Lucia had reached her second man when the struggling figure below Al suddenly kicked a metal pot with his leg, causing it to topple over with a crash.

The sound made the remaining two men jolt awake, and upon seeing the shadowy figures in the cave amongst them, they started scrambling to their feet with a shout. Lucia was on her man in a flash; she had already closed the gap whilst Al had been killing his first target, and she sunk her knife deep into the man's side before he was fully upright. There was a thud and a gasp of pain as the man toppled over, the knife sticking deep into his side and blood pouring from the wound.

Al had jumped upright and charged at the final man with his sword held high, but his would-be victim was already moving towards him, holding an ancient-looking spear with a gnarled and twisted head. He thrust at Al, aiming for his heart, and the young Saxon had to throw himself to the side to avoid the blow, and for a moment he found himself partially standing in the firepit. With a yell, Al jumped back out, but his opponent had pressed the attack. Stars exploded in

Al's vision as he felt a searing pain on the side of his head and caught a brief glimpse of a snarling face as he fell with a thud to the floor, unconscious.

It felt as if Al was wading through water in a dream; his body felt sluggish, and he tried to move his arms and legs, but they did not seem to be responding. He felt panic rising, and then a hard slap to his cheek brought him round to full consciousness, bringing with it a wave of pain. He gasped and tried to raise his hand to his head, but felt rough fingers hold his arm and force it back down to his side.

"Be calm, Al; you need to lie still. You've taken a nasty blow to the head, and you need to rest."

The young man was puzzled; the voice sounded like Carolus, but he did not understand.

"Lucia!" Al cried as he started to try and sit up. His blurry vision was starting to clear, and he saw they were still in the tunnel, but closer to the mine entrance.

The same rough hands gripped him tightly again and forced him to lie back down.

"Enough Alberic!" Carolus commanded. "Lucia is fine, but you are not. And you need to *rest*."

Upon hearing that Lucia was okay but still very confused by the presence of Carolus, Al allowed himself to be pushed back down.

"Carolus? I don't understand. How are you here?" Al asked weakly as he looked to his right, and the friendly old face of his tutor swam into view.

"It doesn't matter right now. Just be calm and try to rest," the tutor said soothingly.

Resting back uneasily, Al felt sleep overtake him and fell into its embrace. He awoke a few hours later to find himself lying in the same spot, but his vision was clear, and the pain in his head had been reduced to a dull ache. Slowly, he drew himself up into a sitting position and looked around. Daylight was streaming into the mine through the entrance, and he could see Carolus and Lucia sitting together just outside. He struggled to his feet and started walking along the tunnel, holding the wall to keep himself steady.

"You shouldn't be up yet!" Carolus said as he jumped to his feet, watching Al approach and looking at him disapprovingly.

"I'm fine, Carolus… Honestly, I just need something to eat and drink," said Al as he dropped to the floor next to Lucia and leant his back against a wooden beam. "What happened?" Al asked the young woman.

"You were hit in the head by the blunt end of a spear; you're lucky it wasn't the other way around, or we'd be burying you." She replied without looking at him.

"I kind of gathered that, to be honest. I meant, what happened after I took the hit?" Al said.

"I killed the last man," replied Lucia simply.

"How?" asked Al, surprised.

"Does it matter?" she snapped back, looking at him for the first time. "He's dead and you're not; that's all there is to it. I checked to see if you were still alive and then dragged you up the tunnel away from the rest. Then I ran back to Carolus and brought him here."

Silence followed these words for a few moments before Al said quietly, "It seems that I owe you my life... and I was the one supposed to be helping you."

She did not reply, but nodded after a moment and turned away again.

"How long was I out for?" Al said, now turning to Carolus.

"It's been about twelve hours; it's early afternoon now. Here, eat up," he said, passing Al a chunk of roasted meat and a cup of wine.

The juice dribbled down into Al's beard as he bit into the meat; it tasted like wild boar, he thought, and it was ecstasy for the young man to finally eat something proper after days of hunger and rations.

"Where did you find this?" Al finally managed to ask, after devouring everything in front of him and downing his wine in one go.

"We found it in the mine," Carolus said with a sidelong glance at Lucia. Al felt ashamed that he had enjoyed the meal now that he knew it had come at the expense of Lucia and her family.

"I think I will be well enough to continue tomorrow," Al said finally, after an awkward silence. "Lucia, can we still count on you to show us the way to Londinium?"

She turned to look at him and nodded. Al saw that her face was no longer expressionless but was now full of sadness. Again, he felt his heart breaking as he looked at her, and a sudden urge to comfort her rose unbidden. He was uncomfortable with this thought. He had known her for less than two days, but it felt like a lifetime. Al was transfixed by her, and even in her grief and sadness, he was taken by her beauty.

"Are you OK?" He asked softly.

She shrugged and then replied, "I don't know. Since that night, there has been such a *rage* eating away at my insides, and I have been utterly consumed by my need for revenge. I couldn't eat or sleep, but now that I have taken it, I feel… empty." She looked into Al's eyes as she said this, and for a fleeting moment, he felt such a connection to this young woman, but she quickly looked away, again and the moment passed. Al knew he would spend a lot of time wondering if she had felt it too.

"I will take you to Londinium; it should only take a couple of days; after that, I'm not sure what I'll do," Lucia said, breaking yet another long silence.

"Thank you, my dear," said Carolus. "You are a gift sent from the gods. We will do everything we can to support you once we arrive in the city."

For the first time since they had met her, Lucilla gave the old Greek the faintest smile, but it was gone in a flash as she suddenly jumped to her feet, looking up in alarm. Al and Carolus followed her gaze, and Al felt his heart drop. Stood on the rim of the pit were a dozen Roman legionaries, looking down at them with weapons drawn. They had crept up the same way that Lucia and Al had, but this time it was they who were caught unawares.

"Stay where you are!" A sharp voice barked out. One of the soldiers dropped down into the pit with a thud and marched towards them. "If you have weapons, I suggest you throw them on the ground."

Having no other choice, Al and Lucia complied and drew their blades before dropping them to the ground with a clang.

Carolus stepped forward and addressed the soldier smartly. "Good afternoon! I hope this pleasant day finds you well. My name is Carolus, and I hail from the beautiful and ancient city of Athens. My companions are Prince Alberic, the rightful King of the Heruli, and Lucia, a noble woman whose home and family were recently destroyed by slaves. To whom do I have the pleasure of addressing?"

The legionary looked taken aback by the friendly and confident nature of Carolus. "Optio Drusus, Victrix Legion, first cohort. What is a Greek, a barbarian, and a Roman citizen doing hiding in a mine in the middle of nowhere?"

"Ah yes, I imagine we must present rather an odd trio!" Carolus said with a laugh. Now that he had been given the opportunity to talk, he was in his element. *This* was his battlefield. "I was hired as the tutor for Prince Alberic over a decade ago; you see, his father and the Heruli tribe have been loyal friends of Rome for many years, and we met in the fine city of Mainz. When Alberic's birth right was stolen from him in the wake of his father's death, his tribe was led in an assault upon our Roman allies, so we set out to provide support to our friends in Britannia."

Carolus had, of course, lied through his teeth as he spoke, neglecting to mention that King Alawar had hated Rome and was the driving force behind the Saxon invasion, but he spoke so confidently and eloquently that the Optio just stared at him without responding.

"It was during our travels that we came across young Lucia here, and upon hearing her recount the terrible ordeal she suffered only two days ago, we agreed to help her seek revenge against the slaves that had murdered her family. Our search led us here, but it was in vain. I'm sure that with your arrival, swift justice will be brought down upon the perpetrators."

This was clearly a lot for the Optio to take in, and he just looked at each of them in turn for a while. Eventually he said, "We captured and killed a gang of slaves this morning; perhaps it's the same ones you were seeking. But that's a hell of a story you've just told, and one I'm not sure I believe. But it's not my place to make decisions on what to do with you. You'll need to come with us to be questioned by my superior. I would much prefer if you came willingly."

Carolus smiled at him and said, "Of course, my good man! We will gladly join your company. Lead on!" Al and Lucia simply looked at each other, not daring to speak at this moment. Carolus had left out the fact that behind them were four bodies lying in pools of blood, and they knew they needed to get the legionaries away from the area. The four of them climbed back out of the pit and joined the small company of soldiers, who immediately set off on a march heading north, the afternoon sun glinting from the tips of their spears.

Chapter 13

Dom and Gereon stood together on the edge of the small camp that the legionaries had built on the other side of the woods the evening after their battle with the Scotti. It was their turn to watch, and they leant on their shields, sweeping their eyes back and forth across the horizon. The evening was clear, and they had good visibility of the fields around them; all was still and quiet as the night marched on. Dom's brief respite from the feeling of constant anxiety that had plagued him since the assault at Bowness ended with the news that Lunt had fallen.

"You're thinking too much again, son," Gereon said, having noticed the frown and prolonged silence from the young man.

"How can you be so calm, Gereon? For all we know, those men behind us are the last true Roman legionaries left on the island. How long can we survive before we're cornered by the forces arrayed against us?" Dom replied, despairing at their predicament.

"Oh, we'll last a bit longer, young Dominicus; don't you worry about that," replied Gereon airily. "I don't think we're the last either; let's think about it." He turned to look back out into the darkness.

"There were five thousand men stationed in Britannia. If every man stationed on the wall died when the Picts attacked, we'd have lost around fourteen hundred. We're already proof that some managed to get away; what's to say we're alone? We know the full cohort at Cornoviorum wasn't destroyed, so there's a good chance there are still at least two thousand men out there."

Dom pondered over Gereon's words, feeling the anxiety in his stomach start to ease slightly. "It's hard not to fall into despair. It seems like every time we have a plan, it falls apart in front of us."

Gereon patted Dom on the shoulder as he replied, "I know, lad. But we must keep going; it's all we can do. Our luck will turn around at some point; it always does. I've been speaking with Callixtus; I think we're going to head for Londinium."

"Londinium? It's been a long time since I was last there." Dom said, thinking of the crowded city, filled with vibrant colours and exotic goods from across the empire—the heart of Roman Britannia. He also recalled the stench of the place, albeit less fondly.

"Any enemy will have a job of taking that city. And once we get the word out of what's happening, the Praetor will be able to call forth the cohorts from the southern forts if they're not already aware. We'll soon be taking the fight to the bastards!" Gereon said confidently, and Dom felt his anxiety ease further.

They spent the remainder of their watch in a peaceful silence and were relieved a couple of hours before dawn. The pair headed towards the tent to which they had been assigned and fell onto the bedrolls at once, not bothering to remove their gear. Dom fell into a quick sleep and was shortly roused by young Magnus, with the light of dawn streaming through the gap in the tent flap. He followed the rest of the men out of the tent and towards the centre of the small camp.

Callixtus stood near the baggage cart, handing out strips of dried meat and skins of water. Dom and Gereon joined the cluster of men at the cart and were soon working their jaws on the tough meat.

"Right then, lads. You're all aware now that Lunt has fallen, as far as we can tell. We could continue in that direction, but the likelihood of finding ourselves standing outside a fort filled with Scotti bastards is high. I propose we head towards Londinium and regroup there. I'm not in charge, though, so I'll listen to any other ideas." Callixtus looked around at the men gathered as he spoke.

Nobody raised any complaints, and Callixtus nodded with satisfaction. "It's a plan. Pack up then, and we'll be on our way in thirty minutes."

The Roman legionaries broke camp with the efficiency they were famed for, and before long, the tent canvases and poles were neatly packed into the baggage cart, and they stood neatly in shining ranks, ready to move out. Dom and Gereon found themselves in the front rank this time, with Callixtus and Gallus. The *de facto* leader of the company raised his hand, and the column started forward. Magnus was again at the rear, leading the ancient donkey by the reins.

The skies were blue and clear once again, and the ground had mostly dried after the downpour a couple of days earlier. The soldiers made good ground and kept a steady pace as they followed the road southeast. At midday, they paused and allowed Magnus to catch up, using the time to catch their breath.

"I think we need to send out scouts again," said Callixtus to his companions at the head of the column.

"I agree," said Dom at once. "And I'm happy to go once more."

Gereon grunted in agreement, and Callixtus nodded. "Very well. Gallus—you take Felix and keep south of the road. Dom, Gereon—you keep to the north. There's a lot more open country between here and Londinium, so you'll need to keep low. If all is clear, raise your sword high—we should be able to see it, and we'll get moving."

A young, short man came jogging up at Gallus' call and joined him as he took off across the fields, keeping the road on his left. Dom and Gereon set off at a trot, keeping the road on their right. Ahead of them, the land was mostly flat. They could see groves of trees dotted around and the odd building standing amidst well-kept pasturelands. They noticed the absence of cattle, and Dom felt uneasy. They had left their enemies behind them, with no sign yet of the Picts moving south or the Scotti moving east. These fields should still be active and full of life, with their farmers having no reason to not have their herds out to graze.

They paused after an hour or so and looked back in the direction from which they had come. The columns were visible in the open country, sunlight glittering from their polished armour. Gereon raised his sword and held it high in the air. After a few moments, when they saw the dark mass in the distance start to move forward, Dom and Gereon turned and continued across the fields. They could see Gallus and Felix to their right, keeping pace with them, their dark shapes popping in and out of view as they moved through the long grass.

"I don't like this, Gereon." Dom said quietly, looking at the low farmhouse to their left as they jogged alongside a sturdy wooden fence.

"It's a bit strange, isn't it, lad?" Gereon replied, casting his eyes over the deserted farm. "Maybe they're just a bunch of lazy bastards, sleeping the day away. Either way, we're in a rush. We can just add it to the list of things to report on once we arrive in Londinium."

The day was nearing its end when the two men wearily climbed to the top of a steep hill, which stood alone on the rolling plains. From its vantage point, they could see the land was starting to rise and fall again, and they would shortly be leaving the flat pasturelands behind. The hill would provide them with a solid, defensible position for the evening, and Gereon turned, raising his sword high once more.

"Make your way back to the column, Dom; your legs are younger than mine," said Gereon. "Bring them here; we'll be able to set up camp on this hill."

Dom set off again at a trot, cutting diagonally across the fields to the stone road, and quickly closed the gap with the marching soldiers.

"We've found a good spot to camp, Callixtus—just on the hill there. It looks like we're about to head into the hills northwest of Londinium; best to do that during the day tomorrow." Said Dom, panting slightly as he spoke.

Callixtus nodded and sent the man next to him to go and catch up with Gallus and bring him to the hill. Dom took the man's place in the front rank, and the company continued down the road for another mile before turning off the track and climbing up the hill. As quickly as they had dismantled the camp in the morning, they rebuilt it on the top of the hill. Hammering long torches into the ground, the first of those on watch took their places in a ring around the tents.

The night passed without incident, and as Dom and Gereon were allowed to skip a night watch after scouting during the day, they awoke feeling refreshed as they joined Callixtus on the edge of the camp as he stood looking southwards.

"Morning, gentlemen," he said as they approached. "Sleep well?"

"We did, thanks. Me and the lad are ready to scout ahead again, and I think it's best for you to hold here until we know the path ahead is clear." Gereon said as he patted the tall legionary on the shoulder.

Callixtus nodded. "I will send out Gallus and Felix again too if they're up for it. We will leave it until one hour after midday; if you haven't returned, we will set off in battle formation and hope for the best."

Dom and Gereon set off a few minutes later, chewing the dried meat that was their breakfast ration, which they were fast becoming tired of. It did not take long for them to reach the hills ahead of them, and they were soon moving between steep valleys with slopes rising either side. The hills appeared deserted, but Dom was reminded of their trip through the wild land in the north and the eyes that had followed them there. He kept glancing up the slopes to either side and every now and then the two men would climb up and see if they could spot anything.

They had been moving for three hours and were preparing to return to the camp to report that all was quiet when Gereon suddenly dropped into a low crouch and dragged Dom down beside him.

"Wait," Gereon hissed, still gripping Dom's arm. "Can you hear that?"

Dom listened for a couple of heartbeats, and then he heard the unmistakable sound of men marching. He nodded towards the slope on their right and started to climb it whilst still crouching, with Gereon following behind. As they rose to the top, they could see the glint of spearpoints moving through a deep valley to the south. Dom felt his gut wrench with anxiety and gritted his teeth. He dropped to his front and began to crawl along the top of the ridge to get a closer look, with Gereon at his side.

"Looks like Roman pila; they must be legionaries!" Gereon said, with relief in his voice. He led the way now, moving along the top of the slope to where they would be able to look down on the men holding the spears. As they got closer and the view of the Roman soldiers came into view, they immediately heard a warning shout as they were also spotted. They saw the legionaries relax an instant later as they recognised the two figures above them as fellow soldiers, and Dom and Gereon jogged down the slope towards them.

"Good Morning! Gereon and Dominicus of Victrix, third cohort approaching!" The old veteran said cheerfully. Dom did a quick head count and saw the company of men numbered around twenty. The legionary closest to them stepped forward to greet them.

"Hello there, Gereon!" He called but with less cheer in his voice. He was a short man with curly blond hair. "I'm Publius, Victrix ninth. I'm glad to see friendly faces. What brings you here?"

"It's a long story, Publius, but me and the lad are with a larger company that's making its way to Londinium. The short version is that the Picts have come south, and the Scotti have crossed from Hibernia." Gereon said, after gripping the forearm of Publius in the legionary's handshake.

Dom saw the men in front of him stir at these words, and he saw glances of worry being exchanged amongst them. Publius grimaced as he replied, "Fucking hell… That's the last thing we need! Picts and Scotti on top of everything else!" Publius exclaimed, raising a hand to his forehead as he started to pace back and forth.

"What do you mean, everything else?" Dom asked, unable to hide the anxiety from his voice.

Publius stopped pacing and turned to face them. "It's another long story, but in short, an army of barbarians has invaded from Gaul, taking the forts at Dubris and Rutupiae."

Dom's heart fell into his stomach, and he felt as if an icy grip had closed in on his chest. This was surely the end of Roman Britannia.

Gereon, however, just swore loudly before replying, "Out of the frying pan and into the fucking fire! What are you lads doing heading north if the fight is to the south?"

"Praetor Vitellianus sent out most of the men stationed at Londinium to engage with the Saxons as they pillaged the smaller settlements southwest of the city," Publius explained. "Not three days had passed since they were dispatched when a barbarian army arrived on the horizon and besieged the city. We tried to hold it, but we were stretched too thin. We abandoned the city when the Praetor fell."

Dom's head was spinning. They were hearing of an entirely different force rampaging across the province that had not only sacked two of the main forts on the south coast but was also in control of the largest city on the island. For once, Gereon was also speechless.

"Around fifty of us managed to get out," continued Publius. "We've set up a base camp of sorts just on the other side of the hills, in an old villa. It's got solid walls and space enough for a few hundred men; we're sending out patrols to find who we can and send them there."

"Well, that's something at least," replied Gereon, finally finding his voice again. "There's around fifty of us as well; it sounds like we need to make our way to this villa of yours."

Publius visibly cheered up at this. "Fifty! That's excellent news. With whom we've managed to find so far, it will bring our number up to two hundred. Don't suppose you've got any officers in that company of yours?"

"We don't, unfortunately; it seems we're in short supply of those at the moment," replied Gereon with a humourless laugh.

Dom and Gereon led the small company of men back through the hills and towards the camp where Callixtus was still holding. Dom felt numb and remained silent as they trotted up and down the slopes. He let Gereon and Publius speak with Callixtus once they arrived, standing to one side as his thoughts whirled through his mind. After a quick conversation, Dom caught a glimpse of the grim expression on Callixtus' face as he signalled to his men to move forward, and the column of now eighty men set off once more, following Publius.

Gallus and Felix joined the company a short while down the road; they had nothing to report, and they too were dismayed at the news from Londinium as they caught up with Callixtus. Although it was a fine, clear day, the men from Cornoviorum were in a grim mood as they marched and continued in silence. Their journey took the rest of the day, and dusk was settling across the land as they finally emerged from the hills. They could see a dark smudge on the horizon, the fires of Londinium sending smoke high into the sky.

Publius now led the column directly south, following the line of hills to his right. Before long, they arrived at the gates of an old villa with solid white walls ringing the property. The wall was only ten feet tall, and they could clearly see the faces of the soldiers standing guard atop it. As they filed into the courtyard, they were greeted by cheers from the men emerging from the main building, who were overjoyed to see their numbers bolstered by the new arrivals.

Callixtus set his men to erecting tents along the wall to his left after Publius advised there was little room left in the old villa. Dom followed Gereon and Callixtus as they in turn joined Publius, entering the building through its handsome wooden doors. They walked through the small entrance room into an enclosed garden, with doors leading off deeper into the main complex. Inside the garden, a large fire was blazing away happily, and the rich smells of cooking meat met their nostrils.

Publius was handed an amphora of wine and quickly filled four cups, handing one to each of his companions.

"To the Emperor, gentlemen," he said whilst raising his own cup to his lips. Dom drained his cup in one go and immediately reached for the amphora and refilled it to the brim. He sat on a stone bench alongside Gereon, and the other two sat on the bench opposite. Gereon and Callixtus began to tell their stories to Publius, and their conversation lasted long into the night. Dom said little, only grunting in agreement when Gereon asked him to confirm a point in the story, and continued to drink cup after cup of the strong wine, hoping for relief in the oncoming oblivion.

Chapter 14

Alberic and Lucia sat alone, a short distance from the group of Roman soldiers. They were camped by the side of a very wide river, which wound its way eastward towards the sea. Carolus was sitting amongst the legionaries, talking to the Optio, whom he had struck up a rapport with during the day's march. It was the second night since they had left the old mine, and they had moved cautiously through the countryside northward.

Al had not spoken with the Optio or the soldiers much, but from the quiet conversations he had shared with Lucia, he knew they were not heading directly for Londinium. Although they had walked together during the march and had spent both evenings sitting away from the rest, they had spoken little. Al had tried a few times to strike up a conversation, but the young woman had responded bluntly or not at all. Instead, he spent his time thinking about the events of the past two weeks and what his future would hold for him if he ever returned to his people. Or if he even wanted to.

Carolus had stood up and removed himself from his spot by the fire and was walking over to where Lucia and Al were sitting.

"Well, you were right, my dear," he said to Lucia as he lowered himself to the ground. "We're not heading for Londinium."

"We're not heading to Londinium? Where are they taking us then?" Al asked.

"I'm not sure. From what I gather, there are several legionaries holed up somewhere near the city, and our gracious hosts are from the same group." She replied to Carolus with a stifled yawn.

"Holed up? I don't understand," Al asked. "Why are they not stationed in Londinium?"

"Londinium has fallen; Al. Broga has moved quickly it seems," Carolus said darkly.

Lucia looked up at this, her eyes wide. "Your people have taken Londinium."

"They're not *my* people anymore," said Al irritably. "What does this mean for us, then?"

"I'm not sure," Carolus said with a frown. "But I think we're even more valuable to them now, with the information we can offer on Broga's forces. At least that is what I've been making the Optio believe."

"And does he believe it?" Asked Al.

"I think so. He doesn't think we're spies, but whether he can convince his comrades of that once we arrive will be another question," the old Greek answered as he raised a water skin to his lips.

They lapsed into silence, and Al stared out into the darkness. Broga had moved much quicker than he had anticipated, and the loss of Londinium as an escape route from the island felt like a punch to the stomach. He was trapped, left with no other options than to seek protection from the Roman soldiers he had been prepared to kill only two weeks earlier. If the Romans continued to lose, Al would fall with them. He had no choice now but to offer what help he could to the legion defending the island and work against his father's dream of a Saxon Britannia.

"And what does this mean for you and your plans, my dear?" Carolus asked Lucia, breaking the peace.

She looked up, startled. "What do you mean?"

"Well… With Londinium no longer an option, do you have any family or friends you could turn to? I'm not sure a Roman legionary camp will be a suitable place for a young lady," Carolus said kindly.

"I have no one," replied Lucia coldly. "And where would you say the right place for a 'young lady' would be, in a country overrun by barbarians?"

"Do we seem like barbarians to you?" Al asked her quietly.

Her face dropped for a second, but it hardened once again. "You helped me, and I am grateful for it. But we are not the same, Prince Alberic," she replied coldly.

Carolus, having spent much of his life in the heart of Rome, was aware of the deep prejudice that ran through their society regarding the tribes living beyond their borders. "Now is not the time to discuss the differences between us; we need to focus on what we will do together to make our way through the difficult times ahead."

Alberic and Lucia were still glaring at each other, but after a moment, Al sighed and looked away. "You can think what you like, Lucia."

Her face softened a second time, and for once it didn't return to the familiar hard mask she wore, but she didn't say anymore.

"So, we'll be sticking together then, for a little longer at least," said Carolus, breaking the silence for a second time. Lucia nodded, then looked away.

The rest of the evening passed in silence as Al brooded on the news that Carolus had delivered. He was not sure how he truly felt about the success the Saxons were having and what it meant for his father's vision. He had always dreamed of being at the heart of their conquest, earning fame for his bravery on the battlefield and proving himself the heir to his father in more than name. And now it seemed as if his very survival depended on him fighting against everything his father had worked towards. Tortured by conflicting thoughts, it took a long time for Al to finally drift off into an uncomfortable sleep on the rough ground.

They were roused at dawn by the rough hands of the Optio, who handed them some hard bread to break their fast. The company set off before the sun had fully risen, following the river upstream to a nearby ford. They were soon on the other side and now heading back east and after an hour or so, they turned north. As they marched along a line of hills to their left, smoke rose from the still-burning fires of Londinium, appearing on the horizon as a dark line.

Finally, after a few more hours, travelling with no rest, Al saw the outline of an estate coming into view. As they drew closer, he could make out the shapes of men lining the walls above its wide gate. The Optio called out a greeting, and the heavy wooden doors began to swing inward. As he walked under the arch of the gate, Al felt as if he were walking into a nest of vipers where one misstep would result in his death.

There were more men in the courtyard than Al could count during his short walk towards the main building, and as he entered the interior garden, he saw it too was filled to the brim with Roman legionaries, who all glared with open hostility at him. He was suddenly very aware of his rough tunic and fur cloak and the bronze arm rings he wore. It was noticeably clear he was not a Roman, and the soldiers who stared at him knew it. As far as they were concerned, the enemy had just walked right into their midst.

Al, Carolus, and Lucia came to a halt in the centre of the garden as the soldiers who had accompanied them filed off to greet comrades. Optio Drusus stood a few yards away, beside a grimy fountain that must have looked quite grand in its heyday. He was talking quietly with a tall legionary, who had a frown on his face as he listened. Alberic looked around the garden as he waited and saw three men enter through a door to his left, making their way through the crowd towards the fountain.

The new arrivals greeted Drusus and listened to his report. One of the men who had arrived was young, Al noticed, and although his armour was that of a standard soldier, he joined in with the discussion with the older men. He could only be a few years Al's senior, but he clearly commanded a level of respect from the legionaries around him. A few tense minutes later, Drusus returned to where the outsiders were standing.

"I was hoping an officer might have arrived by the time we returned, but it looks like I'm about as senior as it gets for now," he said to Carolus with a grimace. "I'm afraid you'll need to be held as prisoners until we've discussed the situation."

"Not a problem, my friend; we will, of course, cooperate," Carolus said lightly, with a wide smile.

"Good. If you follow me, I will show you to your quarters. It won't be very comfortable, unfortunately." Drusus led them back outside to the main yard in front of the villa, then turned left and walked around the back of the building until they reached a cluster of small wooden storehouses built against the estate wall. The closest one to them was empty; the others had already been taken by soldiers, and inside they found fresh straw had been laid.

"My apologies, lady; I didn't mean you were a prisoner too," Drusus said to Lucia, who had followed them. "We will prepare one of the rooms inside the villa for you."

"I would prefer to remain here, unless that is a problem," Lucia replied.

"Here? Are you sure?" The Optio replied, confused. Lucia nodded.

"Er, yes, of course. One of the lads will bring something comfortable for you to sleep on," Drusus said, flustered.

"Some water to wash with and a bite to eat would be appreciated too, if that's ok?" Lucia asked, flashing a rare smile at the officer.

His face coloured, Drusus nodded and stammered something incoherent before closing the door behind him. There was no window inside the small hut, but a few gaps in the wooden planks allowed the last of the afternoon sun to filter through, dust dancing through the beams of light.

"Why would you choose to stay here over a nice soft bed?" Alberic asked incredulously.

Lucia shrugged as she replied, "It doesn't seem right, after what we've been through so far. I will remain with you, at least for now. Unless it's a problem?"

It was Al's turn to redden and stammer a reply that he did not have an issue with her staying with them. There was a knock at the door after a quarter of an hour, and two soldiers entered carrying a small wooden cot that they propped up against the far wall and laid bundles of soft cloth on top of it. A third legionary followed, carrying a bucket of water and a small bag with fresh bread in it. They washed as best they could and ate quickly, and afterwards Lucia and Carolus sat on the low bed, with Al sitting on the floor and leaning his back against the wall. They could see the outline of a man through the cracks in the door and knew a soldier had been stationed outside the hut to guard them.

They spoke little for the remainder of the night; Carolus was relaxed, Lucia was quiet as always, and Al was anxious as he sat thinking about what would happen next. Without an officer or a representative of the Roman government around, they were at the mercy of the soldiers, who hated them and wanted revenge for their defeat at Londinium. Al awoke in the middle of the night to find he had dozed off in his seated position. The hut was dark, and he could see little around him, but as his eyes adjusted, he could see Carolus asleep on the bed and Lucia curled up on the floor. He smiled at the young woman's kindness before lying down and quickly falling back into a deep sleep.

They were awoken by a sudden light streaming into the hut as a soldier stepped in, bringing food. He gave them a handful of apples and some more bread before placing a clay pitcher of water on the ground and leaving. They breakfasted in silence, and Al could see Carolus' good mood had continued, and the old man hummed to himself as he ate. The door opened a second time a while later, with Drusus entering this time.

"I hope you slept well," he said, to Lucia in particular. "If you would all follow me, please."

He turned without another word, and Al and the others scrambled to their feet to follow. The food Al had just eaten seemed to want to make its way back out of his stomach, and he felt anxiety and panic wash over him. They followed the Optio back around the side of the building and into the villa. Instead of heading into the garden, they followed the corridor to the right of the entrance. Drusus led them into a large room, furnished with a long wooden table and an assortment of rickety chairs. Al saw the same group of men who had spoken with Drusus yesterday sitting there, including the young Roman soldier.

Alberic sat down in the seat indicated by the Optio and looked at the legionaries opposite him. The man in the centre was tall, with flaming red hair, and wearing battered armour. To his right was a stocky, well-muscled, and grizzled veteran with good-natured features. To the old soldier's right was the young man, tall and thin but powerfully built, with clever hazel eyes, who was studying him intently. Drusus took the seat to the left of the man in the centre, next to a short, blond-haired man, whom Al remembered as the man Drusus had first spoken with yesterday.

It was clear to Alberic that this group of soldiers were the *de facto* leaders of the men gathered here, in the absence of any proper officers.

"Good morning," started the legionary in the centre as he leant forward and placed his hands on the table. "My name is Callixtus; you already know Drusus; the man next to him is Publius. These two are Gereon and Dominicus, who were stationed in the north. In the absence of officers, we speak on behalf of the legion Victrix."

Al had nodded at each man in turn but was met with cold stares.

"A pleasure, gentlemen," Carolus replied with a smile. "My name is Carolus, of Athens. This is Lucia, a Roman noble woman we met on our travels, whose family has suffered terribly at the hands of rebel slaves."

The Romans looked at Lucia for a moment before their eyes flickered back to the Greek tutor.

Carolus, seemingly unperturbed by their stares, placed his hand on Al's shoulder and said, "Allow me to introduce you to Prince Alberic, the rightful King of the Heruli."

Chapter 15

The trio that sat across the table from Dom looked very strange in his eyes. The young girl was beautiful, her fine features standing out next to the old, stooped Greek. The man the Greek had introduced as a prince was tall, with long braided blonde hair, a full beard, and startling blue eyes. As Dom surveyed the young man in front of him, he felt a wave of hate surge through him as he took in the barbaric attire.

"We're in a tricky situation here, as I'm sure you can imagine," Callixtus was saying. "Every legionary in this place wants his head, and you need to convince us not to take it." He pointed at Alberic as he spoke.

"I understand your predicament, Callixtus," Carolus replied smoothly. "However, if you take the young prince's head from his shoulders, you will lose the knowledge within it."

Callixtus did not reply but scratched his chin absent-mindedly, frowning slightly.

"Drusus has told us your story, but I'm not sure how much of it I believe. I'd like to hear it again, from the top, if you don't mind," said Gereon.

"Of course," replied Carolus with a smile. "Around fifteen years ago, I found myself travelling north from Rome and working for the governor at Mainz. It was there that I first met Alberic's father."

"We don't need your life story!" Callixtus interrupted. "Why are you here if you're not a part of the horde of Saxons pillaging and burning the province?"

"I was getting to that, my good man," Carolus replied, undeterred by the angry interruption. "However, if you would like an abridged version, then I will oblige. Alberic's father, King Alawar of the Heruli tribe, was a good and loyal friend to the Roman empire."

"Enough, Carolus." It was the young prince who had interrupted the Greek this time, and Dom saw a spasm of worry flicker across the old man's face.

"My prince, please allow me to speak on your behalf," said Carolus as he looked hard at Alberic.

"I'm tired, Carolus," Alberic said. Dom thought he looked at it too; there were dark patches under the young man's eyes.

"We will tell them the truth, and they will do what they will," Alberic continued as Carolus spluttered and his calm and wise demeanour was lost. The Romans all stared at Alberic, and Drusus' eyes were narrowed at hearing he had been lied to.

"My father was indeed the King of the Heruli, but he was not a friend of Rome," the young prince said. He continued to speak quietly but looked at each of the soldiers opposite him directly in their eyes as he talked. "It was his dream, ambition, and plan to lead our people into Britannia and conquer it for the Saxons."

The legionaries did not interrupt Alberic, but their faces hardened as they listened. "He took a wound during the first assault at Dubris, which didn't heal. He was dead only a week later, during the next assault at Rutupiae."

Dom saw the young prince take a deep, steadying breath before he continued. "My father had a clear vision for the conquest of the island, and he had strict instructions for how we should treat the people who live here. He wanted to push the Roman forces out but live peacefully alongside those who dwell here."

Gereon snorted at this, and Dom shared his feeling of disbelief.

"Once my father had died, his restriction on the pillaging and plundering of the local towns and villages was lifted by the council. I objected, and my tribe didn't stand by me as my position was usurped by King Broga, who is now the *de facto* leader of the invasion. A cruel man, he cares not for the future of the Saxon people, but only for the riches and glory of conquest."

Dom caught the rise of anger in the prince's voice as he finished but felt no sympathy or pity for the man. He was the heir of the king who had invaded a peaceful island and set the fire that now ravaged across the country.

"So, let me get this straight," said Callixtus. "You're the son of the man who led an entire nation to invade a peaceful island with no reason or justification. And now that another king has kicked you out, you have come running to the enemies you hoped to defeat for safety."

"Britannia was a peaceful island before you invaded, and you did so for glory rather than necessity. What makes Rome any different from us?" Alberic replied calmly.

The legionaries all stirred, and Dom could hear the others' muttering as they also felt anger and disgust at the barbarian's words.

"What makes us different?" Dom said quietly, with barely concealed rage. "Rome brings civilisation, order, prosperity, peace. You bring fire, blood, and chaos! We are nothing alike!"

Alberic just looked back at Dom, with no reaction to the hatred flowing towards him. "Your order and peace were brought at the point of the sword, and you cannot deny it. The world does not end at your borders, and life outside of your empire is the same as life inside of it. We love and we hate; we worship our gods and pray for a good harvest. We want peace and prosperity for our children."

"How is this peace?" Publius said angrily, speaking for the first time.

The young prince now turned to look at him and asked, "Is it peace to let our people starve? Rome has long denied us passage south to richer lands able to sustain our people. You left us with little choice but to fight for a better future."

Carolus' face was deathly pale as he listened to the argument, but he didn't speak.

"I think the events of the last few weeks are evidence enough as to why the emperors have never let you cross our borders and disrupt the safe and peaceful lives of his citizens," Callixtus said with clear disgust in his voice.

"It wasn't the Saxons who murdered my family," whispered Lucia. It was as if she had faded into the walls as the men around the table argued, but she was very much present now, and every head swivelled to look at her. "It was slaves from within our *peaceful* empire."

Dom was at a loss for words momentarily, as were his comrades. The young woman looked up at them, and for the second time, Dom noted how beautiful she was, with long black hair and bright green eyes. With her high cheekbones and unblemished skin, she was a statue of Venus come to life.

"My lady, we offer our deepest condolences," Callixtus said, nodding his head gravely towards her. "And once the current crisis is over, we will bring justice to those who wronged you, I swear. But this is not the same."

"I don't need you to bring justice to those who wronged me," said Lucia, her green eyes flashing as she looked at the tall legionary. "I have already had my revenge, and it wasn't Rome who helped me, but Alberic."

There was an uneasy silence in the room, and Lucia continued, "We do not live in a perfect, safe, and peaceful empire, no matter how much we tell ourselves this. I had always been taught that those from beyond the borders were savage and barbaric, but Al didn't hesitate to help a young woman who was lost and alone in the world."

Dom saw the blonde prince turn to look at Lucia and give her a small smile, but the young woman did not return it. After every strange thing that had happened to Dom in the weeks since the Picts attacked, this was perhaps the strangest. A Roman woman of noble stock, defending a savage barbarian who was a part of an army that had invaded her homeland? It did not make any sense. Dom looked down the table and saw the other legionaries were also quiet and frowning, as confused as he was.

Carolus cleared his throat after a while, and Dom was stirred out of his thoughts.

"I don't think we will be able to solve centuries of preconceptions within these four walls," the Greek tutor said. "However, regardless of your opinion on Prince Alberic, you now share the same enemy in King Broga, and we can help you in your war efforts if you let us."

"Why would you work to betray your father's vision?" Dom asked Alberic. He still distrusted the barbarian, regardless of what he may or may not have done to support Lucia.

"My father's vision died with him," replied Alberic simply. "And I have no future with the Saxons until Broga is dead; I cannot return home, or my life will be forfeit. I do not want to see Britannia burn, which was never my father's intention, whether you believe it or not. I will do what I can to help."

Dom studied the young prince again as he spoke. He could not read the man entirely, but he seemed genuine enough, even if Dom couldn't shake the feeling of natural distrust towards a savage from beyond the border.

"If we accept your offer of help, what do you want in return?" Callixtus asked shrewdly.

"My life," said Alberic with a shrug.

Callixtus looked at each of his companions in turn. Gereon just shrugged, and Publius and Drusus looked unimpressed. When the tall legionary finally looked at Dom, he nodded back.

"What can you tell us then?" Dom asked Alberic. "How many men does Broga have? Where will they strike next?"

"Unless he lost a lot of men taking Londinium, Broga will have at least twelve thousand warriors with him. The Picts promised to bring a further eight thousand south," Alberic replied.

"Wait, the Picts? How do you know anything about those bastards?" Gereon interrupted sharply.

The young man turned his blue eyes to the old veteran now. "My father made a pact with the tribes to the north of your wall to attack at the same time to give us the best chance for success. He also sent envoys to the Scotti tribes from Hibernia, but he had no response."

"Your father sent envoys to the Scotti bastards as well, did he?" Callixtus said angrily, remembering the loss at Cornoviorum. "And how many men did they promise would join this little venture of yours?"

"I cannot give you any information on the Scotti, I'm afraid," Alberic said. "As I said, we had received no response from them before setting sail. I am assuming from your anger that they have also invaded."

They did not answer the prince's question, and Callixtus crossed his arms as he looked away, frustrated at letting his anger get the better of him.

"Well, two out of three ain't bad," said Gereon, his light-hearted nature rising to the surface. "And this pact of your father's explains why the world went to hell in a handbasket in such a short time!"

"So, the Saxons have twelve thousand, and you suspect the Picts have brought eight down south," Publius said, despair heavy in his voice. "We have no notion of how many men have invaded from Hibernia, and we've lost ha."

"Careful Publius," Dom interrupted, looking sharply down the table. With a look of horror on his face, Publius clamped his mouth shut.

"We don't need to defeat them all at once, Publius," said Dom. "We only need to hold out until spring. By now, news of the invasion must have reached the imperial palace. Reserve legions will be sent for sure."

"Holding out until spring is easier said than done, lad," said Drusus, frowning. "If we still held Londinium, it might have been possible."

"If Londinium is the key to us surviving the winter, then we'll have to take it back," Dom replied simply.

Every person in the room stared at him, and he felt a little colour rising into his cheeks. Being in a position of even dubious authority was unfamiliar to Dom, and he could feel the pressure on him.

"You're not bad with a sword, Dom, but how do you propose that two hundred men take a city from twelve thousand?" Gereon asked, amused.

"You won't need to fight twelve thousand," the young prince interrupted. "The Saxon army is made up of independent tribes, which my father spent a decade bringing together through force or diplomacy. But we have warred internally for centuries, and old hatreds still run deep. The council of kings can never agree on the right course of action."

Dom saw Alberic straighten up as he spoke and felt a pang of jealousy. Although they were a similar age, it was clear the man in front had been raised from birth to lead. He did not show the signs of discomfort that Dom felt at holding a position of authority, amongst others.

"Although plans may have changed, the families of the warriors were due to start making their passage across. The army was to remain on the south coast between Dubris and Rutupiae to protect them. I doubt most of the men would have abandoned their wives and children to arrive in a hostile country alone. Therefore, I believe it's likely the force that has taken Londinium is independent of the main army."

"It didn't feel like it when the bastards were climbing the walls," grunted Drusus.

"Did any of you manage to get a rough count of the force that assaulted Londinium, Drusus?" Callixtus asked, turning to look at him.

The Optio sat for a moment, his face screwing up as he tried to remember the details of the Saxon attack. "None of us got a proper head count... But thinking back, I'd hazard a guess at a thousand, maybe fifteen hundred?"

"Fifteen hundred?" Gereon said with a smile. "That's more like it. More and more legionaries are joining us by the hour. An all-out assault is out of the question, of course, but if we're clever about it, then who knows?"

"Well, we know more than we did," said Callixtus. "I suggest we take some time to think it over, but taking Londinium must be the priority, gentlemen. As for you," he nodded at Alberic and his companions. "I'm afraid we'll need to keep you confined to quarters for now."

Carolus began to protest, but the tall legionary raised a hand to silence him. "You have given us much to think about. If your story is true, then we indeed have the same enemy," Callixtus continued. "However, we cannot and will not run the risk of you being false. You are as likely to be spies of the enemy, sent to scout our position, as you are to be friendly."

Alberic nodded, and Dom saw the old Greek's shoulder sag as he bowed his head. There was a loud scraping of chairs, and Drusus led the odd trio back out and towards the hut that was their sleeping quarters. Callixtus, Gereon, and Publius were deep in conversation, but Dom did not join in. He leant back in his chair and looked up at the ceiling. His thoughts were racing, and he felt a flutter of excitement in his stomach as a plan started to form in his mind.

Chapter 16

In the two days since their meeting with the *de facto* Roman leaders, the mood within the small hut that served as their prison had darkened. Since Alberic had turned his plan on its head, Carolus no longer sat with a quiet confidence in his ability to win the Romans support. In fact, the old Greek tutor had barely spoken since their interrogation, and he appeared to have aged a decade in the days since. Lucia continued her preference for silence and spent most of the time sitting in the corner of the room, looking through the cracks in the walls at the grey sky above. Al did not try to force a conversation with his companions and either sat or lay in silence alongside them.

In comparison with the others, Al was calm and content. Although he was essentially in a cell, he had never felt so *free*. His youth had been spent learning how to lead, and he had been forced to follow this path that had been laid before him by his father. In the weeks since the king had died, he had been forced to hide, fleeing across a foreign country, terrified of being discovered and his identity becoming known. But now here he was—no more hiding, no more games. He was Alberic, exiled from the Saxons, and proud of his heritage. The Romans would do what they wanted with him, and he would meet his fate with his head held high. If he only lived one more day, he would be content with not hiding who he was.

He believed his father would be proud, and that thought gave him comfort in his decision to throw aside Carolus' clever charade. Al felt for his tutor and had noticed the weight of age pressing down on the old man's shoulders, but he knew he had made the right decision during the meeting with the legionaries. Al also had a strange feeling in the pit of his stomach that was unfamiliar. Lucia had defended him and his character... He tried to move his thoughts away from the young woman; she confused him more than any of Carolus' ancient Greek philosophies ever had.

Lucia still refused to leave their company for more comfortable lodgings, even after Drusus had reappeared the day before to offer once more. She would not explain why to either the legionary or to Alberic, but she simply declined the offer politely and continued her silent vigil on the straw-covered floor. Al looked up through a crack in the roof and saw the grey sky above, with heavy rain clouds crawling slowly above. The last of the autumn sun seemed to be behind them, and he knew the reputation the island had for constant rain. Their hut would certainly become less comfortable as water made its way through the gaps in the roof and walls, and he wondered if that would finally push Lucia to take the offer of a dry bed within the stone walls of the villa.

There was a knock at the door, and Al was stirred out of his thoughts, ready to tuck into whatever rations would be their evening meal. However, it was not a legionary carrying a cloth sack of bread and cured meat, but Optio Drusus, who had returned for the third time.

"I need you to follow me," Drusus said bluntly. His manner had changed from relatively friendly to cold and openly hostile, in light of the lies Carolus had spun. "We have more to discuss."

He turned on his heel without another word, and the prisoners scrambled to their feet and followed. Within a couple of minutes, they were back in the same room as before, sitting in the same seats facing the same five legionaries. Al noticed they all wore expressions of anger, and a pang of worry flickered in his stomach, finally dampening his good mood. Perhaps this was the end.

"We'll cut to the chase," said the tall legionary in the centre. Al recalled that his name was Callixtus. "Some of your bastard countrymen have captured one of our patrols, and we need you to tell us what you can before we attempt a rescue mission."

"They're not *my* countrymen anymore," Al said, but was ignored as the legionary continued as if there had been no interruption.

"We know where they are camped. We can safely assume they are planning to move their captives to Londinium tomorrow, so we must stop them tonight before they do. How many men can we expect to fight? How will their camp be laid out? What defences can we expect?" Callixtus said, speaking quickly.

Al thought for a minute before responding. Not only was he considering the questions he had been asked, but he realised this was the moment his life might change forever. It had been easy to simply say he would help the Romans fight his countrymen, but there could be childhood friends in that camp, and their blood would be on his hands. *They didn't say a word to help you, so why should you help them?* Said a voice in the back of his head. His resolve hardened, and he looked at Callixtus as he replied.

"I wouldn't expect any more than eighty men. Any larger force would attract the kind of attention the Saxons won't want right now; they will be looking to burn and pillage and be away before any response can reach them." He saw the legionaries in front of him nod at each answer with satisfaction.

"In terms of their camp, it won't be organised. They will be travelling light, so it is unlikely they carry tents, and they should be sleeping in the open. As for defences, only a few men will be placed on watch and a few will be keeping an eye on their prisoners, but with the victories they've had so far, I think it's safe to assume there will be a degree of complacency driven by overconfidence."

Gereon, the old veteran, smacked his fist onto the top of the table. "Told you, Callixtus, they're still the same untrained and undisciplined barbarians as before! We'll catch them off guard and be back with the lads before breakfast."

"Those untrained barbarians have had you on the run for three weeks," Al said quietly, and he heard Carolus groan beside him.

"Listen here, you," Gereon started to say whilst pointing his finger at the young man.

"He's right, Gereon," the youngest Roman said. "We need to plan this carefully."

The old veteran looked at the young man called Dominicus in surprise, then simply grunted and let his hand fall.

"I would like to come with you," Alberic said quietly.

Carolus began spluttering next to him, and the legionaries across the table were shaking their heads and crossing their arms.

"Absolutely not; you're a liar and a savage. And if I'm being frank, I don't trust you as far as I could throw you," Drusus said angrily.

Al ignored the Optio and instead looked directly at Dominicus, the young soldier who seemed to command the respect of his more experienced comrades. "If the Saxons have prepared in a different way than I expected, I won't be much use to you locked up here. How else can I prove that I am no longer a part of my tribe and that we now share the same enemy?"

The young soldier looked at him for a long moment, and Al could see the quick intelligence in the dark eyes that studied him. "I say we bring him along," Dominicus said after a while.

Al nodded at him, but Dominicus spoke again, and his voice was cold as steel. "If there is any sign or hint of betrayal, or you try to alert the enemy to our presence, Gereon will cut off your fucking balls and feed them to the dogs."

The old veteran grinned menacingly at Al as he said, "You've got me hoping he does betray us now, lad; the dogs do love the taste of barbarian bollocks."

Alberic simply shrugged at the threat. "If I alerted the Saxons to your attack and managed to escape your blades, I'd simply be cut down by my countrymen once they realised who I am. I'm on your side, whether you like it or not."

"Drusus, I propose you and Publius remain here whilst me, Gereon, and Dom launch the rescue mission. We'll take my lads and a few of your best if you can get them ready in the yard," Callixtus said. "As the only Optio here, and in the absence of any officers, you are technically in charge, so your word is final."

Optio Drusus shifted uncomfortably in his chair as he replied, "Bloody hell, Callixtus, don't put it on me. I know how to train green recruits into legionaries, but that wooden switch I carry doesn't make me any more of an officer than you. It sounds like a good plan, but I'd rather be out there taking the fight to the Saxon bastards."

"OK, I'll remain behind with Publius then, and you can join Gereon and Dom," Callixtus replied whilst scratching his chin. "I'll send young Magnus along with Gereon; it's about time the lad bloodied his sword."

Gereon nodded, and there was a loud scraping of chairs as the group stood up, with Publius getting ready to lead Lucia and Carolus back to their hut.

"Are you sure about this, Al?" Carolus asked with a look of concern on his weathered face. "Providing information on the Saxons is one thing, but fighting against them…"

"I am sure, Carolus, we have no choice now but to throw our lot in with the Romans," Al replied, trying to ignore the doubt settling in his stomach.

"Well… Good luck, my prince; make your father proud, and you be sure to make it back," the old Greek said with a watery smile and tears filling up in his eyes. Al nodded at him but felt his throat tighten and found he could not muster a response. He realised at that moment he loved the old man like a father, and the emotion threatened to overwhelm him.

"I wish you good fortune, Prince Alberic," Lucia said formally, and a flicker of concern washed over her fine features before it was lost. "Watch out for spears," she added with a small smile.

Al felt his chest swell and he suddenly had the urge to embrace her, but the moment passed, and he just grinned back. "I'll keep two eyes out without you there to watch my back. Don't worry, Carolus; today is not the day I die."

He watched his companions follow Publius out of the room, followed by Callixtus and Drusus, whose loud shouts could be heard echoing through the building as they started to marshal the rescue party in the yard. Al realised he was left alone with the two legionaries from Hadrian's Wall and turned to look at them. The veteran was running his hands over his armour, testing the straps with deft, experienced hands. Dominicus was still watching Al closely, his arms crossed over his chest.

"Why do you want to come with us? These could be friends with whom you'll be fighting. Do you think you'll be able to kill the people you lived with only a few weeks ago?" Dominicus asked, his eyes boring into Alberic's.

"Those *friends* watched and did nothing as Broga exiled me and threw my father's plans into the dirt. Any ties I had to those Saxons are now dead. It's kill or be killed," Al replied firmly.

Dominicus hesitated for a moment, then nodded at him and did not say anymore.

"I'll need a weapon," Al asked.

Gereon snorted as he replied, "That's going to go down well with the lads, a Saxon prince strutting about with a sword."

Dominicus, however, strode to the other side of the room, where Al noticed his stolen gladius lay against the wall, the dried blood of the slave he had killed still on it. The young legionary handed it to Al, and Gereon sighed before making his way out of the room. "I'll go and warn the lads, so our young princeling here isn't slaughtered the moment he steps outside."

It was now only Dominicus and Alberic in the room. "Thank you. For allowing me to fight and for giving me back my sword," Al said awkwardly.

"Don't thank me yet. And don't think it means that I trust you," Dominicus replied gruffly. "Come on, we'd best get out to the yard; we'll be setting off soon."

"Where are the Saxons camped?" Al asked as he fell into step alongside the young legionary.

"Near the Thames. About 3 hours march south." Dominicus replied shortly.

As the two men entered the courtyard in front of the old villa, Al could see a column of Roman soldiers lined up and ready to march. He quickly counted seventy men, stood perfectly still in fourteen ranks of five. The light from the torches on the walls glinted from their polished armour, and Al thought for the first time that this was the Rome about which he had heard. The finest fighting force in the world, these were the men who had conquered all before them and carved out an empire from Britannia to Egypt. He was amazed at how the Saxons had achieved such victories against these men of iron and steel. The element of surprise was lost now, however, and the Saxons would have to meet the might of Rome sword-to-sword in the field.

Al joined Dominicus, Gereon, and Publius at the head of the column, alongside a towering brute who glared at him as he joined.

"Did they teach you to march in those uncivilised lands you call home?" Gereon asked.

Al ignored the insult and said, "Yes, I know how to march."

"We'll see," the old veteran said. "Double time, lads!"

With a surge, the column started moving forward, and Al struggled for an instant to match the stride of the men alongside him. He could hear curses from behind as the legionaries struggled to find their rhythm because of him. After a few seconds though, he settled into the legionary's trot, and the column smoothed out. Again, Al felt amazed by the soldier's surrounding him. He had believed he was physically fit but now realised his stamina was nothing to the men around him. By the end of the march, Al would be exhausted if they kept at this pace, and he was not even wearing any armour. The Romans, however, would be ready to fight a pitched battle by the time they arrived, hardened by years of rigorous training.

The evening drew on, and the land was dark. The column continued to move south at pace, keeping the line of hills to their right. Al's breathing was heavy, and he could feel a tightness in his chest, but he refused to let the legionaries see his weakness. He stiffened his resolve and carried on, praying they would reach their destination soon. As he marched along, he felt a pang of sorrow for his countrymen, sleeping unaware somewhere in the darkness ahead. They had no idea what was about to be unleashed upon them.

Chapter 17

The grassland around the soldiers lay flat and open, but the heavy cloud cover of the day persisted into the night, resulting in a sky void of all stars and moonlight. They could not have picked a better night, thought Dom. Around a mile in front of them, on the crest of a small hill, they could see a dozen torches in a circle, a handful of figures illuminated by the light. The Roman soldiers had reached the area an hour ago, and after a brief discussion on the plan led by Dom, they continued to crawl through the tall grass on their stomachs, inching ever closer to the unsuspecting enemy.

The legionaries had moved at a snail's pace, ensuring their armour did not clink as they crawled and alerted the enemy. His plan of attack was, in the end, a simple one. It appeared Alberic's information had been sound; the Saxons had placed no more than four men on guard, and the rest were either asleep or drinking themselves into a stupor at the centre of the camp. All the Romans had to do was approach silently, towards the dark spaces in between the torches. Dom and Gereon would take down one sentry, and Drusus and one of his men would take down another, thus opening a gap in the line wide enough for the rest of the legionaries to gather before launching their attack.

Dom grinned to himself as he started forward again, following a brief pause to make sure the advancing Romans remained undetected. Either the barbarians were as overconfident as Alberic assumed, or they were as undisciplined as Gereon believed. Either way, the lack of any alert sentries would make the legionaries job much easier. He thought to himself how a Roman camp in hostile territory would have been neatly organised, with tents in rows and small trenches dug around the perimeter; usually, two guards were posted every ten metres and replaced often. *And that young prince wants us to believe they are no different,* Dom thought to himself. Here was the proof of how different they truly were.

The column had come within two hundred yards of the nearest guards now, and the four men handpicked to take down the sentries started forward on their own. Dom watched as Drusus and his companion prowled towards the shadowy figure on the right, prompting him to move towards the sentry on the left. Now that he was close enough to see the enemy standing by the torch clearly, he almost laughed aloud. The man was practically *asleep*. He was leaning heavily on a tall wooden spear, his head drooping onto his chest. Dom suddenly had a vivid recollection of his first week at the fort in the faraway north. A sentry had been found asleep on watch, and his penalty was to be beaten to death by his comrades. Sentry duty was a sacred trust, and woe to anyone who broke it.

Gereon had halted just outside of the ring of light cast by the torch, slowly bringing himself up from the ground and into a crouch, watching the figure ahead. Dom followed suit and quickly scanned the area. Their unsuspecting victim was still dozing, his eyes closed. There was no sign of anyone else nearby, and looking to his right, he could see Drusus and his comrade had circled around their target and were looking at Dom, waiting for the signal. Dom raised his hand for a moment and then dropped it.

He saw Gereon step forward at once and clamp his hand over the guard's mouth as he slid his gladius in between the man's ribs. The sentry's eyes jumped open for a second before they lost focus, and Gereon gently lowered the lifeless body to the floor. Dom looked over to his right and saw Drusus kneeling over a corpse, and he nodded at him. The four men stood still for a few seconds, their ears strained to catch any sign of movement from the dark shapes huddled on the floor around a large fire. A few heartbeats later, Drusus and Gereon started to signal for the rest of the men to move up.

Dom's heart was in his mouth as the sound of armour softly clinking rang through the night, with the legionaries now moving quickly to close the gap to the camp. He saw the young prince Alberic at the front of the men joining him, but his mouth was clamped shut and his face looked resolute. The legionaries were now gathered between the two torches, and the camp was still quiet, the only sounds being those of soft snores and the crackle of the fire. Dom raised his gladius high and swept it down in the direction of the enemy.

The legionaries did not charge in with a cry but swept towards the Saxons like vengeful spirits in the night. They were amongst them in seconds, and the slaughter began. Dom thrust his gladius down into the first dark mass he came across and was met with a soft gurgle and a groan as the man below him died almost instantly. He stepped over the body and thrust his sword into the next man, and the next. He was moving to his fourth when the cry finally went up.

There was an almighty commotion as the Saxons on the far side of the camp roused themselves, jumping to their feet and grabbing weapons.

Dom saw the remaining sentries from the edges of the camp, and those who had been standing watching over a group of huddled shapes came charging over whilst brandishing weapons and screaming incoherently. He leapt forward to meet them, catching a vicious spear thrust with his shield. He felt the weight of the spear and knew it must have gotten stuck in the wood. Thrusting his shield to the ground, he advanced on his now unarmed opponent and swept his sword up and into the man's stomach, spilling his guts as he ripped it back out. The barbarian fell to the ground, screaming, trying to hold his insides as they spilled out over his fingers.

The world was suddenly flipped upside down, and Dom felt the air forced out of him as he landed flat on his back with a crash. His legs had been swept from under him, and he saw a huge man wrapped in thick fur standing overhead with a giant double-bladed axe. With a roar, the man swept the axe up and brought it down towards Dom. Rolling to his side at the last moment, he felt the heavy axe collide with his shoulder, but it did not punch through the metal plate of Dom's armour. His shoulder throbbed painfully as he scrambled to his feet and turned to face the barbarian.

The Saxon, however, was just standing there looking stupid, his mouth open and revealing rotting, brown teeth. Slowly, like a great tree being felled, the huge man fell backward with a crash. Alberic stood just behind where the figure lay, his gladius wet with blood. He was panting, and his blue eyes were bright with battle lust as his gaze settled on Dom. They stared at each other for a second, and for a wild moment, Dom thought the young prince was going to attack him, before Alberic turned and disappeared into the gloom, looking for another opponent.

Dom felt his left shoulder gingerly with his right hand, testing the armour and moving his arm in wide circles. It ached terribly, but it was only bruised. Looking around him, he saw the fight was already over. Drusus and a handful of his group were busy cutting away the bonds of the captured patrol, whilst Gereon and the Cornoviorum cohort were stripping the dead Saxons of anything of value. Dom could see a handful of legionaries lying amongst the dead, tears coming unbidden as his eyes found young Magnus.

The boy lay as if asleep, a peaceful look on his face. A dagger protruded from his chest. Dom knelt by the body and gently closed his eyes.

"Poor kid…" Gereon had found Dom still kneeling by Magnus. "He was a good lad; he would have grown into a fine soldier."

Dom looked up at the sound of approaching feet, and his rage threatened to explode out of him at the sight of the young Saxon prince. Jumping to his feet, he advanced on Alberic but found his arm being held by Gereon.

"It wasn't him who killed Magnus," the old veteran said quietly.

"He's as good as responsible!" Dom spat furiously, tearing his arm out of Gereon's grip and pointing first at Alberic, then at the boy's body behind him. "Look! This is what your father's grand plan has led to! His blood is on your hands."

He saw the young prince's eyes move towards where he pointed, and sadness filled the Saxon's face. The battle frenzy from earlier was long gone.

"It's the way of war, Dom; you know this. How many Saxon boys died tonight or will die tomorrow? It's a damn shame, but the man who killed Magnus is dead, and we move on," Gereon said gruffly.

"It might be the way of war, Gereon," Dom replied angrily, "But it's a war that didn't need to happen!"

"And what of the wars that Rome has started? Of the countless young boys cut down in the name of your emperors?" Al said, anger in his voice.

Dom glared at the Saxon standing before him, fury coursing through his veins as he struggled to free himself from Gereon's grip. The anger that had flashed across Alberic's features had passed as suddenly as it had appeared, and the young man looked truly saddened as his eyes fell on the small body lying at Dom's feet.

"I'm sorry about Magnus," Al said quietly, after a pause. "I don't think there's any point in discussing whether this war did or did not need to happen. But I promise you, I will help end it. Too many boys will lie dead upon the fields from both sides before it's over."

Dom snorted and, turning on his heel, marched away from Alberic as he wrenched his arm from Gereon's grip at last. He could still feel fury running through his body, and the ache in his shoulder was forgotten completely. He clenched his fists, and even though he had just fought a battle, he desired nothing more than to hit something. In his blind haste, he stumbled over a crumpled figure almost hidden on the dark ground.

He looked down to see what he had tripped over and saw the face of a boy, younger even than Magnus. Wrapped in the thick furs of the Saxon people, he could have been mistaken for a man from a distance, but the youthful face told the truth. The anger ebbed away as Dom stood looking at the young boy's face. *What a terrible waste of life,* he thought to himself. Alberic was right; fate would be cruel to both sides, and many a young life would be cut short, long before their time.

The sun was creeping over the horizon, battling through the heavy clouds to supply a dim light for the morning. The death toll for the Romans stood at twelve, and they counted seventy-two dead Saxons. They piled up the barbarian corpses and left them for the crows and wild dogs. The dead legionaries were placed on makeshift stretchers, built with spears and cloaks taken from their enemies. The rescued patrol stood ready to carry their fallen comrades and honour them for their sacrifice. Alberic did not protest the treatment of his fallen countrymen but stared sadly at the unceremonious pile of bodies that were already attracting flies.

The Roman column set off northwards, back the way they had come, and towards the villa. They moved slowly, a few having snatched quick moments of rest after the battle, but most had been unable to. They were exhausted and walked in silence, dreaming of a hot meal and a soft bed back at camp. Dom dropped back through the ranks to the rear of the column, where he found Alberic marching alone, a few paces behind. The young Saxon looked up as he approached and began to speak.

Dom held up his hand, however, and cut him off. "I just came to say thank you. I wouldn't say you saved my life, but I appreciate you taking down that big bastard."

The young Saxon's wary expression changed to a look of surprise before he said, "Look, about that young boy, Magnus." Alberic started before being cut off a second time by Dom.

"There's no point. Gereon was right; it's the way of war. I don't think I'll ever understand the reasons why your people came here, but it is what it is. You've proven yourself to be on our side, and that's enough for now."

"Thank you, Dominicus. The realities of war are often ignored in the schemes of the powerful, and now I have seen firsthand the result of the invasion... My father's vision has become increasingly blurred for me. I know why he believed we had to come here but at this cost? In this fashion?" Alberic's fine features were marred by doubts and anxiety as he spoke, and for the first time, Dom felt pity for the young man. He was as lost as any of them, his father was dead, and his people had abandoned him. Whoever the man had been before the invasion, he was certainly someone different now.

"Gereon would say you're thinking too much," Dom told Alberic, smiling as he spoke.

"It's not the first time I've been accused of that," Alberic replied, returning the smile.

The two men continued their march at the rear of the column in a comfortable silence. The day drew on, although it was difficult to tell with a little hint of the sun through the dark clouds above. A fine rain was falling as the column finally approached the villa, the estate standing out in the empty countryside around it. The aftereffects of the battle and a lack of sleep conspired to make his body ache, and the grief he felt for the loss of young Magnus gnawed at him as he marched. Despite this, Dom felt his mood lightening as he thought about the importance of their rescue mission. Not only had they saved valuable Roman lives, but they had also struck their first blow against the Saxon invaders. Dom vowed to himself that it would not be the last.

Chapter 18

Alberic felt as if his tired legs could go no further, and in his mind, he thought of the straw-covered floor of the cold prison hut as if it were a soft feather bed. He was shocked out of his dreary daydreaming by a cheer from the men at the head of the column. He felt the young legionary beside him start to speed up, and he kept pace with Dominicus as they trotted up the line. The villa was straight ahead of them, but the land immediately around the walls was no longer empty. Dozens of tents had been erected in the shadows beside the estate.

The size of the Roman force had grown considerably in the hours since they left, and the tired soldiers from the rescue party cheered at the turn in their fortunes. The legionaries going in and out of the tents grinned back at them, cheering their safe return just as loudly. The column entered through the gates and found the yard bustling with activity and noise. More cheers erupted as the rescued patrol greeted old friends and the tired heroes were welcomed back. Al saw Callixtus come striding out of the main building with a wide smile, and he was accompanied by someone Al did not recognise.

A well-built man wearing exceptionally fine armour with a red paludamentum over his left shoulder, his olive skin glowed in the light of the torches. His black hair was cropped short and oiled, and strength and good health seemed to exude from the man. To Al's immense surprise, he saw Carolus following behind in the wake of the newcomer. He noted with pleasure that the age and despair that had weighed down on the old tutor's shoulders appeared to have lifted, and the Greek walked lightly down the steps towards the legionaries.

"It gladdens my heart to see you return safe, my young prince," Carolus said as he pulled Al into an embrace.

"So, this is the latest prodigy of Carolus the wise, is it?" The man in the fine armour said.

"Ah yes, let me introduce you properly. Al, this is Tribune Maxentius, a former pupil of mine from my days in Rome. Maxentius, this is Prince Alberic of the Heruli tribe, who I was hired to tutor for the last decade or so." Carolus said with a broad smile.

"A decade!" Maxentius exclaimed with a mock grimace. "Three years was enough Plato and Aristotle for me!"

"Plato was not so bad... It was worth sitting through to get to Homer," Carolus replied with a grin.

"Well, who doesn't love a bit of Homer every now and then? Come, I will have wine brought to my quarters; there is much to discuss." Maxentius patted Al on the shoulder and started to make his way back towards the main building complex whilst calling out to the tall legionary who was currently mixing with the returned soldiers. "Callixtus! Join me in my quarters when you can; bring Optio Drusus and the two men from Hadrian's Wall you were telling me about, if they still live."

Al followed the Tribune into the villa, with Carolus beside him. As they walked through the corridor, Al whispered to his mentor, "Can we trust him?"

"Yes, I believe so. I knew his family well; the patriarch is an honourable man. I last saw him when he was a young boy, of course, but he seems to be of the same stock as his father," Carolus said quietly.

They had entered a wide room at the back of the building, where a large bed stood against one wall and a long wooden table occupied the other side. On top of the wooden surface, there were scattered maps and scrolls. Al took a seat beside Carolus on one side of the desk, and Maxentius sat facing them. A moment later, Callixtus entered, followed by Drusus, Gereon, and Dominicus, with the former carrying an amphora of wine. The Tribune took it from Dominicus and started to fill up half a dozen wooden cups, and topped each with water from a clay jug.

"To the Emperor!" He called, draining his cup in one long gulp. Al didn't join in on the toast but drank deeply all the same. It was a good vintage, he thought, as the sweet wine warmed his stomach.

"Take a seat, gentleman; we'll be here a while," Maxentius said as he gestured to the empty seats.

Once they were seated, the Tribune began to speak again. "Firstly, congratulations are in order. An excellent job rescuing the captured patrol," he nodded and raised his cup towards Gereon and Dominicus. "For those who don't know me, my name is Maxentius, military Tribune for the province. I was

117

stationed at the fort in Lunt before the Scotti decided they wanted it for themselves."

"Lunt!" Callixtus exclaimed, "But hasn't Lunt fallen, sir?"

"Oh yes, we had to abandon the fort, unfortunately, but it wasn't a complete disaster, if I may so myself. We managed to retreat in formation until the Scotti tribes gave up the chase and returned to their plunder. Two hundred men all told so it could have been worse." Maxentius replied.

"Now then, I have received the full breakdown of events from Callixtus upon my arrival this morning. It was a tough pill to swallow hearing about the fall of Hadrian's Wall and the deserters at Eburacum, but they will have to wait for now. Our most pressing concern, as I see it, is the Saxons." The Tribune refilled his cup as he talked and drained it again in one.

"I have also spoken at length with Carolus. I know your story, Alberic. I will admit, in different circumstances, we would not be drinking together, and you wouldn't live to see another sunset." Al felt his stomach tighten as he listened. The Tribune was still smiling, but he did not miss the threat within his words.

"However, if Carolus vouches for your character, then I will trust him. You have already proven yourself an ally with the information you have freely given and by fighting alongside us, regardless of your stance prior to the invasion. Therefore, I name you a friend to Rome, and you may come and go as you please throughout the empire, by my word, as the Emperor's executive."

Al felt light-headed as he listened to these words, relieved that the threat in the Tribune's voice had passed, and he thanked him.

"As an exiled prince, I think we can offer you more suitable accommodation," Maxentius said before he barked out an order and a legionary entered the room. "Have the lads make one of the bedrooms available for the young prince here; I believe they also have a young woman in tow, so three beds will be needed."

The legionary nodded and marched back out, the door closing with a thud behind him.

"On to our next order of business. I have received a head count from Callixtus a total of four hundred and forty-seven men, which includes those I have brought with me and those sadly lost in the rescue operation. As a result, there will need to be some reordering. You have done an admirable job so far, but the men will always need discipline and structure." Maxentius placed his cup down and started to shuffle through his papers.

"I am reordering the men into a new cohort of five centuries. And we can't have centuries without centurions, now can we?" he said with a small smile before finding the papers he was looking for and handing a scroll of parchment to each of the four legionaries. "Congratulations, gentlemen. You have proven yourself loyal and intelligent soldiers. I am promoting each of you to the rank of acting centurion, to be ratified by Rome once the crisis is over."

"It's an honour, sir. Thank you," Al heard Dominicus say as the others murmured their thanks in awed voices, turning the scrolls over in their hands.

"Well deserved, my good man. And I'll accept only the best from each of you." Maxentius replied as he set about refilling each of their cups again.

"Excuse me, sir, if I may ask a question? Have you heard any news from elsewhere in the country, sir?" Gereon asked the Tribune, and Al was surprised to hear the rough veteran speaking so formally.

Maxentius nodded before replying, "The cohorts in the southwest are intact; thank the gods. However, they have their hands full with a full-blown slave revolt that has swept the province. They have had some encounters with the Scotti tribes but are keeping them at bay for now."

"Finally, a bit of good news! Thank you, sir," Gereon replied.

"I believe there are still a lot of our men scattered throughout the province, so we will continue to send out patrols to find them—in larger numbers this time, I think," Maxentius said, with a wry smile. "But now for the real matter at hand. It is crucial that we retake Londinium; without it, we will not make it through the winter, and we need to take it as soon as possible before the main Saxon force arrives."

"Sir, if I may?" Al heard Dominicus say, and he leant forward in his chair to look sideways at the young centurion.

"Fire away, Dom," said the Tribune genially.

"If Alberic's estimation is correct, which I think we have every reason to believe it is, there is still a force of up to fifteen hundred waiting behind the walls at Londinium. Even with our bolstered ranks, they outnumber us three to one," Dominicus said, setting his own cup down on the desk. "I believe I have a way of reducing their numbers."

The Tribune raised his eyebrows and gestured at Dominicus to continue.

"Alberic has advised that the overall aim of the Saxon force now is to plunder and take everything they can get their hands on. I say we offer them a prize they won't be able to ignore and lay a trap in doing so," Dominicus said. Al thought he could hear a faint note of anxiety in the young soldier's voice as he spoke.

"I suggest we let the Saxons know that we're planning to move the legionary treasury to the south coast, to get it away from the island and keep it out of their hands. We let them know the route, and we tell them a spot that would be perfect to ambush a slow-moving baggage train. As they send out men to capture it, we ambush them instead." Al noticed a flush of colour creeping up Dom's cheeks as he talked through his idea.

"Well, I don't have a problem with the idea itself; it's not bad, actually, but how do you suppose we get this information to the Saxons without them knowing it's a trick?" Maxentius asked whilst scratching his chin.

Dom did not answer, and his cheeks reddened further.

"Merchants," Al said quietly. The men in the room all swivelled to look at him in surprise, and although he could not see it, Carolus smiled to himself as he drank the last of his wine.

"Merchants?" Gereon repeated, nonplussed. "Did you take a blow to the head, lad?" His formal tone had dropped at once; now he was not addressing an officer anymore.

"Thank you for your concern, Gereon, but no, I did not take a blow to the head. We can use merchants to relay the information to the Saxons. It's how my father gathered information from Britannia; he paid travelling caravans for news and rumours. The men in Londinium won't suspect foul play if they hear it from their usual sources," Al said confidently.

"Merchants, eh? It is not a bad idea at all, but it will take some planning. I wonder if there is anybody left on the island mad enough to still be travelling across country flogging their wares," Maxentius replied.

"Lucia might know?" Al prompted.

"Is that the young woman you arrived here with? She's a local, yes? It's worth a try. I will leave that in your capable hands for now, Alberic," the Tribune said whilst draining yet another cup of wine. The man seemed to be a bottomless pit for the strong drink.

"There's a lot to think about, but for now, I suspect the men will want to congratulate their new centurions. Dismissed." At the Tribune's command, the new officers left the room, chatting and patting each other on the back. Al had made to stand up, but Carolus placed a hand on his arm, and he sat back down.

"Maxentius, I must thank you for your generosity and support. It's more than we could have asked for," Carolus said to the Tribune.

"Don't mention it, Carolus; you're more of a family friend than a tutor," Maxentius said with a wave of his hand. "Young Alberic here seems a good sort, but please make sure you don't make me regret my decision. Have you given any thought to what you will do next?" This question was directed at Alberic.

Al took a moment to ponder before he replied. He thought about the skirmish with his own people, the blood he had spilled, and the guilt starting to build up within him. Unbidden, the face of Broga came to the front of his mind, his guilt being replaced with anger in a flash. His hand had been forced when his people had abandoned him, and he knew he would never be safe in a Saxon Brittania.

"If you will allow it, I would like to stay and help until the island is at peace again. I was part of the spark that set Britannia on fire, and I will do everything I can to put it right," Al said as he looked directly at the Tribune.

"Glad to hear it. With insights like what you supplied earlier, I believe we will need you," the Tribune stood up after he finished speaking and made his way to the door. He called out, and the same legionary from earlier rapped smartly to attention. "Is their room ready? Good, if you can escort our guests there, please."

Al and Carolus bowed to the Tribune and followed the legionary out into the corridor, making their way up a flight of stairs before reaching their new accommodation. It was certainly an upgrade from the cold hut outside, and Al saw three beds lined up, one against each wall. On the one closest to the door, he saw Lucia, who looked up as they entered, a smile flickering across her face. The legionary left them to it and backed out of the room, closing the door behind him.

"Welcome back, Alberic. How went the battle?" Lucia asked as she handed him a scrap of cloth and a bucket of water.

"Is it that obvious I'm in need of a wash?" Al said with a grin before splashing water over his face and washing the grime of the previous day away. He dried himself and sat on the bed opposite Lucia, with Carolus taking the one in the middle. The old scholar wasted no time and was soon fast asleep. Al and Lucia had one of their longest conversations yet, although it lasted barely ten minutes, as the young prince gave a detailed account of events. Lucia listened to him speak and gave him an update on events at the villa in his absence.

Once they had exchanged news, however, they broke off into an awkward silence.

"I am glad you returned safe, Al," Lucia said quietly after a few minutes. "Good night."

She had laid down and turned her back to him before he had finished replying, and he was left with the now-familiar feeling of confusion in the pit of his stomach. He found himself thinking increasingly of Lucia when he wasn't in her company, but as soon as they were in the same room, he felt as if his tongue was glued to the roof of his mouth. He did not ponder over these emotions for long, though, as the exhaustion from the battle and the subsequent march finally took their toll, and he fell into a long, deep slumber.

Chapter 19

Running his hands over the tough horsehair dyed red, Dom felt as if his heart would burst from his chest with pride. *Centurion*. He could hardly believe it; this was more than a man of his age could hope for. He felt a pang of sorrow as he wished his father had been alive to share this moment with him. He heard the trumpets blare out the rise of the sun, and he pulled his new centurion's helmet over his head, tying the strap under his chin. He strode out of the room he was sharing with Gereon and Callixtus and out into the inner garden, where the older men were already breaking their fast.

"I don't think I'll ever get used to seeing that," Gereon said with a grin. "It's a good thing Maxentius promoted me as well, because there's no way I'd be calling you *sir*."

Dom grinned back at him; the old veteran's mood was infectious. "I would have loved to give you ten lashes for insubordination, shame."

Callixtus tossed Dom a chunk of hard bread as he sat down. His jaw was aching by the time he had chewed it through, and Dom washed it down with a long drink from his canteen. Drusus had joined them whilst he was eating, and shortly after, a fifth centurion unknown to Dom arrived, sitting next to Callixtus, and pulling off his helmet.

"Morning! My name's Fabian," the newcomer said. He was a short but extremely broad man, with a wide face. Dom felt his stomach lurch as he looked at the man. Missing his left eye, with a scar that ran from his scalp to his jaw, Fabian was no pretty sight. Callixtus introduced each of them in turn to Fabian, and they shook hands with the scarred centurion.

"Busy day ahead. I've been with Maxentius this morning, rearranging the men into new centuries. Here, the names are written down for you." Fabian handed each centurion a roll of parchment. Dom glanced through the list and only recognised one name, Publius.

"Your century is mostly made of men from Lunt, Dom. They're good boys, but I'd pick your Optio carefully to keep them in check," Fabian said.

Dom nodded and stood up, feeling nervous. "Time to introduce myself, I think."

"We'll join you; let's get them formed up," Callixtus said as the five officers made their way into the yard. They hailed the trumpeter to join them, and upon command, he fired three long blasts into the air.

"Form up!" Fabian called, his voice carrying over the estate.

The legionaries came spilling out of every tent, both from behind the main villa and from within the stone building. Due to the size of the force now camped at the estate, they had the soldiers line up in the fields just outside the gates. There was a lot of jostling and shoving as the centurions moved them into their new centuries. After a hectic few minutes, silence fell, and the new cohort stood smartly to attention in five long columns, with one centurion at each head. Dom heard yet another trumpet call behind him and saw Tribune Maxentius standing above the gates.

The silence grew as Maxentius swept his gaze over the assembled troops, and after a while, he raised his voice to address them. "Legionaries! As I look upon you, I see the soldiers of Scipio, of Caesar, and of the divine Augustus! You are the men who forged the greatest empire in the world." The army in the field cheered at the Tribune's words, and Dom felt pride surge through him as he listened.

"Today is the turning point, gentlemen; today we start to take the fight to the bastards that surround us, and today we remind everyone of the might of Rome!" The Tribune raised his sword high into the air to emphasise his last point, and Dom found himself cheering as loudly as the men around him. The Tribune descended from the wall, and Dom turned back to face the men in front of him.

"For those who don't know me," he called out, happy to hear his voice strong and clear and carry out across the column. "My name is Dominicus, your new centurion. My expectations are simple: that this century will be the toughest group of bastards the legions have ever produced." The men in front of him grinned, and he knew he had struck the right chord.

"Publius!" Dom called and saw the short, blond-haired man break rank from the centre of the column and come trotting up to the front, snapping smartly to attention. "I'm appointing you, Optio; don't go easy on them." He handed

Publius the tall, hostile staff that marked his position, and the man nodded gravely as he took it.

Dom spent the remainder of the morning walking amongst his new legionaries, getting to know them as best he could, learning names and back stories. Nearly every one of them was older than him, and he felt their doubt and uncertainty about following a younger man. He would have to prove himself, he knew, but his role in the rescue mission had somewhat boosted his reputation. He picked a group of thirty men and gave them the task of heading west into the hills to round up any legionaries they could find and return before dawn the following day.

Dismissing the rest of the century, Dom and Publius made their way to the villa complex and into the large room that had been used for their interrogation of Alberic. Inside they found the other centurions and new optios, and the large table was now full of scrolls and wax tablets. In the hours that followed, Dom soon realised that there was a lot more to being a centurion than leading men in battle. Led by the experienced Fabian, the new officers set about tallying supplies, calculating wages, and solving the myriad of logistical issues that came with keeping a large body of men in the field.

His head was spinning by the time Dom left the room, and he had a dull headache behind his right eye. He took a seat in the inner garden and let the frosty night air flow over him. The breeze was pleasant after the stuffy heat of the officer's room. He heard footsteps from behind him and turned to see the young Saxon prince Alberic heading towards him.

"Congratulations, Dominicus. I hope you're enjoying your new position." Alberic said as he took a seat on a stone bench opposite Dom.

"It's not come without it's headaches, both figurative and literal," Dom replied as he pressed his knuckles into his eyes, trying to dull the pressure he felt building up behind them.

"Heavy lies the crown—or the helmet in your case. My father often said there was no greater joy than leading people and no greater trouble," Alberic replied.

"I'd say he was a wise man if he hadn't destroyed half the country," Dom said.

Alberic smiled at the response: "Even the wise make mistakes, despite their intentions. Anyway, I've come with news. Lucia believes she knows someone who would brave the trip into Londinium. And apparently, he would do anything for a few coins."

Dom looked up at once, his tiredness vanishing. "Let's call a meeting at once; Maxentius needs to hear this."

The two men quickly made their way through the complex to the Tribune's quarters, and after waiting a moment upon knocking, they were admitted into the room to find Maxentius sitting over a map at his desk. Word was sent to the other centurions and to Lucia, and Dom sat fidgeting in his chair as he waited for them to arrive.

Once all had arrived, Maxentius turned to Alberic. "So, you have good news for us?"

"I do; Lucia knows of a trader who lives nearby who is a likely candidate for our plan," Alberic said, and he turned to look at Lucia, prompting her to speak.

"He lives in a small settlement a few hours away; if you head to the Thames and follow it downriver, you will come across it. It's well defended, so it's likely the Saxons have avoided it. My father always said the man had a poor reputation and would sell his own mother for a handful of coins. His name is Bedwyr." Lucia spoke confidently and straight to the Tribune, undeterred by the room full of men.

"Excellent. Gereon, take whatever men you see fit and find this Bedwyr. Before you leave, however, we need to choose where we will lay the ambush." The Tribune stood up and placed his hands on either side of a large map of the surrounding area. "Any suggestions?"

"Here, between our position and Londinium, is a deep valley." Dom said at once as he placed a finger on the map he had memorised. "It's northeast of the city, and a road runs right through it. If we let the Saxons believe the baggage train is trying to avoid the city and is heading through this valley, they will undoubtedly head straight for it."

The other centurions stood up and clustered around the map, nodding and murmuring assent. Maxentius looked towards Alberic, and the young prince nodded.

"Excellent. It's settled, then. Gereon, take five pounds of silver from my treasury; it should be enough to keep this merchant on our side. Make sure he knows exactly what he is supposed to relay. Tell him the 'baggage train' will be making its way through the valley in three days' time. Dismissed."

Dom made his way into the outer courtyard with Gereon, patting the older man on the shoulder and wishing him good luck. He watched as a group of ten men ran out of the gates and into the darkness. Dom made a final loop of the walls, stopping by the sentries he recognised from his century and building relationships as much as he could. Retiring to his quarters, he fell into a deep, unbroken sleep without much trouble, the efforts of the day finally taking their toll.

Waking refreshed, Dom spent the following day drilling his new century, starting the morning with an eight-mile run and noting with pleasure that every man accomplished it in good time and few looked tired at the end. Splitting them into groups of ten, he had them lock shields and take turns advancing and defending. The legionaries ran through the manoeuvres with ease, and Dom felt confident in the soldiers he would be leading into battle; they would not let him down. Not that he had expected any less from the finest fighting force in the world, of course.

The rest of the day passed like the previous, with his afternoon taken up with paperwork and planning, and he was enjoying a cup of wine with his fellow officers in the evening when a young legionary knocked on the door. Upon entering, he requested they report to the Tribune, as Gereon had returned from his mission. Quickly making their way through the complex to the now-familiar Tribune's quarters, they entered to find the old veteran sitting with Maxentius, both men looking pleased. Alberic was also present again, sat away from the other two men.

"The girl's information was solid. Gereon has relayed the information to the merchant and left him on the outskirts of the city. All that's left for us to do is prepare the ambush and hope the Saxons take the bait," Maxentius said once all were seated once more.

"We won't know how many men the Saxons will send. Do you have any thoughts, Alberic?" The Tribune asked the young prince.

"For a prize that lucrative, they will send out a formidable force. I would expect no less than three hundred, perhaps more," Alberic replied.

"Three hundred..." Maxentius said, rubbing his temple absent-mindedly. "With the element of surprise, three centuries should be more than enough. Callixtus, Dominicus, and Fabian—your men will lead the attack. Drusus and Gereon will hold our position here and continue to scour the area nearby for stray legionaries." Maxentius eyes were bright as he spoke, and he barely concealed the excitement within his voice. "I will lead the ambush personally; we will break camp in the morning to ensure we find the best position possible before the enemy arrives."

"If I may, Tribune? I would like to accompany you and fight alongside Rome once more," Alberic said.

"You are more than welcome, Prince Alberic. You shall be attached to Dom's century as an auxiliary, and I expect you to follow any orders he gives," the Tribune replied.

Dom nodded at Alberic and saw the battle frenzy shining in the Saxon's face once more. He was a good fighter, and Dom was happy to have him along. The centurions filed out of the room and made their way back to their makeshift office to start preparations for the ambush. It was the middle of the night by the time they finished, with Dom handing Publius a list of final tasks to take up with the quartermaster in the morning. His fellow centurions were feeling the strain, and each man slept fully clothed, exhausted in their new roles.

It was a bleak morning that saw the three centuries lined up again in the field outside the villa. The rain that had been threatening for the previous few days was sure to break any moment, and the battle ahead would be a slog in the mud, Dom thought. He saw Alberic standing awkwardly to the side of Publius, fidgeting in the new breastplate and helmet that had been provided to him as an auxiliary of the legions.

"You'll get used to it, and you'll be thankful when it stops a sword from punching into your gut," Dom said as he approached the Saxon.

"I don't know how you fight in these things; I feel like I can barely move!" Alberic protested as he tried to twist his torso from side to side.

"We'll make a soldier of you yet, Al," Dom said with a grin.

"I'm already a warrior, *thank you*," Al replied irritably, and Dom sensed his comment had needled an old wound.

"That you are. But there's a difference between a soldier and a warrior. And that armour is only the start," Dom said as he patted Al on the shoulder.

The Tribune arrived a few minutes later, his fine armour shining despite the dim morning sun. He marched to the head of the column, and with a raise of the arm, he started the men forward. The Romans took their time as they marched, keeping in close formation. At the back of the ranks was an empty cart covered by furs and cloaks being pulled by an old war horse past its prime. Not wanting to arrive tired or give their position away to a Saxon scouting party, they picked their way through the countryside with caution. It was late in the evening by the time they started to climb a steep hill, and upon reaching the top, they saw a deep, green valley open up below them.

Chapter 20

Heavy rain lashed down upon the men who sat huddled together, holding cloaks above their heads in a vain attempt to keep dry. Al felt utterly miserable as the night dragged on, cold and soaked to the bone. He was with Dominicus' century at the end of the valley, where the road bent to the southwest. Maxentius remained on top of the slope to their left with Fabian's men, and Callixtus had led his men down to the start of the valley, a few miles north of Al's position. The Tribune expected the Saxons to come pouring over the hill to the east, and the three centuries would close in and trap them on three sides.

There was no sign yet of any movement, and the Tribune had given strict orders not to send out scouts in case they gave their position away. If no Saxon force appeared the following day, the Romans would retreat to the villa at nightfall and try a different approach. The uncertainty of not knowing if his former countrymen would take the bait was twisting a knot in Alberic's stomach. Waiting for a battle he didn't know would happen was worse than fighting in one. Although he could barely see the men sitting around him, the anxiety in the air was palpable.

Dawn finally arrived with a break in the downpour, the heavy rain rescinding to a soft drizzle. They could see the valley was now half flooded, with the small lakes and ponds having burst their banks during the night. Dominicus gave orders for the men to move away from the road and partially up the slopes on either side, leaving one man on the lookout crouching behind a sad-looking bush that grew alone by the side of the road. Al continued to fidget with the straps of his new armour; his shoulders ached from the unfamiliar weight, and without a good night's sleep, he felt exhausted.

"With weather like this, your people must have been mentally ill to come here," Dom said grumpily as he squatted down beside Al.

"How long will it last for?" Alberic asked.

"The rain? About six months, on and off," said Dom.

"You're joking, right?" Al said, his heart sinking.

"Partially," Dom replied with a smile. "At least that's what it feels like."

"Brilliant," Al said moodily.

"Chin up, Al; we'll soon be back inside the villa and drying off," Dom said as he stood back up.

"Any sign of the Saxons?" Al asked him, also rising to his feet as his cold and tired joints ached.

"Nothing yet," Dom replied.

Al started to walk absent-mindedly through the group of men who were waiting impatiently on the slope of the hill, stretching his tired limbs and loosening up. The sun was rising but brought with it no warmth, and his wet clothes felt like ice on the skin. Without warning, Al suddenly heard feet splashing towards him, and his heart started to beat faster as he saw the scout scrambling into view and running towards Dominicus.

"The enemy force spotted sir, on the hill to the east," the man panted as he came skidding to a stop.

Dom nodded and raised his hand to signal to the men on the other side of the road to make ready. Al and Dom started to creep slowly forward to the edge of the slope and looked towards the hill opposite. They could see hundreds of shapes milling around the top of the slope, and looking down the valley, they saw the shape of a small man leading a horse-drawn cart slowly along the road. Callixtus must have caught sight of the Saxons earlier than Dom's man and had sent the carriage along to convince the barbarians that the rumour was true.

Even though Al knew the man who had volunteered for this suicide mission was someone who had suffered terrible injuries during the rescue mission and was missing his left arm, his heart went out to the lone figure who was being sacrificed for a Roman victory. A wild howl went up from the Saxons on top of the hill, and like a great flood, they came streaming down the steep slope towards the lonely cart now in the centre of the valley. Al saw the poor legionary make a show of trying to mount the decrepit horse and try to escape, but the tribesmen were amongst him in seconds.

A trumpet call blared out from behind the hill to Alberic's left, and he saw ranks of shining Roman legionaries appear on the crest. They came forward in a wide line, two men deep, marching methodically towards the Saxons, who were turning to face this sudden threat. When the tribesmen realised they greatly outnumbered the force that was advancing upon them, jeers echoed out across the valley amidst the sound of spears on shields as they whipped themselves into a frenzy.

"Not yet!" Dom hissed next to him as an eager legionary began to move forward. "Wait for my signal, lads; if we don't time this right, we'll give the Saxons too much time to reform their lines as we charge."

The soldiers marching down the slope had reached a relatively dry patch between two ponds and were shortening the line as they started to head through. The Saxons surged forward to meet them, and the sounds of battle exploded as the front ranks engaged. The numerical superiority of the enemy was temporarily negated by the narrow strip of land they fought on, but it would not last for long.

"Now! Forward men! Kill the bastards!" Dom screamed as he jumped to his feet and started sprinting forward into the heart of the valley. Al was right beside him and could feel the battle lust start to descend. His senses felt heightened; he could hear the blood pumping in his ears, and his mouth was dry. The discomfort from a few moments earlier was forgotten, and his only desire, his only thought now, was to kill. He saw dark shadows pass over his head as the legionaries behind him threw their pila in high arcs into the men crammed together.

He saw dark shapes spilling into the valley from the northern end, but they came quietly and were for now unnoticed by the warriors in the heart of the valley. The arrival of a new force to the south, however, had sent ripples of fear throughout the ranks of the Saxons, and as their left wing tried to reform to face the new arrivals, the Roman javelins punched into them. Scores of men died instantly, and their line was in disarray as the legionaries smashed into the flank of the enemy.

Alberic threw his left shoulder into the man directly in front of him, allowing his momentum to send his opponent staggering backwards into the men behind him. He thrust the gladius straight forward and into the chest of the dazed man, killing him instantly. Pain jolted through his left arm, and Al hacked wildly at the man who had struck him, his sword slicing through fur, leather, and skin with ease. This time, pain came from his right leg, and upon looking down, he saw blood trickling freely from a cut in his thigh. He whipped the sword around and into the side of a wiry Saxon holding a vicious-looking dagger. The man screamed in pain, and blood spurted over Al's face, blinding him.

A rough hand grabbed Alberic's shoulder and started dragging him backwards. Vigorously wiping his enemy's blood away from his face and eyes, Al saw Publius glaring at him.

"Do you have a death wish?" He shouted over the din of battle. "That's not how we fucking fight here! Now get back before our whole line crumbles around you!"

Al felt himself being jostled out of the way and soon found himself stood behind the legionaries, a wall of iron and steel in front of him. A moment later, he found himself being pushed back once more as the Roman line in front staggered backwards. There was a second of blind panic where Al was overwhelmed with the desire to flee, but it passed once it became clear the movement had been caused by Callixtus' century smashing into the Saxon right. Al watched with a mixture of horror and awe as the unruly and less equipped Saxons panicked and began to fall under the unrelenting machine that was the Roman army. The bloody skirmish ended abruptly, as the tribesmen suddenly broke and fled, being cut down by legionaries on all sides. Al saw a handful of men scrambling up the hill, but he knew very few Saxons would leave that valley alive.

As he stood panting, the pain in his left shoulder became clearer, and his thigh ached terribly. The cold clothes seemed to reappear on his body in an instant, and he found himself shivering and feeling light-headed. Nevertheless, Al felt pride coursing through him. He had fought in and survived a second battle. For a fleeting moment, he thought about how proud his father would be. But he then remembered who it was he had been fighting, and a wave of emotions flooded over him. His chest started to tighten, and his breaths came in short gasps of air. He doubled over and fell to his knees, his hands sinking deep into the mud.

He was supposed to be leading the Saxon people to glory and conquest over the might of Rome, and here he was taking the very lives of the men he had known since birth. They spoke the same language, worshipped the same gods, shared wine with him on feast days, and now they were his enemies. How could he make his father proud if he were doing all he could to undo a decade of his life's work? Al felt as if he were falling through an abyss with no bottom.

"Alberic? Are you okay?" Dom's voice distorted as if from a great distance. "Al?" The voice sounded clearer a second time, and Alberic struggled back to his feet and took deep, steady breaths.

"I felt proud," he said finally, as the tightness in his chest began to ease.

"As you should! You fought well, if a bit reckless and not in Roman fashion," Dom replied with a grin.

"How can I feel pride, Dom? I'm killing the men I was born to lead; I should be dead in that valley alongside them, cut down by Roman swords." Al felt his eyes filling with tears and quickly rubbed them.

Dom studied him for a moment before replying. "I can't imagine what you're feeling, Al. If I was told to pick up a Saxon spear and fight the legions…" His voice trailed off, and he looked uncertain on how to continue. "But you must remember, those men didn't stand by you in your hour of need; you said it yourself."

Alberic nodded but did not reply. He wanted desperately to believe in the words Dominicus said, but the positive memories of his childhood were replacing the enmity he had felt towards the men who had betrayed him. Dom patted him on the shoulder and left him alone once more, striding back to his century and shouting out commands. Al felt calmer now after the short exchange with the young Roman, even if his thoughts still swirled and battled within his mind.

The Saxon dead were tallied at some three hundred, at the cost of only forty Roman lives. It was a sound victory, but the legion needed their men more than the invaders, and upon hearing the death toll for the legionaries, Maxentius cursed the will of the gods. The Romans buried their comrades and once again left the corpses of their enemies to rot unceremoniously. It was a grim mood in which the soldiers formed up and prepared to return to the villa. Al fell in alongside Dom, and the columns set off at a trot, eager to return and rest.

They marched in silence, and dusk was falling by the time they arrived back at the estate. They were cheered upon arrival, and their grey mood was finally lifted as they reunited with friends and began to tell the full story of the battle. Maxentius gave orders for every man to receive a double ration of wine, even those who had not fought, and the mood was lifted higher. Al did not linger in the yard; he made his way through the crowd to the old stables that were acting as the legion's armoury. He sighed with satisfaction upon freeing himself from the heavy armour and rooted through the barrels to find a new tunic.

Clean and dry once more, Alberic made his way through the villa complex and up to his quarters to find Carolus and Lucia waiting for him.

"Our hero returns!" Carolus cried as Al entered and moved across the room to embrace him.

"Another successful battle?" Lucia said, with a smile that, for once, did not flicker but remained there, lighting up her features, causing Al's stomach to do a summersault.

"Successful, yes. But a hero? I'm not sure," Al said as he sat down on his bed. "A hero to the Romans, maybe."

Carolus' smile faded as he looked at his pupil and was replaced by a frown of concern. "What is it, Al? This is a joyous occasion; you are turning into the warrior your father always dreamed you would be!"

"And did he also dream that my status as a warrior would come at the deaths of his people?" Al replied quietly. "Did he see his son as a soldier of Rome instead of a warrior of his people?"

"Perhaps not. But he also didn't dream that his people would abandon his son for a bloodthirsty usurper. The Saxons have forced your hand, Alberic; you know this. You cannot return, and you cannot stay in Britannia without helping Rome defeat her enemies," Carolus reasoned.

"I wish it were that simple, Carolus," Al said as he placed his head in his hands. "I'm not just fighting against men who betrayed me; I'm fighting against the future of my people. Our culture, our way of life—this is all at risk. It's the reason my father led us here in the first place!"

"Then you need to save them," Lucia interjected.

"Save them? From myself, from Rome? How can I do that when they will kill me on sight?" Al asked.

"Every single Saxon man would kill you on sight? Do you really believe that's true? How many were caught up in the moment. How many were afraid for the safety of their own families over the safety of their prince?" Lucia replied, her voice soft. "I don't know much about your people, Alberic, but if you're anything to go off, I doubt you have as many enemies amongst the Saxons as you think."

"I don't doubt you, my girl, but you must understand that the tribes have been commanded by the king's council to kill Alberic if he tries to return; regardless of their own feelings on the matter, they won't hesitate to follow their orders," Carolus said gently.

Lucia scoffed, and her hair danced across her face and shoulders as she whipped around to look at the old tutor. "I'm not proposing that Al march up to the gates of Londinium and ask them politely if he can come home. What I am saying is that once this Broga has been defeated, and he *will* be defeated, Al will have more support than he thinks. As the tide turns in this war, the Saxons will look for new leaders, and not all will have forgotten the son of their great king."

Al looked up at the beautiful Roman woman, with her long, thick hair shining in the candlelight and her green eyes sparkling. "Thank you, Lucia, truly. You're right; I have let my grief and despair cloud my view, and in doing so, have judged my countrymen too harshly. In the aftermath of this war, if I can save my people, then I will," Al said.

Lucia smiled at him and nodded happily as she saw the change in Al's demeanour. After telling them she was off to find food and wine, she swept out of the room, placing a hand on Al's shoulder briefly as she passed.

"A special girl that one, she won't lack for suitors when this is over," Carolus said, smiling to himself as he saw colour rising in Al's cheeks.

Chapter 21

The moon shone bright and full, peaking through a rare gap in the clouds above to illuminate the dark stone walls of Londinium. Dom's heart thudded painfully against his ribs as he looked up at the high walls towering over him, amazed that the men above could not hear the pounding in the quiet night air. He swept his eyes over the men he had picked for his mission; the confidence he had felt in the Tribune's offices back at the villa was wavering. His legionaries were all huddled directly against the wall, pressing their bodies tight against the cold stone as they waited for the signal. He could see them testing the rungs of their ladders in their agitation.

He turned his head and looked west into the heavy darkness that his eyes could not penetrate, waiting for the signal from Maxentius to begin their attack. When the Tribune had told them his plan the previous evening, Dom had happily accepted the dangerous task of scaling the high walls in the dark, slaughtering the guards, and opening the tall wooden doors that made up the Cripplegate. Situated in the northern stretch of the wall, it led directly into the old stone fort. Once open, the rest of the legion would come pouring in and secure the northwest area of the city. From here, the Romans would be able to retake Londinium step by step until the Saxons were defeated.

It had seemed so simple when Maxentius explained, and Dom understood the urgency that was driving the assault. A flurry of arrivals at the estate had bolstered their numbers but had added considerable strain on the supplies at the villa. The soldiers had scoured the nearby countryside, emptying every farm and small settlement they came across. The Tribune had brought provisions with him from the secure Roman southwest, but they were now down to only a few days rations. Retaking the city with its supply routes to Gaul via the wide Thames river was the only solution to their immediate problems.

Dom now felt as if he had been sent on a suicide mission. They had no idea how many were waiting for them on those high walls. Surely the barbarians would be on high alert after the men they had sent out to capture an easy prize a week earlier had not returned. Cold sweat trickled down Dom's spine, and he shivered. His palms felt clammy, and he wiped them on his legs to dry them. The seconds crawled by, until finally a small light illuminated the night sky. From Maxentius' vantage point in the hills to the west of the city, an arrow with its head dipped in tar now burning brightly arced high and seemed to hang for a moment before falling to the earth and vanishing.

"Let's go, quick and quiet now, lads," Dom whispered to the soldiers.

The two ladders were quickly raised against the walls, and the top of the struts was wrapped in soft cloth to prevent the usual clattering of wood on stone. Dom tested the first rung with his foot; it appeared solid, so he began to climb as quickly as he could, a nimble and thin legionary leading the way up the second ladder to his left. As he neared the top, he found the ladder was three feet short of the battlements; he would have to scramble and pull himself over. He grimaced as he knew the sound of his armour scraping across the stone would likely alert anyone nearby to their presence.

He popped his head over the wall and looked around. There was nobody directly in front of him, but there were three men standing around a torch, roughly twenty yards to his right. Looking to his left, he caught the nimble legionaries' eyes and indicated, with a free hand, the number of guards nearby. They would have to be quick, or the whole fort would be aware of the attack in moments. Standing on the tips of his toes to bring the edge of the wall as close to his waist as possible, Dom pressed his palms down onto the smooth stone and hoisted himself over, rolling in one fluid motion to land lightly on cloth-covered sandals.

Immediately he started sprinting towards the guards, not waiting to see if they had heard the rustle and clink of his armour as he had climbed or if his comrade was following. The three Saxons turned with wide eyes to see a Roman ghost sweeping along the wall towards them, and before they could shout, Dom was amongst them. He charged into the man closest to the edge and barged into him with his left shoulder. The man stumbled, and with a cry of surprise, he toppled over the edge into the gloom, landing with a sickening crack. Dom sliced his sword at the man in the middle, the blade cutting deep into the startled sentry's neck.

The remaining man had raised his spear, opening his mouth to shout, but the only sound that escaped was a soft hiss as the second legionary appeared and plunged his sword deep into the exposed throat. The Saxon fell with a crumple, and Dom held his breath as he waited for the sounds of alarm. Surely they must have heard the cry of the falling man and the sound of his body hitting the hard floor. If the element of surprise was lost, the Romans had to move quickly, so without wasting any more time, Dom leant over the battlements and hissed at the remaining soldiers to climb the wall and join them.

His breaths came in short gasps of air as he fought to steady himself whilst desperately trying to hear the first, inevitable sounds that the Saxons within the fort were being roused. When the remaining soldiers had completed the ascent, Dom set off along the smooth, wide walkway in the direction of the gatehouse ahead of him, its high towers illuminated by torches running alongside him. A horn blared out into the still night and was shortly followed by shouts and the sound of running feet. The game was up, and the Saxons were finally aware that something was amiss.

Dom sped up and charged into the gatehouse tower, driving his gladius into the stomach of a sentry who turned around looking bewildered as he entered the small room.

"You five, take the other tower and meet us by the gate. The rest of you with me!" Dom instructed as he started bounding down the spiral stone steps, taking two at a time. He burst through the wooden door into the open space behind the closed wooden gates. There were a dozen Saxons milling around the courtyard who all stared open-mouthed at the legionaries streaming out of the tower. The Romans dispatched the nearest barbarians with brutal efficiency, and the remainder fled into the darkness of the fort, their shouts of warning and panic echoing all around.

"Lift the bar!" Dom shouted as he threw himself against the rough wooden gates and put his shoulder underneath the heavy plank of wood in its bracket. At first, there was little movement, and he felt a wave of despair that they would not be able to open the gate. But as more men joined him, the plank started to slowly creak upwards and suddenly toppled into the Romans as it tipped over the iron brackets holding it. Curses rang out into the night as the heavy bar thumped into shoulders and thighs. They dragged the bar out of the way, hearing hundreds of men approaching from within the darkness behind them.

With a groan, the thick wooden gates slowly opened as the legionaries dragged them inwards. The way was open, and Dom heard a cry of triumph from beyond the gloom ahead, followed by the sound of armour clinking and iron-shod sandals pounding as the main Roman force swept forward to take the city.

"On me!" Dom commanded. "Form the line! Lock shields!"

In the narrow space between the two towers, under the arch of the gateway, Dom's small force formed up into four ranks, five men deep, and prepared to meet the Saxon force.

"We *must* hold lads!" Dom shouted over the din of the two approaching armies. He braced his legs, leaning into his shield and gripping his sword tight. He could taste bile in the back of his throat as he fought to contain a sudden surge of fear. If their reinforcements did not arrive in time, then he knew these could be his last moments alive.

The wind was knocked out of him momentarily as the Saxons threw themselves at the Romans like stampeding horses, with screams of unintelligible rage. He felt his back pressing into the shield of the man behind, and for a few seconds, the Romans were pushed back inch by inch before they were able to dig their heels in and hold against the immense weight being pressed upon them. With significant effort, Dom pushed his shield into the mass of churning bodies ahead and freed up a small space for his sword. Settling into the legionary's dance of death, Dom felt his world shrink to the size of a few small yards. He was aware only of the man to his left, to his right, and the enemy in front.

Thrusting his sword repeatedly into any gap that appeared, he cut through his enemies mercilessly. A heavy axe glanced off his helmet, causing bright lights to explode in his eyes, but he managed to remain on his feet, thanks to the man behind him keeping him in place. Spears were darting in under their shields, and Dom felt one grace his ankle. His right leg trembled from the pain, his right arm felt heavy, and he knew his strength was failing. Still, the Saxons came on, pressed tight up against the Roman line, screaming and hacking away. Suddenly, Dom felt the pressure to his left ease, and his insides turned cold as he saw the legionary next to him falling backwards, a spear stuck deep into his chest.

The line buckled, the Saxons surged into the opening gap, and Dom felt himself beginning to turn as the enemy tried to push through. As suddenly as his panic had risen in his throat once again, he felt relief course through him. The Roman reinforcements had arrived at last, smashing into the gap in the line like a battering ram. Dom saw the tall figure of Callixtus at the head of the column, using his immense strength to force the barbarians back into the fort. The arrival of the main Roman force was too much for the Saxons, and they broke, streaming backwards into the darkness. Most of them had been asleep minutes before, and now they were running for their lives.

Dom stood panting, exhausted and in pain, as his adrenaline began to ebb away. He stood by and let the column pass, hearing the battle continue beyond his vision. Looking around the gate, he could see a jumble of bodies, mostly Saxon, with a few legionary red cloaks lying amongst them. They had been seconds from annihilation, and Dom felt giddy at the gift of life the reinforcements had provided.

"Well done, lads," Dom said to his tired troops, of which only twelve remained. His men grinned at him; they knew how close they had come to destruction and now felt the ecstasy of having achieved the impossible.

"No rest for us yet, though; we need to rejoin Publius and the rest of the century and get the fort secure," Dom said. "I need you to head to the Tribune and let him know we were successful and that the legion is in the fort," he commanded an old veteran with a nasty gash in his side, who would have been little use in the remaining battle. The man nodded gratefully, his hand holding tight to the wound as he marched off into the darkness.

The battle dissolved into a bloody mess as the Romans advanced through the fort, fighting room by room to remove the Saxon invaders. It did not take long, however, as most of the enemy had abandoned the fort to regroup with the warriors who were lodging within the city proper, and a new force was gathering in the streets of Londinium, preparing to counter the Roman advance. Dom found his Optio by the walls of the fort that faced into the city.

"Damn fine job, sir; they'll be talking about this one for years!" Publius said as Dom approached, punching him on the shoulder enthusiastically.

"Easy, Publius; I've just been crushed by a hundred Saxons, you know," Dom said with a grin. "How are the men? Any casualties?"

"A few," Publius said, his smile fading. "A dozen were cut down as we took the mess hall, so with who we lost at the gate, I'd say we're twenty men down."

Dom nodded; it was a blow to lose a fifth of his men only a matter of days after taking the position. He heard hoofbeats behind him and saw Tribune Maxentius coming into view.

"Excellent work, Dominicus! The Emperor will be hearing of your bravery," Maxentius said as he jumped from the saddle.

"Thank you, sir; you honour me," Dom replied as he bowed low. The Tribune patted him on the shoulder before sending off runners to bring the remaining centurions to his position.

"The task is only half-finished, gentlemen; we have a foothold, but we need to take the city as soon as possible," Maxentius said once the officers had arrived. "It will be a bloody business, but there's no point in delaying. Reform your men and take to the streets. Kill every Saxon bastard you can find until you reach the Arx Palatina. Dom's century will hold here at the fort, to provide a secure position to fall back if necessary."

Nodding with grim expressions, Gereon, Callixtus, Fabian, and Drusus each marched off, shouting commands and orders for their men to assemble in the yard. Dom gave orders for his men to take to the walls of the fort that faced into the city before following Maxentius up the stone steps and coming to a stop on the section of wall above the gatehouse. He could see the city of Londinium sprawling ahead of him. Fires and torches allowed them to see the hundreds of dark figures moving in between the houses and buildings closest to them. Dom did not envy the task ahead of his comrades; in those close quarters, the discipline of the legionaries would only count for so much.

With a blast of a trumpet, the Romans marched out of the gate and down the gentle slope towards the narrow streets of the city. The din of battle reached Dom's ears as he saw the columns enter the alleyways, but he was not sure if it was going well or not for the legion. An hour passed in this state of anxiety and frustration, and the Tribune stood next to him, saying nothing. Fires would suddenly flare up in a new section, and the sounds of battle would follow before the night quietened down and signs of the next clash would come from a new area.

Finally, they saw a small group of filthy, blood-stained legionaries come trotting out from between two buildings and make their way up to the fort.

"Report," Maxentius said, with an impatient edge to his voice once the legionaries had climbed the wall.

"The city is secure, sir; we have captured a large number of Saxons, and the remaining enemy force has fled through the Aldgate," the exhausted legionary said as he stood trembling.

"Excellent. Dismissed," Maxentius said, satisfaction written across his wide face.

Orders were given for the remaining supplies and men from the villa to make their way to the city, and the Tribune strode through the gates to take stock of the situation and station himself at the governor's palace, or what remained of it. Dom leant on the battlements and sighed. His tired body was demanding sleep, but he knew it would be a long while before he would finally be able to rest. He straightened up and started to make his way down into the fort, calling for Publius to join him.

Chapter 22

Prince Alberic stood on the wharf, watching the Thames frothing as it raced between the stone arches of the great bridge connecting Southwark to Londinium proper. The piers around him were largely empty, just a couple of leaky fishing tubs rocking in the swell. In the past, there would have been dozens of boats lined up here, tall warships and wide merchant trading vessels. Now the docks were deserted, the bustling and noise of men and goods coming and going from the ships a mere memory. Al sighed to himself, his heart was heavy from the sight of hundreds of dead Saxons piled high beside the Ardgate, ready to be taken outside of the city and buried.

Footsteps echoed from the hard wooden planks of the wharf, and Al turned to see Carolus making his way towards him.

"Tribune Maxentius has requested your presence, my prince," the old Greek said as he came to a stop beside Al.

"Any idea what it's regarding?" He replied to his tutor.

"He hasn't said, but I would assume it must be linked to the Saxon prisoners they captured during the assault," Carolus replied. "I suppose this is the opportunity Lucia spoke about, but I wouldn't get your hopes up for a positive outcome."

"Let's go then. I don't doubt that it will be tough, but I will do what I can to save them," Al said as the two men started to make their way back towards the city, passing through the stone arch of the Belins gate.

The city was quiet, with most of the Roman forces either recovering within the fort in the northwest corner or patrolling the stone walls. The citizens who had survived the original Saxon assault were finally leaving their homes, albeit cautiously, and were picking their way through the stone streets to check on family and friends. Others were visiting the temples to offer sacrifices to thank the gods for the deliverance at the hands of Maxentius' troops. The Saxon prisoners were being held within the large amphitheatre that was situated near the fort, close enough to the legionaries to keep them in check.

Maxentius had set up a table within the large forum at the centre of the city, and a large crowd had gathered there to speak with the Tribune as he worked to set straight the affairs of the city. As Al entered the wide space, decorated with white marble columns and lifelike statues, he was reminded of the splendour of Rome and wondered how his father believed they could have achieved victory here. The Romans were blessed by the gods, and the forum was built to remind everyone who was the true master of the world.

Taking a seat alongside Carolus, Al waited for a few hours before he was called to come forward and speak with the Tribune. As he fidgeted in his seat, he heard the many problems and grievances the people of Londinium brought to Maxentius and marvelled at the political skill the Tribune showed. He listened to every case brought forward, showed no favourites between the rich and the poor, made promises where he could, and offered gentle condolences where he could not supply immediate support. The main topic on everyone's lips was food. The grain supplies within the city were running dangerously low, and Maxentius had the clerks next to him busy calculating what would be needed to see the city through the approaching winter.

When Al was finally called to approach the Tribune, he saw the man looking exhausted with dark patches under his eyes.

"Prince Alberic, thank you for coming. We have much to discuss," the Tribune said with a tired, resigned voice. "Fabian, clear the forum, please. This will be the last bit of business today, for those who have not yet had their opportunity to speak with me, tell them we will reconvene in the morning."

The centurion nodded and set about dispersing the crowd. After a few minutes, the only people left in the area were Al and Carolus, who stood before Maxentius, and his two clerks, still seated behind the wooden desk.

"Now then..." the Tribune said as he leant back in his chair and rubbed his tired eyes. "What am I to do with two hundred Saxon prisoners? The prudent approach would be to have them executed and send their heads to Rutupiae; I think."

Al was horrified by the Tribune's words; he had expected the worst-case scenario for his countrymen to be slavery, not mass slaughter.

"This is your opportunity to provide me with an alternative, Alberic," Maxentius said, looking at the young prince.

"I would have you show clemency, sir. I hope I have shown you from my actions over recent days that the Saxons are honourable people," Alberic said whilst maintaining eye contact with the Tribune, his hands clasped behind his back. "The men you captured during your victory have only been following orders, as any good soldier would."

The Tribune did not respond, and Al knew he had to pick his next words very carefully. The lives of the tribesmen lay on the edge of a knife, and a misstep on Al's part would result in a terrible loss of life.

"I would have you offer the prisoners the chance to swear fealty to me, and I will take on responsibility for them. If I fail to keep them in check, you can proceed with your prudent approach and take my life alongside theirs," Al said. He heard Carolus gasp behind him at the last point, and Maxentius' eyes widened slightly.

"You're placing a lot of faith in your countrymen, Alberic. Are you sure you want to do this?" Maxentius replied.

"I have every faith in both the Saxon people and Alberic's ability to keep them in line," Carolus said quickly, and Al nodded in agreement.

"Very well. I will allow you to speak with them; if they swear fealty to you, they will keep their heads… For now. We will assign them a portion of the city to reside in, but they must remain restricted to this area until the crisis is over. We can discuss further once you have their answer," Maxentius said with a wave of his hand.

Al and Carolus bowed and set off for the amphitheatre to speak with the Saxons. As they left the forum, Al could see people watching them from doorways and windows; every face had the same expression of hatred and mistrust. He walked with his head held high, but he knew the following days and weeks would be extremely dangerous for him and his people. The Roman citizens would be looking for any opportunity to exact their revenge. It did not take long for them to see the tall white building standing high above the smoke-blackened houses around it, and they were soon walking through a decorated archway into the dark interior of the theatre.

They were stopped by two legionaries who stood just inside the doorway, and once Al had explained they had been given the Tribune's permission to enter, they were ushered through another door and back out into the open. Stone benches rose on either side in a wide semi-circle, all looking down upon a wide sandy pit in the centre. A wooden stage stood at the back of this open space, and the Saxon prisoners were milling around. Some were sitting on the benches, others on the edge of the stage, but most were pacing up and down anxiously. A murmur of interest broke over the crowd of people at the sight of Alberic and Carolus, and they all gathered to hear what the young prince had to say.

"I'm sure most of you will recognise me if you don't know me personally," Al began, his voice echoing around the theatre. "My name is Alberic, son of King Alawar and former prince of the Heruli. I am here to relay Rome's offer, and I implore you to take it, or the consequences will be dire."

He swept his eyes over the crowd of people, and his heart sank as he realised that he did not know anyone personally. A few faces were familiar, but none were from his tribe. He would not be able to rely on a friend or distant relative to convince the group to make the right decision.

"The offer is this. Swear fealty to me as your king, and you will be allowed to live. The Romans will provide us with an area of the city to settle in as we wait for the crisis to be resolved. Once the war is over, we will be allowed to return to our homeland," Alberic said, his heart rising into his throat with anxiety.

"If we swear fealty to you, Broga will kill us!" A voice shouted from within the crowd; Al could not see who had spoken.

"Our families will be exiled or thrown into slavery!" Another voice called.

Al raised his hands to quiet them before speaking again. "I know that this is not an easy choice to make. By swearing fealty to an exile, you and your families will be exiled as a result. But Broga will not be long for this world, the Romans will soon retake the island. As far as the remainder of the tribes know, you are being held as prisoners, and by the time they're aware of your new allegiance, the war will be over and Broga will be dead."

There was an outbreak of murmuring at his words, but no more outbursts. The Saxons were looking at each other, and fear was on their faces.

One man stepped forward; his face was covered in old blood, and his left eye was partially closed from swelling. "And what if the Romans lose? We've had them on the run for weeks! This is a temporary setback," he said defiantly.

Carolus shook his head sadly as he stepped forward to stand beside Al. "I have lived amongst you for a decade. The Saxons are undoubtedly fine warriors, and the war started as well as it possibly could have. But without King Alawar, I'm afraid the outcome will most certainly be a Roman victory. Their forces are no longer scattered, and their army in the southwest is largely untouched. In the spring, new legions will arrive and reassert Rome's dominance over the island."

The old Greek surveyed the crowd as he continued, "You must swear fealty to Prince Alberic; it is the only way you will make it back to your families."

The air was thick with tension as the Saxon prisoners mulled it over. Al observed the men before him exchange worried glances, and he felt the anxiety start to creep into his gut. It lingered for a moment before the men closest to Al finally dropped to one knee, the men behind them following suit. Alberic's throat tightened at the sight; they were not the Heruli, and it wasn't the return of his crown and his rightful place, but it was a start and a momentous occasion for the young man. He was finally taking his first steps down the path his father had laid out for him. Carolus recited the oath of fealty, and the warriors repeated it back as one.

"I swear to each of you that I will do everything in my power to ensure your protection and safety, and when the crisis is over, I will lead you home to your families, and there will be peace for the Saxons once more," Al said. It was not greeted with cheers, but the men nodded. "For now, I need you to remain here until I have worked with the Tribune on the next steps, before we move to our designated part of the city."

Al and Carolus left the amphitheatre a short while later, heading for the house the Tribune had assigned them the morning after the battle. It was a small house; its previous owner was either dead or fled when the Saxons took the city. Inside, it was simply furnished, but anything of value had been stripped. All that remained were a few soft couches in the main room and old wooden beds in the adjoining bedrooms. However, it was comfortable and private, and Alberic found the house peaceful after the cramped quarters at the villa. As they entered, they found Lucia lying on her side on one of the couches, sipping wine.

"I think that's the happiest I've ever seen you, Al," Lucia said as she sat up, smiling at him.

"I think it's the best I've felt in weeks, and it's all thanks to you," Al said as he returned her smile and sat on the couch opposite.

"All thanks to me?" Lucia replied, cocking her head to one side.

"What you said back at the villa… You were right, Lucia! I have convinced Maxentius to allow the prisoners to live, and they have just sworn their fealty to me." Al said as he reached for the amphora on the floor, grinning from ear to ear.

Lucia's green eyes had widened at this as she said, "So, you're a king now? Do I need to bow and kiss your hand?" Her eyes sparkled as she teased him. Al's heart had skipped a beat at the word 'kiss.'

"Bowing will not be necessary," he replied. "I'm not a king yet, though; that can only be decided by a majority vote of the tribe and ratified by the elders. The men captured here come from several separate groups."

He sipped the wine in his cup before continuing, "But I am a leader of men now. With all the responsibility that comes with it."

Lucia's expression softened at the frown on Alberic's face. "You will excel at this, Al; those men are lucky to have you leading them."

"He certainly will! I have no doubts in your ability or your character, Alberic; you are your father's son." Carolus' eyes were shining with emotion as he looked at his pupil. "He would be proud."

Al felt tears rising unbidden at these final words and gave Carolus a weak smile. The three of them spent the rest of the evening in pleasant conversation, with Lucia coming more out of her shell. She had a sharp wit and was quick to laugh. Al felt himself becoming entranced by her presence. In the time he spent in her company, the worries and anxieties of the coming days were forgotten. As the young prince retired to his bed, he resolved to himself that he would confess to Lucia the feelings that were growing in his heart, even if the idea of it was more daunting than the thought of leading ten thousand men into battle.

Chapter 23

There was a nasty silence in the Tribune's office, deep within the Praetorium, where he had taken up residence. The centurions had arrived in the early morning as ordered by Maxentius and had entered to find the young Saxon prince Alberic seated with the Tribune.

"The men won't like this, sir," Gereon said.

"The men will do as they're told, Centurion. If you cannot keep them in line, I will find someone who can," Maxentius replied coldly. His demeanour had changed considerably in the days since their victory. Gone was the friendly, good-natured officer, replaced by a calculating senator.

"My apologies, sir. I will keep them in line, sir," the old veteran replied, staring at a spot on the tiled wall above the Tribune's head.

"Good," Maxentius replied. "We will be assigning them the northeast of the city. It is sparsely populated, and those citizens that remain in that area will be moved into empty houses elsewhere. Compensation will be given to the displaced at the end of the crisis when the Saxons leave the city."

"How many shall we assign to guard them, sir?" Callixtus asked.

"None, Callixtus. We are stretched thin and cannot afford to leave gaps in our sentry lines on the wall. They are sworn to Prince Alberic, and it is his responsibility to keep them confined to the area. If they disobey, we will kill them," Maxentius said, without looking up from his maps of the city and the surrounding area.

"Fabian, I will leave it with you to clear the area, ready for Alberic to lead them from the amphitheatre. It goes without saying, gentlemen, that our key concern is keeping peace within the walls; we have enough enemies in the field around us without trouble between the citizens and the tribesmen. Keep people away from the Saxon quarter. If anyone has complaints, they can raise them with me. Dismissed," the Tribune waved a hand through the air, and the centurions snapped a salute before leaving the office.

When they were out of earshot, Gereon cursed loudly and pounded his fist into his palm. "What the fuck is he playing at? How can any of us sleep soundly knowing there's two hundred savages prancing about unguarded within the city walls?"

"Careful, Gereon, Sounds a lot like treason that. The Tribune has made his decision, and it's not our place to challenge it," Fabian said warningly.

Dom nudged Gereon in the ribs and shook his head to warn the old veteran to hold his tongue. Fabian was a good man, but he had served under Maxentius for some time, and his loyalty to the Tribune was absolute.

As the group reached the fort, Fabian marched off, calling for his Optio to assemble their century. Callixtus and Drusus headed for the officer's quarters, taking the opportunity to sleep before the night watch. Dom and Gereon made their way up the stone steps and onto the tall, wide wall that enclosed the Roman city. Their men were currently on watch, and the two centurions occupied themselves with a circuit of the walls, stopping to speak with each man they came across. In the gaps between each legionary, they spoke about the Tribune's decision to not only spare the Saxon prisoners but allow them to take up temporary residence within the walls.

"I don't like it as much as you, Gereon, but we have to trust both Maxentius and Al," Dom said.

"He's a boy! They threw him out on his backside only a month ago; why will they listen to him now?" Gereon replied.

"He's only a few years younger than me," Dom argued. "And he seems to be mature beyond his years."

Gereon scoffed, but they broke off their conversation temporarily as they approached the next sentry.

"I know you think highly of the lad, but don't forget who he is—or *what* he is," the veteran said once they had continued along the wall a few moments later.

"Wasn't your father born to a tribe beyond Roman borders?" Dom replied. "Surely you know better than most that not everyone born outside of the empire is a mindless savage."

"He was, but he also had the good sense to fight *for* Rome, not against her," Gereon said. "And you've changed your tune; I've never heard you say one positive thing about the bastards from beyond the borders. You were all out for blood when that prince first strutted into the villa!"

Before Dom could reply, however, the sound of trumpets came from the north side of the city. Swivelling around, the two men set off on a run back along the wall until they reached the legionary holding his brass instrument.

"What is it?" Dom asked at once, staring out into the rolling hills north of the city.

"Men are approaching, sir, on horseback. They should come back into view momentarily," the legionary said as he pointed northwards.

A few seconds later, Dom saw a small group of people rising from the hills. There was no sign of any standard, and they did not appear to be armoured. Dom and Gereon made their way down from the steps and back to the fort. Gereon called for horses to be brought and for a handful of his men to mount up to join them. They trotted out of the Cripplegate ten minutes later, heading north to intercept the newcomers. As they approached, they could see blood splattered across the flanks of tired horses, and more than one rider was sporting cuts and bruises.

"Halt!" Dom called as he pulled up in front of the group. "State your business at once."

The man closest to him, with dark skin and thick, curly hair, raised his hands in the air as he spoke. "We're Roman citizens; we come seeking aid."

"Roman citizens, eh?" Gereon said, having not forgotten the crucial piece of intel from Alberic regarding the Saxons' use of spies. "You won't have any issues telling me the name of the Emperor, then?"

"Which one? It's Valentinian in the west and Valens in the east," the main replied irritably.

"Anyone who thinks Valens does anything other than what his brother tells him is a fool, but it will do for now," Gereon replied with satisfaction. "What brings you here to Londinium?"

"War!" the man grunted. "We come from Camulodunum. Barbarians overran the city three days ago; we barely made it out in time."

Dom nodded gravely. "If you could follow us, please, the Tribune will want to hear of this personally."

The two centurions led the refugees back to the city, heading straight through the fort and into the streets beyond. Their horses' hooves clattered from the smooth stone paths, echoing around them. Dom could see people peering around doorways and through windows as they passed, worried expressions on their faces as they watched. Dismounting in the yard of the palace, they announced their arrival to the clerk, who came hurrying out of the building. The man's eyes widened as he took in the sight of the bloody and injured travellers that Dom and Gereon had brought with them, but he said nothing as he rushed back inside to inform the Tribune.

A moment later, the clerk reappeared, gesturing for them to follow. They made their way into the same office from the morning meeting and saw Alberic was still present, undoubtedly still working through the headache of housing his people within the city.

"My name is Maxentius, military Tribune for the province. I hear you have come from Camulodunum. What news of the province capital?" Maxentius said, looking up from his mountain of scrolls and wax tablets.

"The city fell after a brief struggle three days ago. It was inevitable after the Praetor abandoned us for the safety of Londinium. I am surprised not to be greeted by him." The man who had spoken with Dom outside the city had stepped forward as he replied to the Tribune. Dom noticed the man did not show any nerves when speaking with Maxentius and knew he must be either rich or had held a position of authority within the capital.

"Praetor Vitellianus is dead," Maxentius said as he narrowed his eyes. "Who are you? I will not tolerate any criticism of the Emperor's chosen officials, alive or dead."

"I am Jovinus," the man replied stiffly. "I will say no more regarding the decisions of our former Praetor."

"Good," the Tribune said as he sat back in his chair. "What can you tell me of the force that took Camulodunum? I will confess, I was expecting this news sooner rather than later, but I was hoping for more time."

"You were expecting this news but sent no aid to protect the citizens that live there?" Jovinus said, his voice rising in outrage.

"Watch your tongue!" Gereon snarled, stepping close to Jovinus.

"Calm, Gereon. The man has no idea what we have faced in recent weeks, and I believe he is letting his emotions get the better of him," Maxentius said, his eyes glinting with malice as he raised his hand, gesturing for Gereon to stand back.

Jovinus must have realised the danger he was in and bowed to the Tribune. "My apologies, Tribune. I am sure you would have supported Camulodunum if you were able to."

"The enemy army numbered in the thousands; the household guards of the merchants and priests that lived in the city were no match for them," Jovinus continued now that the tense moment had passed.

"What about banners, or standards?" The Tribune pressed. "We need to know which enemy it was that took the city."

"Which enemy was it?" Jovinus replied, visibly confused. "Are you saying there is more than one army of savages loose within the province?"

"Unfortunately, yes. It seems that news has travelled slowly to the capital. The island is under attack from a coalition of tribes from beyond our borders. We need to know which of these tribes took the city," Maxentius replied rather calmly.

"I've spent some time trading beyond the wall. They were Picts, I'm sure of it," Jovinus said, dismay at the Tribune's words etched across his face.

Dom felt as if his insides had turned to ice. Somehow, in the chaos of the previous weeks and days, he had forgotten about the northern savages entirely. He had been so intent on fighting and defeating the Saxon menace that the events that had led him here had been pushed to the back of his mind. Memories of fire and blood came leaping to the fore as he recalled the terrible night at Hadrian's Wall when their prefect's treachery had led to the slaughter of his comrades. He felt Gereon tense up next to him and knew the old, grizzled veteran was recalling that evening with the same vivid detail as he was.

"Well, they were bound to head south at some point and meet up with their allies," Maxentius said with a shrug. "They're still a few days hard march from Londinium, and I would expect them to remain in Camulodunum and enjoy the luxuries of the city for some time, potentially for the winter."

"I'm sorry, but I'm afraid that's not the case," Jovinus cut in.

Maxentius' eyes narrowed once more, and he leant forward in his chair. "You have more to tell me, Jovinus?"

"After the walls fell, we fled through the south gate. We paused a few miles from the city, hoping to catch our breath and decide where to head next," Jovinus said, shuffling on the spot. "But as we looked back to the city, we saw a part of the enemy had already left and was marching southward. We didn't hang around to see exactly where they were heading or if they were following us here, but it was clear the Picts are not content with remaining in the capital."

The room was silent as Jovinus finished speaking. Dom could feel anxiety clawing at his insides as the confidence from their victory at Londinium was shattered by the reminder of how dire their situation was. If the Picts brought their full number down upon their position, the small Roman force would be wiped out.

"Very well," Maxentius said after a while. "I assume you are tired from your journey and in need of good rest. One of my clerks will support you with temporary accommodation." The Tribune clicked his fingers, and a short, fat man appeared, the same person who had greeted them in the yard. Jovinus and his silent companions all bowed before following the clerk back outside.

"It appears we have some work to do. Gereon, I need you to send out scouts. We need to find out where this Pict force is heading, and if they're on a collision course with Londinium. It is also imperative that we get some idea of the numbers we're up against." The Tribune had returned to pouring over the papers on his desk, shuffling through scraps of parchment.

"We will need to step up our preparations and prepare the city to withstand an assault. The latest inspection showed the walls are in decent shape, and with the arrival of the Dubris contingent yesterday, we have recuperated somewhat the losses sustained when we took the city. But even so, we can put no more than five hundred men on the wall if they attack in numerous places…" Maxentius' voice trailed off as he flickered through a sheaf of hastily scrawled notes.

"If I may interject, Tribune?" The Saxon prince said, who had largely gone unnoticed up until this point.

"Fire away, Alberic," Maxentius said without looking up.

"I believe I have a solution to your shortage of manpower… Allow my countrymen to fight alongside you in the event of an assault upon the city," Alberic said.

Dom fought to choke back an angry retort, and he could almost feel the heat coming from the rage burning inside Gereon beside him. The young man had proven himself capable and a good ally. But suggesting they provide weapons to the same savages who had killed so many Romans in the past few weeks was madness.

"I think not, Prince Alberic," Maxentius said softly, turning to look at Alberic. "I trust you, to some degree. But I do not trust any one of the men who have only recently sworn fealty to you. They will remain confined to their quarters, or I will have them killed."

Alberic's cheeks reddened at the rebuke, but he did not reply. Gereon and Dominicus left the Tribune's office once again a few moments later and remounted their horses in the yards before speeding off back to the fort. Gereon did not waste any time, and he sent four men through the Cripplegate out into the hills to find the enemy. Dom busied himself with preparing the city for attack, organising his century back into ten contubernium of eight men each, a task he had not yet completed, and assigning them sections of the wall to guard that evening.

Exhausted, Dom retired to his bed in the late evening. His head was spinning with the hundreds of tasks he felt were outstanding, and he struggled to switch off his brain in order to sleep. The anxiety that was sparked during Jovinus' account in the Tribune's office had intensified over the last few hours. Dom could not see any hope for the small Roman force if the Picts attacked. They could hold two, maybe three, stretches of the long wall, but if the barbarians launched several attacks on different sides of the city, the legionaries would be stretched too thin to offer any real resistance. He fell into an uneasy sleep, with thoughts of impending doom twisting his dreams into nightmares.

Chapter 24

The heavy rain had returned, and the sky was dark with thick clouds as Alberic made his way towards the Saxon quarter of the city. His boots splashed through deep puddles, and his waterlogged fur cloak weighed heavily on his shoulders. The previous few days had been exhausting for the young prince as he worked through the details of settling his people within Londinium. He felt the pressure of his new role, with the lives of two hundred men dependent on his decisions and ability to keep them safe and fed. The buildings housing the tribesmen loomed out of the darkness, and Al made his way to the largest, a two-story house with a handsome façade decorated with faded scenes of a long-forgotten battle.

Al entered to the sound of angry voices and found a group of Saxons huddled around the firepit, built into the tiled floor, all facing the Greek tutor, Carolus.

"It's not enough!" The tallest man in the centre of the room was shouting. "We'll starve before winter ends!"

"We are doing everything we can, Thrax. Please remain calm," Carolus replied as he raised his hands.

"Thrax?" Al asked, puzzled by the Latin name.

"It's a nickname," the tall man grunted. "I earned it after defeating a Thracian legionary."

"Well-met, Thrax. Please tell me, why are you hassling poor Carolus here?" Al said as he peeled the sodden fur cloak from his shoulders.

"I will do more than hassle him if our rations continue to be this poor," snarled Thrax.

"Carolus has nothing to do with the quality or quantity of your rations. At the moment, this is all the Romans can afford to provide for the imminent threat of a siege on the horizon. Everyone within the city is suffering the same," Alberic reasoned.

"Lies!" A stubby man with a filthy beard shouted out. "They want to keep us weak and hungry whilst they grow fat and laugh at our expense! They mean for us to starve."

"Exactly! If the Romans won't give us our fair share, then we will take it for ourselves," Thrax said as he massaged the knuckles of his right hand with his left palm.

"If you try to take anything by force, then we're all dead," Al said calmly.

"Still a coward, I see," Thrax replied with a sneer.

Al bit back his response, anger flaring up within him as he felt a strong urge to punch the man. "Understanding that two hundred unarmed men stand little chance against five hundred legionaries does not make one a coward, Thrax," Al said after a few moments, through gritted teeth.

"The last thing any of us needs is further bloodshed within the city walls, when a huge army of Picts is likely marching straight for us," Al continued. "I have put my own neck on the line to keep you all alive, and you need to trust me."

The tall Saxon warrior waved his hand through the air contemptuously at Al's words and stormed out of the room with his companions following in his wake.

"I should have let Maxentius kill them all, the ungrateful sods," Al said to Carolus grumpily.

"It is always the way, my prince. You will find that men do not care about the time and effort you put into securing a future for them if they have empty bellies," Carolus said as he flopped down on an old couch.

"They're hardly empty," Al protested. "It might not be glamourous, but it's enough to keep them going. Do they think the Romans are all eating roast boar and drinking fine wines?"

"Pretty much," Carolus said with a shrug. "The grass is always greener on the other side of the fence, or so it seems."

"How do I keep them from tearing the city apart, looking for food that isn't there?" Al said, as he put his face into his hands.

"You need to keep them busy. And this Thrax seems to be their *de facto* leader; if you can get him on side, the rest will follow," Carolus replied.

"*I'm* supposed to be their leader. They swore fealty to me, not Thrax," Al argued, looking up indignantly.

"They did. But their choices were between bending the knee or being cut down. You will have to earn their respect now," Carolus said. "I would suggest we speak with Maxentius about giving them something to do."

Alberic thought over the scholar's words as he listened to the crackling of the fire. Earning the respect of the tribesmen in such challenging conditions seemed to be an insurmountable task for the young man.

"The legionaries are currently working on strengthening sections of the north wall where the brick has come loose. I will propose that we repair the section closest to us, and I will have Thrax direct the men if the Tribune gives the go-ahead," Al said finally.

Carolus nodded but did not respond. After a few moments, Al could see the older man starting to nod as he fell asleep. Standing up and making his way over to the couch, he gently helped the Greek lie down and covered him with dry blankets. Al considered for a moment making the journey back through the heavy rain to the house he shared with Lucia, but decided against it. Not only would he be arriving late in the evening, but even if she were still awake, he would no doubt find his tongue glued to the roof of his mouth. It would be better to stay here and sleep on a spare couch, warm and dry.

The morning was bright, the sky had cleared, and the downpour ended as Al and Carolus made their way through the muddy streets towards the Praetorium, in the southeast of the city. They passed Roman citizens hurrying up and down the roads, fear etched in their faces. Al knew they were all waiting to hear the dreaded sound of warning trumpets, signalling the arrival of yet another force that wanted to destroy their homes and lives. More than once, the people passing would spit at Alberic's feet as they caught sight of the Saxon, and their fearful expressions would be replaced with open hostility.

Alberic continued with his head held high, ignoring them. Inside, he felt a cold fury at the pit of his stomach, but he refused to let it show. Their meeting with Maxentius was short, and Al was pleased when the Tribune confirmed he would provide the timber and tools necessary for the Saxons to repair the section of wall closest to their quarters. The Roman senator hesitated over the idea of providing hammers to the Saxons, but eventually relented. His scribes scurried out of the palace with notes and orders to arrange the movement of supplies to the northeast corner of the city, and Al made his way back to his people with Carolus alongside him.

"Well done, Al. You're turning into a fine diplomat," the old tutor said as they walked.

"I fear that was the easy part. Now it's time to convince Thrax to spend the next few days repairing the Roman wall," Al replied.

It was in fact a much easier task than Alberic had expected, and as he gathered the tribesmen and told them of their new task, they merely grunted their ascent and trudged off towards the wall to get started. Their supplies arrived shortly after, with the young centurion Dominicus leading a handful of legionaries through the streets. Each soldier was guiding a cart laden with freshly cut timber and cloth sacks of iron nails. When it came time for the legionaries to hand over a dozen rusty-looking hammers, they did so warily. Al saw Thrax take one of the blunt instruments and grip it in his right hand, sizing up the legionary in front of him.

After a tense moment, Thrax grunted and turned on his heel as he started shouting orders to the Saxons to start unloading the carts. A small crowd of citizens had followed the carts through the streets and were now standing around the legionaries, looking mutinous.

"Who the fuck gave them weapons?" A voice called out from the crowd, followed by jeers.

"A dozen hammers are hardly weapons," Al called back. "We're repairing the wall that keeps you safe; surely you can't begrudge that?"

"We won't be safe until your lot are dead!" Another voice called out.

"Kill them all!" A third voice screamed.

Alberic looked at Dominicus for help and was met with a cold look. The centurion just stood with folded arms, refusing to intervene. The Saxons had stopped their tasks and were looking at each other nervously. Most of them could not understand Latin, but the murderous expressions and angry voices were enough to warn them that the crowd of Romans had not come here peacefully.

"Look," Al said as he raised his hands to the crowd. "If you have a problem, you need to take it up with the Tribune. You shouldn't be here."

Alberic was cut short as trumpet calls blared out across the city. The crowd of citizens all flinched and started scurrying back through the streets to their homes. Al told Thrax and Carolus to lead the Saxons to their buildings and wait for news. He then tore off in the direction of the Cripplegate, in the wake of the young centurion who was leading his men in the same direction. Al was furious that Dom had refused to intervene and disperse the crowd, despite clear instructions from Maxentius that the Roman citizens were to be kept away from the Saxon quarter. He had considered the young man an ally after their time spent at the villa, but those days now seemed like a distant memory.

A call to open the gates came from above, and Al felt a wave of relief that the trumpets had not heralded the arrival of the Pict army. He stood at the back of the courtyard, just inside the gate, panting slightly. The Tribune Maxentius came trotting into sight atop a fine stallion, followed as he always was these days by his two scribes, who came jogging along behind the horse. The large gates creaked open as legionaries pulled them inward, and Al saw a large force of Roman soldiers come into view, marching towards the city. Even from a distance, they looked in rough shape, with some of them limping or wearing bandages, and all were covered in mud and dried blood.

They came to a halt, looking exhausted and breathing heavily. Al could not count them easily from his spot, but it was clear there were hundreds of them. A battered centurion stepped forward to speak with Maxentius, taking his helmet off before bowing low to the Tribune.

"Welcome to Londinium. To whom do I have the pleasure of speaking?" Maxentius said as he dismounted in front of the officer.

"Centurion Gaius, fifth cohort, Victrix legion. Stationed at Eboracum," the centurion said.

There were angry mutters from the men on the walls and around the yard, and Al saw Dominicus start marching towards the Tribune with a look of fury on his face.

"Eboracum?" Maxentius repeated with a frown. "I'm afraid we have heard some concerning stories from the city."

Gaius looked terrified, and Al knew why. He remembered Dom and Gereon discussing the traitors at Eboracum with disgust back at the villa, and he could tell the man was hoping that news of their transgressions had not made it south to the rest of the legion. Whatever support they were expecting was quickly disappearing.

"They're traitors, sir. They murdered the Emperor's chosen representative in the city," Dom said with disgust as he approached the Tribune.

"I recall your story well enough, Dominicus. There is no need to interrupt," Maxentius said coldly.

Al felt a savage pleasure as he saw the colour rising in Dom's cheeks at the rebuke.

"What do you say to these charges, Centurion Gaius?" The Tribune asked.

"It wasn't us, sir! It was a small group of centurions who led the rebellion, and they threatened to kill us in our sleep if we didn't fall in line," Gaius replied, his words coming out in a rush.

Al heard Dominicus snort and turn away. "One more outburst, Centurion, and I will demote you back to the ranks," Maxentius snapped at him.

"I swear to the gods, we were only following orders!" Gaius hesitated, then continued speaking fast: "The Picts arrived shortly after and besieged the city. We held out for a couple of weeks, but their force was too large. When they breached the walls, we retreated south and have been on the run since. We headed for Camulodunum but saw the city in flames, so we continued south but were spotted and chased as we made for Londinium."

"And the leaders of your rebellion?" Maxentius asked. "Where are they?"

"Dead. They fell in the first few days, defending the walls. I was the last officer alive; I made the decision to retreat," Gaius replied.

Maxentius did not respond at once; he simply studied the man in front of him whilst he scratched his chin.

"In normal circumstances, I would have you beaten to death. However, these are not normal circumstances, are they..." Maxentius said. "Instead, I will offer you the opportunity to regain your honour by defending the city. A chance of an honourable death is more than you deserve."

Gaius took an involuntary step back, fear written across his face. "Defend the city, sir? But we need to leave! Britannia is lost; our only hope is escaping to Gaul."

"Britannia is not lost, Centurion. Not whilst we still defend it. Must I add cowardice to your list of infringements?" The Tribune asked, his voice like ice.

"N-no, sir, sorry, sir," Gaius stuttered, dropping to one knee.

"How large is the force following you? How many days behind are they?" Maxentius asked.

"At least two thousand, sir. I would expect them to be here within a day," Gaius replied, speaking to the hem of the Tribune's toga.

"Dominicus, gather your fellow officers and report to my quarters. Centurion Gaius, you and your men are to set up camp beside the fort, and not within it, to await my orders," the Tribune said as he remounted his stallion. He looked around the yard and caught sight of Al. "Prince Alberic, I would have you join us. But first, please ensure your people are focused on their work; we will need the wall as strong as possible."

Al nodded at the Tribune and set off at a jog back towards the Saxons. He called Thrax towards him as he arrived at the tall building and saw the imposing man walking out of the front door.

"Get the men back to work; we need the wall strengthened as soon as possible; the Picts will be here by tomorrow," Al said.

"We?" Thrax repeated, his eyes full of malice, "Are you with the Romans now, Prince Alberic? And when the Picts attack, how are we to protect ourselves?"

"I'm with every living person within these fucking walls, Thrax!" Al exploded, and the fury that had been building within him finally burst out. "Do you think the Picts will give a damn that you're not a Roman if they take the city? We will do whatever we can to support the defence of the walls, and if that means following Roman orders, then so be it."

Thrax did not reply; he just stared back with open hostility.

"You bent the knee and swore fealty to me, Thrax. And you will follow my orders, or I will have you killed. Get the men back to work and keep your mouth shut," Al finished.

He thought for an instance that the tall man was going to hit him, but the moment passed, and Thrax simply nodded before turning on the spot and stalking back within the building. Alberic took a deep breath as his anger started to ebb away. Either Thrax would respect him for his tough stance, or he had just sown the seeds of a new rebellion. It was not something he could think about for now; however, there were more pressing issues at hand. He turned and started running towards the Praetorium to join the war party gathering with the Tribune.

Chapter 25

Beads of sweat dripped down Dom's face as he thrust his sword forward and into the chest of a snarling barbarian climbing the ladder. He ripped the blade back, blood spraying across the stone battlements. Thrusting his shoulder into the top of the ladder, he heaved forward and heard a satisfying cry of terror as it toppled backwards, crushing the men still on its rungs. The Pict assault was in full flow, with savage warriors swarming up and over the Roman wall like flies. Dom used the brief respite to take a few deep breaths and wipe his forehead free of sweat and blood. He looked along his stretch of wall and saw his men were holding. How the rest of the Roman defence was faring was another question. The ladder clacked against the wall, raised once more by the barbarians below, and Dom hefted his gladius, ready to kill the next man to appear.

The Pict army had arrived the previous evening, only a few hours behind the traitors from Eburacum. Maxentius had assigned five centuries to sections of the northern wall, with the remainder of his force keeping watch east and west for any signs of a flanking attack or the arrival of a new threat to the city. Dom was holding the stretch of wall to the northeast, near the Saxon quarter. He knew the bulk of the enemy force had attacked the Cripplegate, and Gereon had been tasked with crushing the assault with the aid of Gaius and his men. The Tribune had no grand strategy or clever tactics for this battle; his orders had been simple: hold the wall at any cost.

The attack had been launched at dawn, and the barbarians had attacked numerous spots along the wall, hoping to overrun the thin Roman line. It had worked for the Saxons a month earlier, but the Picts were finding it a much harder task. The legionaries were putting up a staunch fight and they struggled to gain a foothold atop the walls. The battle had raged for almost three hours at this point, and with every savage the soldiers cut down, two more rose to take their place. Atop the wall, every legionary that fell only put more pressure on the remaining defenders as their line grew thinner. Dom shoved the ladder back for what felt like the tenth time, and exhausted, leant heavily against the battlements.

He did not know for how much longer he could keep this up, his arms were heavy and his back ached, and he prayed to the gods for the ladder to remain down even for a minute, so he could catch his breath. It appeared the gods were listening, as the ladder did not reappear as quickly this time. In fact, it didn't come clattering against the wall at all. Dom looked up and around him and felt a wave of relief as he saw the Picts running back to their tents lined up on the hills to the north. Trumpets blared out, signalling that the battle had ended, for the moment.

"Optio!" Dom called out, as he straightened up.

"Sir?" Publius replied, snapping a salute.

"Send for water, bandages, and whatever else can be scrounged up for the lads. They'll have to rest against the wall for now, until the Tribune sends out the message to stand down," Dom told him. "Pick a dozen of the least tired and have them remain on watch, as spread out as they can be."

Publius nodded and marched off, snapping out orders and calling for runners to relay his centurion's orders. Dom made his way to the wide stone steps descending to the ground, and walked as quickly as his tired body would allow towards the fort where the Tribune was based. As he made his way along the wall, he could hear cries of pain from above, as the battlefield surgeons were treating wounded legionaries. He grimaced at the thought of what they were going through. A lot of the men who survived the battle would live the rest of their lives as cripples, begging for coppers in the gutters. *A poor exchange for ensuring the safety of the empire,* Dom thought.

"Your luck is still holding out, I see?" Gereon said with a grin as he saw Dom arriving at the fort.

"Just about. Don't think I could have lasted much longer if the bastards hadn't retreated. How did you fair at the gate?" Dom replied, patting the veteran on the shoulder.

"Was touch and go, lad. But we held them off, that's all that matters," Gereon said as he wiped a grimy cloth down the blade of his gladius.

Together, the two men made their way deeper into the fort into what had been the senior centurion's office, now commandeered by Maxentius as his base of operations.

"Report," the Tribune said, without looking up at them.

"Sixty-three dead, eighteen injured." Gereon said as he saluted the senator. "The gate remains undamaged."

Maxentius nodded and gestured for Dom to report.

"My apologies, sir. I didn't have time to make note of our losses, but I will have Publius check and report as soon as I leave. The wall remains secure," replied Dom, a sinking feeling in his gut.

"Not good enough, Centurion. I am beginning to doubt my decision to promote you," said Maxentius coldly.

"I will do better, sir," Dom replied nervously. The idea of being stripped of his rank so soon after attaining it was galling, and he knew it would be the death of his career if he was demoted to the ranks at his age.

"If we assume that Dominicus lost a third of his men, as seems to be the average, I would gauge our remaining numbers at around four hundred and fifty," the Tribune mused as he flicked through his notes. "We will have to pull the remaining century from the east and west walls to face the next assault and plug the gaps in the line."

Dom felt his heart sink at the Tribune's words. Less than five hundred men to hold a wall almost a mile long, against an enemy force at least double their size. Add to that the fact the legionaries were exhausted, the future looked bleak to the young Roman.

"There are no changes to my orders for now. Return to your centuries and help your men recover as best you can. Hold the wall gentlemen, whatever it takes." Maxentius waved a hand to dismiss them, and the two centurions left the office.

"Not looking good, is it son?" Asked Gereon, as they trudged back through the fort.

Dom did not reply as he feared his words would come across as cowardice to the older man. He knew this was likely his final day, and the prospect of his impending demise terrified him. They walked in silence to the Cripplegate and Gereon patted him on the shoulder as they parted. Dom continued alone, returning to his section of the wall.

"Any news from the Tribune?" Publius said as his centurion climbed the last few steps to join him against the battlements.

"Nothing new," Dom said. "Have you done a head count? How many did we lose?"

"Twenty-two dead, six injured." The Optio replied with a grimace. Dom knew his men would be at breaking point, with so many of their comrades lying dead upon the battlements amongst them. He forced his own despair down and locked it away, knowing his men needed him now more than ever.

Dom nodded and looked out across the fields, at the no-man's land between the wall and the barbarian camp. There were hundreds of bodies littered across the ground. Dozens of corpses were twisted into grotesque shapes and lay close to the foot of the wall where they had fallen during the attempt to take the city. Sighing, Dom lowered himself to the ground, leaning with his back against the cold stone. His head drooped to his chest, and he fell into an exhausted sleep within seconds.

He was shaken from his nap by Publius, to find evening had enveloped the land. It was clear night, and the moon was full and bright in the night sky.

"How long have I been asleep?" Dom asked, as he rose to his feet and stretched.

"About six hours, sir. Thought it best to let you get some rest. No sign of the Picts," Publius replied as he handed Dom a cup filled with water.

Before Dom could bring the cup to his lips however, he heard a scream rent the night air to his right. Swivelling around he stared along the wall, his neck and shoulders groaning in protest from the day's battle, and his heart thumped painfully as he saw black shapes swarming across the battlements, between the pools of light cast by the torches, moonlight glancing from their weapons. He heard movement below him and looked over the battlements to see men rising from the dead. Not all of the bodies Dom had seen were truly dead. He marvelled for an instance at the willpower and strength of these savages, that some of them had lain in twisted shapes pretending to be corpses for hours, waiting for the chance to surprise the Romans.

"To me!" Dom cried, drawing his gladius, and charging along the wall.

He slew his first opponent with a vicious slice across the man's chest, feeling his blade jar against bone. Moving towards the nearest ladder he went to push it back as he had done some many times that morning. As he leant against one of the poles, filthy hands gripped his face and started dragging him back. In blind panic, Dom bit down hard on the hand clamped over his face, tasting iron as blood spurted into his mouth. He heard a cry of pain and kicked his heel back into his attacker's shin. The hands disappeared and Dom wheeled around to see a black figure tumbling backwards from the wall into the darkness below, followed by a sickening crunch.

"Sound the alarm! They've got to send more men, or we're fucked!" Dom shouted to Publius, and watched as he raised a horn to his lips and hears the harsh notes blare out into the night.

Suddenly, a blaze of light and heat swept over him. One of the houses closest to the wall inside the city had gone up in flames, and Dom saw men running from building to building. He realised with a sudden rush of fear that the Picts were already over the wall and inside Londinium. Spitting blood from his mouth, he started running down the nearest stone steps towards the ground, and as he jumped the final few, he felt a great weight collide into him, sending him crashing into the stone wall. Stunned, Dom tried to raise his shield and locate what had hit him when warm liquid sprayed across his face. Sputtering, he wiped furiously at his face to rub the blood away.

The wide, fat barbarian warrior that had been advancing on him, had come to a halt with a comical expression on his face, his mouth open in shock. The point of a blade was protruding from the scarred belly that was sticking out from under his furs. The man toppled sideways, and Dom found himself face to face with Alberic, the young Saxon prince had saved him for the second time.

"We need to arm my people!" Alberic roared over the sounds of battle.

"Have you lost your fucking mind?" Dom shouted back, furious at the suggestion. He ducked under a wild swing and tripped a Pict warrior who had come running towards him.

"They're going to slaughter us! You've lost the wall and my people will die if they can't defend themselves!" Al replied, as he thrust his sword down into the fallen Pict.

The chaos that swirled around them seemed to come to sudden stop, as Dom looked into Al's bright blue eyes. The battle for Londinium was balanced upon a knife edge, and without support the Romans would surely lose the city for the second time, and as a result the entire island. Concern for his men clashed with every fibre of Dom's being, which resisted the idea of arming the people he had sworn to fight. Memories flashed across his mind, of his parents lying dead in a muddy street, cut down by savage barbarians, but they were suddenly replaced with memories of Al saving him from certain death, not once, but twice.

"You have to trust me, Dom!" Al shouted over the din that seemed to return like an explosion around them.

A roar came from their left and Dom saw a tall Saxon come charging out of the nearest building, holding a Pict warrior by the throat a foot off the ground. He marched straight to the wall and smashed his opponents head against the stones, blood and brains bursting on impact. The Saxon picked up the fallen Pict's spear, hefted it in one hand and took aim. The weapon flew straight up into the crowd above and Dom saw a man wrapped in furs topple from the wall, the legionary he had been battling cheered and jumped back into the fray out of sight.

"There are barrels of *pilum* on the walls," Dom said to the Saxon prince, his mind suddenly made up. He had finally come to understand what Al had been trying to tell him for weeks, that the world was not as black and white as he had believed. The Saxon prince was evidence enough of this reality.

"They're designed for throwing but can be used as spears in a pinch, your people will have to make do with whatever else they can find from those that have fallen," Dom said, as the massive barbarian nodded and moved towards the wall.

"Thrax!" Alberic called to the tall man. "There are bundles of javelins on the wall as well, grab them and anything else you can find and distribute them to the men!"

The tall Saxon nodded again, this time with a vicious grin and started bounding up the steps taking them three at a time.

"The Tribune will kill me for this," Dom said.

"He needs us. You've no chance of retaking the wall without help. Come on!" Al replied, setting off at a sprint back towards the buildings of the Saxon quarter.

The two men charged into a tall house to find a dozen men struggling and wrestling in the gloom. Dom hesitated, he could not distinguish Saxon from Pict in the gloom, they were all barbarians in his eyes. Alberic however, danced through the room like the god of death, cutting and slicing down his enemies before they were even aware of his presence. Within moments he was stood panting in the centre of the room, the Saxons were nursing wounds and leaning against walls catching their breath.

"Al, that was-," Dom started to say, amazed at the Saxon's skill.

"No time, Dom!" Al said, straightening up and heading deeper into the house to save his people.

As they moved from building to building, their task became easier as the weapons collected by Thrax found their way into the hands of Saxon warriors.

The Picts went from hunters to prey within minutes, and soon the area closest to the wall was clear of invaders. The sounds of sword on shield still clanged out from above them atop the wall, and Dom knew his comrades couldn't hold out much longer.

"We need to retake the wall!" Dom shouted to Alberic, who stood next to him, his chest heaving.

The Saxon prince nodded and called out in his strange language. Dom saw warriors coming out of every building to join them near the wall, some holding javelins, others holding swords and spears taken from the dead. With a roar, Al led them up the stone steps his sword held high. The battle did not last for much longer, the arrival of a hundred bloodthirsty Saxons was too much for the Picts, and they were cut down in waves as they tried to scramble back down their ladders. Legionaries and warriors raised their weapons to the night sky as they cheered. But their cheers were cut short almost instantly. The Romans took notice of who had arrived to save them from certain death, and the sight of cold steel in the hands of men they had fought only days before brought looks of cold fury to their faces.

"Alberic, tell your men to disarm," Dom said as he stepped in between the two groups. "I will tell the Tribune of how you saved us, but for now I need you to trust me, as I trusted you."

Al looked at him, uncertain. The air was thick with tension, but then Al turned to the man he had called Thrax and spoke to him in their own language. Dom wasn't sure what was said, but he could tell the tall man didn't like it. After a brief but heated exchange, Thrax threw his sword down with disgust and the remainder of the Saxons followed suit. Dom took a deep breath, relieved that further bloodshed had been avoided. As the Saxons started to make their way back down to their buildings, he saw a blood-spattered legionary trotting along the wall towards him.

"The Picts have retreated once more sir, and the city remains secure," the man said as he came to a halt in front of Dom. "The other officers are gathering at the fort, sir, and have asked if you would join them?"

"I'll be there shortly," Dom replied. "I just need to do a head count for Maxentius before I leave."

The man hesitated for a moment before responding, "I'm afraid the Tribune is dead, sir."

Chapter 26

Alberic felt a strange sense of déjà vu as he looked down upon the body of Maxentius, wrapped in a splendid white toga. Although the Roman senator looked nothing like his father, the steady trickle of people coming in and out of the palace to pay their respects transported him back to the tent outside Rutupiae. *Had it really only been two months since they had arrived on Britannia's shores?* Al thought to himself. It felt like he had lived an entire lifetime, and he certainly felt like a completely different person to the boy who had stood beside his father, watching the white cliffs of Dover approach.

His body ached from the battle two days earlier, when the Pict assault had broken upon the walls of Londinium. The northern tribes had melted back into the hills after their second attempt to take the city, and legionary scouts had returned that morning to advise that the enemy force had retreated in the direction of Camulodunum. Al didn't share the delight of the Romans with their victory; his concern for his people was all-consuming. With the passing of Maxentius, their position was more precarious than it had been prior to the arrival of the Picts. There was no senior figure in place to hold the Romans in check, preventing them from tearing the Saxons into bloody pieces.

"He was a good man," Carolus said over his shoulder. The old man had arrived unannounced, and Al jumped a little at his sudden appearance. "I will write to his family; they will be proud of what their son achieved here."

"I fear he will not be the last of your former students to die within the walls of this city," Al replied gloomily.

"Former?" Carolus chuckled. "I have much more to teach you yet, my young prince. I do not believe your gods are done with you yet."

"I'm not sure the gods will be much use against Roman steel," Al said, determined not to be stirred out of his dark mood.

"Perhaps not, but I think your friend Dominicus will be a good enough shield," Carolus said, patting Al on the shoulder. "Come, Thrax has sent word. He would like to speak with you."

"Great!" Al grumbled. "Just what I need—yet another battle with Thrax. What does he want now? A roast ox and a barrel of ale?"

Carolus laughed and steered Al through the Praetorium and out into the weak, early winter sunshine. They made their way through the now-familiar roads and streets of Londinium, with Carolus chatting away in an attempt to cheer up his ward. Al did find himself feeling slightly happier as he arrived at the two-storey building that Thrax resided in. As he entered, he saw the dark stains that marked the spots where he had killed the invading Picts, and Al felt strange as he looked at them. In those exact spots, there had been living, breathing men only a couple of days ago. With dreams, ambitions, and families, their lives were cut short at the point of his sword in an instant. Shaking his head to clear the confusing thoughts, he looked up at the tall Saxon standing beside a couch with a long tear in it.

"You have something you would like to discuss with me, Thrax?" Alberic said bluntly, getting straight to the point.

"We're leaving." Thrax replied, equally blunt.

"I beg your pardon. What do you mean, leaving?" Al said, nonplussed.

"We mean to leave Londinium. I've been speaking to the men; there is nothing for us here. We live on scraps the Romans throw at us, like dogs." Thrax spat on the ground as he said these words before continuing, "Even when we pulled their arses out of the fire, they still treat us like criminals."

"Well, you did sack their city a month ago, Thrax. How short do you think their memories are?" Al retorted with a snort. The man was a fearsome warrior, but Al despaired at the lack of brains inside the thick skull. "And how many times do I have to tell you about the supplies within the city?"

"It's not about the fucking supplies, Alberic! We came here for riches and plunder, but all we have done is bury our brothers, our sons." Thrax started to pace up and down as he talked. "We have nothing to show for the blood spilled, and our people are already losing ground. No, it's time for us to return home."

"Home? Back across the channel?" Al asked, amazed at what Thrax was saying. It was the very last thing he had expected the tall man to say.

"Yes." Thrax said simply. "Will you join us?"

"Will I *lead* you? I think you mean," Al said irritably, tired of having to remind the man he had sworn to follow him.

Thrax simply shrugged as he replied, "We're leaving with or without you. If we have your blessing and you come with us, we will continue to honour our oath to follow you, but our path is set."

Carolus raised his hands and stepped forward to speak, "Patience, Thrax. You can't just get up and march out of the city, even if Al is leading you. We will need to discuss this with the Romans first."

Thrax snorted before responding to the Greek, "Why? Their leader is dead. Surely, they'd rather we left?"

"Not if they think you're going to head straight back to Broga." Carolus explained.

"We'll fight our way out if we have to!" Thrax said, his voice rising angrily.

"Don't be stupid, Thrax! Even with their losses, they outnumber us almost four to one; we'll be cut down in minutes." Al said, his voice rising in equal measure. "Carolus is right. It will take some convincing for the Romans to let us leave."

Although Thrax had seemed to be ready to battle both Al and Carolus a moment before, his shoulders sagged as the fight went out of him. "We're tired, Al. We have no intention of returning to Broga and continuing this pointless war. We just want to return home to our families."

"I'll do everything I can, Thrax. You have my word," Al said, surprised by the first hint of softness within the man who had given him so many headaches over the last few days. The tall man nodded and left the room.

As Al and Carolus made their way to the Roman fort, the Greeks again tried to strike up a conversation, but the young prince was entirely lost in his thoughts, and they continued in silence. The prospect of leaving Britannia and returning to his homeland would have been enticing only a few weeks ago, but now he was not sure he was ready to leave so soon. But how could he justify abandoning his people as they made their journey back across the country? And why did he want to stay in a country where people spat at his feet and hated his very presence?

"Hey Al! Carolus! Wait up." A voice called out from a side street, pulling him out of his thoughts.

His stomach did a somersault as he saw Lucia running down the road towards him, her black hair wild and free in the wind, her green eyes shining as she smiled at him. *That's why I want to stay*, Al thought to himself. It was ridiculous, but he knew he wanted to be wherever Lucia was, even though he still had not told her his true feelings. He was torn by a deep fear of rejection and a burning passion that only grew hotter every time he saw her.

"Hello, my dear!" Carolus called out happily, as she embraced the old man. "And what are you up to on this fine day?"

"I've been helping the Therapeutae of Asclepius with the wounded," Lucia replied, as Al noticed for the first time the blood staining her clothes.

Carolus grimaced as he responded, "A nasty job. And not one for a young lady such as yourself!"

"I've seen my share of battle wounds, Carolus, it doesn't bother me," she chided the older man.

"Given a few battle wounds as well," Al said, grinning.

"A few," she said with a smirk. "And where are you two off to? I thought you were at the palace."

"We need to visit the fort; we have business with the officers," Al said vaguely.

"Oh, I'm sorry, your royal highness; forgive me for asking such impertinent questions!" Lucia said mockingly, giving Al a low bow. "Are you too high and mighty to share your grand plans with a mere woman now?"

"Of course not! And don't call me that," Al said, scowling. "My people have decided they want to leave, and I need to see if the centurions will let them."

Lucia's eyes widened. "Leave? As in, leave the city."

"More than that, they want to leave Britannia completely," Al replied.

"What about you?" She asked, cocking her head to one side.

"What about me?" Al asked warily.

She rolled her eyes as she said, "Are you leaving too? With your people?"

"I don't know…" Al said, watching her closely, but if she was feeling a certain way about that idea, she was showing no sign of it to him.

"Well, it's certainly an interesting turn of events… I won't hold you up any longer. Let me know how it goes!" Lucia said brightly, promptly turned on her heel, and set off back to the healing houses.

"I have a feeling she'd prefer you to stay," Carolus said softly.

Al spun around to face him, "What? How can you tell?" He said sharply and then added quickly, "Not that I care."

"Experience." The old man said with a smile.

They set off again in silence, but this time Alberic's thoughts were entirely on Lucia. Arriving within the fort, they were led by a legionary to the centurion's office, where they found four men working away at a table littered with cups and scraps of parchment.

"I wasn't expecting to see you today, Al. How are you doing?" Dom said as he looked up from a wax tablet.

"Not bad, Dom. Yourself?" Al replied as he took an empty seat across from the young centurion.

"I've been better," Dom grunted. "Winning the battle was supposed to be the hard part, but I think I'd rather fight a hundred Picts alone than try and deal with all this paperwork."

"Where are the other officers?" Al asked as he looked around the room. He saw Gereon, the old veteran, who was sitting with a short, fat man that Al recognised as one of the former Tribune's scribes. Next to Dom sat Publius, his Optio.

"Fabian died alongside Maxentius," Gereon grunted without looking up. "Drusus is on watch; Callixtus is in the infirmary, but he'll live. Without Julian here, we'd be fucked."

The scribe nodded weakly towards Al before returning to the mountain of paperwork in front of him.

"If there is anything non-legion-related that I can do to help, I would be more than willing. As would Carolus," Al said.

"Once the dust settles, we'll certainly take you up on the offer. I barely know how to keep eighty men supplied, never mind an entire city. Julian has proposed we put together a council of sorts to see us through the winter. But that's for another time; did you need something in particular, Al?" Dom said as he took a deep gulp of wine from his cup and leant back in his chair.

"I've come to request something of you," Al said cautiously. "As a gesture of goodwill for the Saxon support in the battle."

Dom frowned but did not respond, so Al continued.

"My people have expressed a desire to leave both the city and the province. I am here to ask for your permission to allow them to leave as the highest-ranking officers within the city." Al said.

"Fuck off!" Gereon burst out angrily. "We had to fight tooth and nail to take this city back from your lot, and you want us to send a hundred or so warriors right back to the army rampaging across the country?"

"They don't want to fight anymore, Gereon, trust me. They're tired. All they want to do is return home," Al said to the veteran.

"Gereon has a point, Al. If they're not being truthful, we could be bolstering our enemies ranks whilst giving up key information about the city's defences and, more importantly, our numbers," Dom said as he sat forward and leant his elbows on the desk. "It's too big of a risk."

Al thought for a few seconds before replying; he knew he only had to convince Dom, and the young centurion would bring the veteran round. "I asked you to trust me during the battle, Dom. I didn't let you down, did I? You asked my people to disarm, and they did so at once."

"I trust you, Al; I just don't trust your people," Dom said sadly.

"If I may interject, Dominicus?" Carolus said, speaking for the first time since they entered the room. "I lived with the Saxon people for a decade. I understand their way of life, as few outsiders do. They are passionate and emotional people; when they want war, they do not hide it. And when they want peace, it is the same. If the Saxons within the city are saying they only desire to return to their lands across the Rhine, there is no reason to doubt them."

"No reason, he says!" Gereon fumed. "Thousands of dead soldiers and citizens are reason enough, you old git!"

Dom and Al stared at each other for a long time as the older men bickered beside them.

"Please, Dom. Let them leave and return to their families." Al said quietly.

"You keep saying 'them,' Al, and not 'us'? Do you not intend to lead your people?" Dom replied.

"I've… I've not decided yet," Al said as he looked away.

"Well, of all the Saxons within the walls, you at least are welcome to stay." Dom refilled his cup as he spoke, adding water to his wine. "I say we let them go, Gereon. The gods know the last thing we need is fighting in the streets, and if the food rations get tight in the winter, then a hundred less mouths to feed will suit us."

"If my opinion is worth anything," piped up the fat scribe, his voice high and squeaky, "I agree with Dom. I think the smartest thing to do is to let them leave. Less pressure on our supplies and peace within the city walls. The city is ready to blow."

Gereon looked from Julian to Dom, then shook his head. "If you two think it's best, then go for it. But we best run it by Drusus first."

Al and Carolus thanked the centurions and made their way out of the room. The sky had already grown dark as the days became shorter, and they had to take care on the slippery cobbled roads as they headed for their home within the city. As they arrived, they saw Lucia waiting for them. She lay on a couch, sipping wine. Al let Carolus tell her the full story of what had transpired at the fort, watching her closely. He decided to make his decision in the morning and swore to himself that if he chose to stay, then he would tell Lucia exactly how he felt about her.

Chapter 27

Wrapping his cloak around him, Dom looked out from atop the Belins gate in the chilling morning air, watching the Saxons cross the great stone bridge to Southwark. Winter had arrived with a bitter Easterly wind, and he was already dreaming about returning to the warm office within the fort, even if it meant tackling the never-ending pile of tasks waiting for him. He heard someone approaching from behind and turned to see Prince Alberic climbing the stone steps to join him. The young man was holding his fur cloak tight about him, but he looked less uncomfortable than Dom felt.

"It must feel strange watching them leave," Dom said as Al drew up alongside.

"It is, but my mind is made up," Al replied. "I'm not finished with Britannia just yet."

The two men stood in a comfortable silence as they watched the group grow smaller in the distance. Dom realised he was happy that Al had decided to stay. Not only had he come to respect the man's ability on the battlefield and his intelligence, but he also considered the young prince a friend. He snorted suddenly to himself. How times had changed—that he now considered a barbarian from beyond the empire's borders to be anything but an enemy. They had their disagreements, but Dom was not too proud to understand that he would not be here if it were not for Alberic.

"What's so amusing?" Al asked suspiciously.

"Nothing…" Dom replied with a grin, "How's Lucia?"

Al's head spun around to look at him so quickly. Dom was surprised the man hadn't broken his neck. "She's fine, as far as I know. Why?"

"Have you plucked up the courage to tell her how you feel yet?" Dom said, grinning wider still at the Saxon's expression of horror.

"How do I feel? I don't know what you're talking about," Al said quickly. "Oh gods, is it that obvious?" He finished, shaking his head.

"Only to someone who has spent about thirty seconds within your company," Dom said. "What kind of barbarian are you? Don't you lot go stealing your wives?"

"That's rich, coming from the people who stole the Sabine women," Al retorted.

"Who the bloody hell are the Sabines?" Dom asked, frowning.

Al shook his head exasperatedly as he replied, "Honestly, Dom, how is that a barbarian knows more about your history than you do?"

"Because I wasn't born a privileged princeling, that's why," Dom said irritably. The young man was clever, but he didn't need to always shove it in everyone's face.

It looked as if Al bit down an angry response, but his face softened a moment later. "Sorry," he mumbled. "It's easy to forget that not everyone grows up to be the son of a king."

"Don't worry about it," Dom replied awkwardly. "Anyway, Lucia. What's your plan?"

"Still on that, are you?" Al grumbled back. "I don't know how to approach it; what if she spurns my advances?"

"Maybe you should have spoken to her before your people left," Dom said. "It looks like you've taken a bit of a gamble, mate."

"Despite what you think, Lucia wasn't the only reason I decided to stay," Al said as he pulled his cloak even tighter around himself. "There's something about this country… A wildness, a sense of life that I've not felt before. I want to see it in the spring."

"Well, that will be worth staying behind for. You've not seen anything until you've seen Britannia in the spring. I don't think there's a greener place on earth," Dom said wistfully, thinking of his first sights of the rolling green hills, fields filled with brightly coloured flowers, and the woods teeming with wildlife. "That's if there's still anything left alive to grow by the time spring arrives."

"My people are fearsome in battle, but they're not used to long campaigns. My father's plan centred around securing as much as possible prior to the arrival of winter and settling it immediately," Al said. "From talking with Thrax, it seems like most of the families didn't make the journey across as planned. He won't be the last soldier wanting to head home."

"I hope you're right, Alberic," Dom said. "Now then, let's talk about your lady problems."

As winter set in, bringing with it icy cold rain, thick snow, and a wind that chilled to the bone, Dom found himself feeling at peace for the first time since his final days at the fort alongside the Solway Firth. He had the responsibility of helping to keep the entire city running, with no experience or knowledge of government, and the pressure of this role often left him with migraines in the evening. But the immediate dangers had passed for now; the enemy forces had settled into their conquered cities to wait out the winter. Scouts were still being sent out daily, ranging further afield with each trip, but there was no sign of any enemy force threatening the city.

The removal of raiding parties from the countryside had allowed communication channels to be reestablished with the Roman forces in the southwest. Reports came through that they had repelled all attacks from both Saxon and Scotti war bands, and the forts in that part of the country were secure. They had not been able to send anyone senior to Londinium to oversee affairs, but just knowing they were not alone on the island was deeply comforting to all within the city. Small fishing vessels and wide river trading boats had returned to the docks, and the markets had started up again, albeit a shadow of their former selves.

With the city having open supply routes and a sense of normality returning, it allowed Dom and his fellow centurions to take a step back from the emergency council they had formed in the wake of Maxentius' death. Julian had been voted as city mayor by unanimous decision, and with the advice of Alberic and Carolus, he was doing a fine job with the city's administration. Dom happily settled back into the legionary life he loved. He knew his position as centurion was tenuous at best, and the arrival of the Roman response force in the spring could see him demoted back to the ranks, but he tried to push that thought to the back of his mind. The more concerning thought that he struggled to ignore was the prospect that the Emperor would decide that the distant province of Britannia was not worth retaking.

It was the morning after the feast of Saturnalia, and Dom was nursing a nasty hangover when he heard hard knocks on the outside of his bedroom door. With a groan, he dragged himself to his feet, swaying slightly.

"By the gods, Gereon, not so loud!" Dom groaned as he opened the door to find the old veteran standing in front of him.

"Feeling tender, lad?" Gereon said with a grin.

"I'm never drinking again," Dom said with a moan as he sat down on the edge of his bed. "Why have you woken me up so early?"

"I Just received news of a ship heading down the river, towards the city," Gereon said excitedly.

"You've come here to tell me a fishermen's boat is on its way back? I don't think fish will sort my hangover out," Dom said irritably.

"I didn't say boat; I said *ship*. It's flying a legionary banner," Gereon replied, still grinning.

It took a few seconds for Dom's brain to process the words, but they eventually clicked into place, and he started hastily pulling on his boots.

"That's the reaction I was waiting for. I'll wait for you in the yard," Gereon said, closing the door behind him.

Dom dressed quickly, strapping his armour on and pulling his centurion's helmet over his head. He found Gereon waiting around the gate that led from the fort and into the city proper. They walked quickly; the cold air on Dom's face made his head spin, but he forced himself to continue. If the ship had come from Gaul, they may finally have heard what response the Romans were planning. His stomach churned, but he wasn't sure if that was the previous night's wine or nervous anticipation of what awaited him at the wharf. The city was silent as they made their way through, the citizens of Londinium sleeping off the previous day's revelry.

As they marched under the Belins gate and towards the docks, they could see a tall ship being hauled to the shore by dockworkers. From atop its single mast, a banner was flying, scarlet red with a golden eagle in the centre. A thin man was standing at the prow of the ship; he wore a white toga trimmed with blue, his olive skin glowed, and his thick, curly hair was cropped short. Dom stepped forward to greet the man as he disembarked a few minutes later.

"Good morning, sir. Welcome to Londinium. My name is Dominicus; this is Gereon," Dom said with a salute.

"A pleasure, Centurion. I am Dulcifies, Dux for Britannia." The thin man said, casting his eye around the wharf. "Please take me to the Praetor."

"Er, I'm afraid the Praetor is dead, sir. There are no officials within the city; I can take you to the mayor, who is currently residing in the Praetorium." Dom replied.

The thin man didn't seem to be shaken by the news and simply nodded. Dom and Gereon led him quickly through the maze of streets to the grand palace, rousing a slave to wake Julian. In the meantime, other attendants showed them to a small office area and brought bread and wine whilst they waited. Dom's stomach did a flip as he smelled the strong spirit, and he politely declined a cup from the slave who tried to offer him one. The room was pleasantly warm; a fire had been kept alight during the night, it seemed. The fat scribe-turned-mayor came bustling into the room, bowing low to Dulcitius.

"It is a pleasure to have you within the city, sir. I hope your journey was a comfortable one," Julian said.

"Crossing the channel during the winter is anything but comfortable, but Neptune allowed us safe passage," Dulcitius said as he settled into a soft couch, cradling a cup of heated wine. "Now, I need a full report on the state of affairs within the province."

Between the three of them, they told the Dux everything that had happened since the Picts assaulted Hadrian's Wall towards the end of autumn. His face was expressionless as he listened, and Dom found it hard to figure the man out. He had thought he understood Maxentius, but the former Tribune's easy-going attitude at the villa had been replaced by a cold, calculating senator. Was this man the same? A man of two faces, one for the soldiers in a time of crisis and one for the people, when he was in a position of power? Dom knew he would have to tread carefully, as his relationship with Maxentius had soured towards the end and almost cost him his rank.

"A dire situation indeed," Dulcitius mused when they had finished their tale. "You have done as well as can be expected; I see no reason to counter the former Tribune's orders, but I cannot ratify your promotions to centurion. I will pass on my recommendation to the general when he arrives."

"The general, sir?" Dom said eagerly. "The Emperor is sending reinforcements."

"Naturally. I have been sent here before the campaign is launched to gather information and prepare the city," Dulcitius said, sipping his wine.

"When will the legions arrive, sir?" Gereon asked.

"As soon as the waters calm, if they can travel before spring, Theodosius won't hesitate to take advantage," the Dux replied.

"Theodosius!" Gereon exclaimed, smiling wide. "A fine man, sir, a fine man! He'll have these barbarians on the run soon enough!"

"I'm sure the general will feel gratified to know you think so highly of him," Dulcitius said sarcastically. Gereon blushed, and Dom felt himself disliking the man.

"Julian, you were a scribe prior to your elevation to mayor, correct? I will offer you a place on my staff if you're willing. The role of mayor is defunct now I have arrived," Dulcitius said, and Julian nodded, a little crestfallen.

"Dominicus, Gereon, you are to continue in your roles until the arrival of Theodosius. I will send for you if I need you. Have your men unload my baggage and send my slaves here," the Dux said, dismissing them with a lazy wave of the hand.

The two centurions left the Praetorium, heading back to the docks.

"Charming man, isn't he?" Dom said to Gereon as they walked.

"Typical bloody politician; he makes Maxentius look like he was one of the boys," Gereon grumbled.

As they arrived back on the wharf, they saw a dozen haughty-looking soldiers standing beside the ship, wearing gilded armour, and looking around them with expressions of distaste.

"*Scholae Palatinae*," Gereon muttered.

"Imperial bodyguards?" Dom asked. "Just what we need."

They approached the well-dressed legionaries and directed them to the Praetorium. They didn't respond but looked at them with disdain before marching off to join the Dux. It took a few hours for them to fully unload the ship; it appeared Dulcitius had brought three homes worth of possessions with him to the island. They arranged for ox carts and helped with the loading of the goods. Gereon set off, leading the caravan towards the palace, a huddle of slaves, scribes, and attendants following in his wake. Dom sighed and looked up at the grey sky; it was threatening to snow again. But even the snow couldn't melt the fire now burning in his heart. Theodosius was on his way, and the war for Britannia had only just begun.

Chapter 28

Alberic stood in front of the Dux, his hands clasped behind his back. He tried to read the thin man's expression, but his face gave nothing away.

"I believe you have provided a service to the Emperor," Dulcitius said, his hands clasped together on his lap. "However, I have also heard that your heritage provides us with a problem."

"Do Romans believe that a son should be punished for the deeds of the father?" Al replied.

"It depends on the son," Dulcitius replied smoothly. "Your father, King Alawar, led the invasion force, correct?"

"He did, and he paid for it with his life. My people banished me, and I have devoted my time to helping the legion expel them from the province," Al said, fighting to remain calm. The man was infuriating, but losing his temper here was likely to result in his death.

"Hmm," Dulcitius murmured, watching Al with a less than savoury look in his eye.

"You may remain in the city in your current lodgings. However, if you leave Londinium without my permission, I will have you hunted down and killed. Any role you had in the administration of the city ends immediately," The Dux said after a while. "It is for Theodosius to determine your fate."

Al felt his anger bubbling away and fought to keep his voice calm. "I am to be a prisoner? After fighting in defence of the city in the name of Rome?"

"Few prisoners have the luxury of their own home and a city to explore in their free time. You should be grateful I am not putting you in chains, not that I haven't completely decided against the idea just yet." The thin man's eyes glinted with pleasure at the thought. "You have my verdict. Go," Dulcitius said, flicking his wrist towards the door.

One of the Dux's guards escorted Al out of the palace, as if he hadn't spent the last two months coming and going from that very building, as he supported

Julian in keeping the citizens of the city fed. He walked blindly, in a foul temper, through the streets with no real destination in mind. His feet had followed the familiar path back to the humble house he called home, and he blinked with surprise as he saw the decorated door in front of him. He hadn't planned to return so early, but with no real business to deal with after his meeting with Dulcitius, he headed inside. He found Lucia sitting on the couch with a needle in hand.

She placed the needle, thread, and toga beside her when she saw Al enter and noticed the expression on his face.

"What's happened, Al?" Lucia asked, her voice full of concern.

"Dulcitius has determined that I am not trustworthy," Al replied bitterly. "I am to remain within the city walls unless I receive the express permission of our new Dux."

"Oh, I'm sure he'll come around. There's not a Roman you haven't managed to impress yet." She said it with a smile and leant forward to place her hand on his knee.

Al jumped as if he had been struck by an arrow, and his knee tingled from where she had placed her hand.

"I don't bite, you know," Lucia said, scowling as she sat back on the couch.

"I know," Al said quietly. It had been six weeks since his people had left, and despite the constant teasing from Dom, he still had not told her how he felt. He felt heat rising up his cheeks, and his tongue seemed to swell as he looked at her. She smiled at him, and her bright green eyes met his.

"Look, Lucia. There's something I've been meaning to talk to you about…" Al started to say, but his throat had gone bone dry, and his words faltered. He suddenly felt the urge to be sick and almost ran from the room.

"Yes, Prince Alberic?" Lucia said as she ran her hand through her thick, brown hair, pulling it to one side over her shoulder. Al felt his pulse quicken, and he wondered if he was about to faint.

"Erm, well, over the last few months, I've started to, to…" Al stammered before faltering once more.

"Oh, for the love of the gods, Al!" Lucia suddenly burst out, and she began to laugh. "You'll run headfirst into a battle without a second thought, but you can't tell a girl that you love her."

Al felt his mouth drop, and he quickly closed it. He could have sworn that the air had been sucked out of the room, and he was struggling to breathe.

"You knew?" He finally managed to croak out.

"Of course, I knew. You're not the first suitor I've had, you know," Lucia said, smirking at him.

"Oh gods," Al whispered, and he put his face into his hands. "I've made such a fool of myself."

He heard her move from her spot on the couch, and a moment later, he felt her soft hands wrap around his, pulling them down as he looked up. She was kneeling before him, their eyes level with each other.

She began to speak so softly that it was barely audible. "After what happened to my family…to me, the only emotions that I felt were hatred and disgust. I couldn't see past my revenge. I gave you no reason to help me, and yet you did."

Al could see tears forming in the corner of her eyes as she continued, "Without hesitation, you came with me. You helped me kill the men who had destroyed my life, even if it meant risking your own."

"I'm not sure how much I helped; I seem to recall you having to save my life in the end," Al said uncertainly.

"That's not the point, Al. The point is that when I was at my lowest, you were there for me when you had no reason to be. The truth is, I don't think I've ever met someone quite like you." Lucia whispered, and she placed her hand on his cheek.

"But I'm a barbarian; you said so yourself." Al protested, convinced that his heart was going to burst from his chest at any moment; surely this was a dream.

"If you're a barbarian, Alberic, then so am I," she said with a soft smile.

Before he could react, Lucia had kissed him. As her soft lips met his, everything around him seemed to melt away. He could no longer feel his dry throat or swollen tongue, and if he still had a beating heart, he could no longer feel that either. The only thing that existed was Lucia. Their arms wrapped together in a tight embrace, and they fell to the floor.

Carolus entered the courtyard, heading towards the door, and as his hand touched the rough wood, he suddenly heard giggling from the other side. He smiled to himself as he turned away. *About time,* he thought.

Dom, Gereon, and Carolus were sitting at a wooden table, playing dice, as Al entered the inn. The warmth from the fire hit him immediately, and he shrugged off his wet cloak after closing the door behind him. He slapped a few copper pieces on the bar, and the innkeeper bit them suspiciously before pouring him a mug of beer. He dropped into the empty seat beside Carolus and drank deeply.

"He's alive!" Gereon exclaimed mockingly. "Come up for air, have you, lad?"

The others laughed, and Al grinned. Carolus exclaimed in Greek as he rolled his dice and happily scooped the coins from the centre of the table towards him. It still amazed him to find his tutor in the company of rough soldiers, but their shared love of gambling had made Gereon and Carolus fast friends.

"Have you heard the news, Al?" Dom said as he flicked a coin into the middle, ready for the next round.

Al shook his head and took another deep gulp from his mug.

"Theodosius has managed the crossing earlier than we expected. He's not shipped the full legion over yet, but he took the Saxons at Rutupiae by surprise and retook the fort," Dom said excitedly.

It felt as if someone had punched him in the stomach; he had not thought about his countrymen in weeks, wrapped up as he was in his budding romance with Lucia. And to hear the name of the place where he had said goodbye to his father, he had to quickly steady himself before tears could form in his eyes.

"It won't be long until he's here," said Gereon happily as he rolled his dice. "Then we can take the fight to the Saxon bastards properly! Er, present company excluded, of course."

"Are you ok, my prince?" Carolus said. Even though it had been long since Al was the prince of anyone, his old tutor persisted in using the old title.

"It feels strange," Al replied. "Don't get me wrong, I'm happy to hear the end of this war is in sight. But how many of those who died at Rutupiae were planning to leave as soon as the weather turned?"

"Shouldn't have come in the first place, then, should they?" Gereon grunted.

"They still have families, Gereon. How many wives and children have now lost husbands and fathers who had already given up the cause?" Al said he was not sure why he was feeling angry.

"And what about the families they've murdered and raped since they invaded, eh?" Gereon said furiously, looking up at Alberic.

Dom raised his hands and said, "Calm down, both of you. I'd rather a clash of swords didn't interrupt my dice game, thanks."

The old veteran snorted and angrily stacked a coin onto the small pile in the middle.

"It's only natural to feel conflicted, Alberic," Carolus said kindly. "But you know this was always a potential outcome for your people. Few men invade Roman territory and manage to escape with their lives."

"I wish you had given my father that advice ten years ago," Al grumbled.

"Ah, well, your father was unique. If he had lived, you may have sat at this table with three Saxon warriors, sharing tales of battle. But you would not have met Lucia. Our future is written for us by the gods, Al. There is no use in thinking about what could or could not have happened," Carolus said as he patted the young man on the hand.

"A wise man, your tutor," Dom said with a grin.

"What else would you expect from a man of Athens?" Carolus replied as he spread his arms wide.

Al pondered over the scholar's words. It was true that if events had not played out the way that they had, he would not have met Lucia. And the more time he spent with the Romans, particularly Dom, the less he understood his father's hatred. But if he wasn't a Saxon, then what was he? Dulcitius had reminded him that, in the eyes of most Romans, he would always be considered a threat. And if he were still a Saxon, how could he feel anything but dismay at the news of his people being slaughtered? His mixed emotions swirled inside of him, competing and clashing in a way that they had not done for months.

"You're thinking too much," Dom said, noticing Al's expression. "I know how you feel, in a way. If someone had told me six months ago that I would be drinking with a barbarian and considering that man a friend, I would have told him to jump off Hadrian's Wall."

Al scowled at the use of the word barbarian, but before he could speak, Dom continued. "Whether it's your gods or mine, they've put us on a strange path. Like Carolus said, all we can do is walk down it and enjoy the life the gods give us."

Dom's words were soothing to Al, and he felt himself unwinding. He drained the last of his mug and dug into his pouch for a couple of bent coppers, ready to join in the next round of dice. The four men spent the rest of the evening drinking and gambling, sharing stories and songs. Al realised as he stumbled back home through the gathering gloom, guiding Carolus, whose pockets clinked with his winnings, that he had found a comradery he had not realised he needed. He had friends growing up, of course, but he could never tell if they liked him for who he was or just wanted to get close to the future king of their tribe. But here in this foreign city, where he should have been truly alone, he found himself in the company of people he truly cared for. Whatever fate had in store for him next, Al knew he would not have to face it alone.

Historical Note

The events of 367 AD are known to historians as "The Great Conspiracy". Our main contemporary source for this period of Roman history was written by Marcellinus, who was writing from Antioch at the time, and it is likely that most of his information was second-hand. We know little of the true chronology of events, but what we do know is that a coalition of Germanic and Celtic tribes launched a joint invasion of Britain during a time when the province was severely understaffed. There are accounts of garrisons along Hadrian's Wall allowing the tribes from Scotland, known as the Picts, to pass without hindrance; other garrisons revolted (likely due to a long delay in their payments), and escaped slaves roamed the countryside as brigands. Tribes from Ireland known as the Scotti invaded from the west, whilst several tribes (including, but not exclusively, the Saxons) invaded from the east. It is understood that by the winter of that year, there were only a handful of forts still held by loyal soldiers. The rest of the country was being pillaged from north to south by war bands of different nationalities. It was the darkest period that Roman Britannia had faced since the rebellion of Queen Boudica.

For ease of narrative, I have combined the numerous tribes from mainland Europe under the same name, and I have them invading via Dover, when it is likely they landed in the north-east first. Aside from this, I have kept as close as possible to the limited source material we have and focused on what I believe life for those involved in the crisis would have been like. The characters within the story are entirely fictional, until the arrival of Dulcitius and Theodosius, who were the two men responsible for reconquering the island in the name of the Emperor. It was a crucial moment in Western history, as until this point, the Saxons were only one of the many wild tribes that lived beyond the Rhine frontier and had rarely appeared in the historical record. Marcellinus writes that the tribes that invaded in 367 AD were only interested in looting and the spoils of war. However, the fact that the Saxons would return less than a hundred years later to settle the island and to build the foundations of England after the Romans had officially abandoned it raises the question of whether there was a greater scheme at play from the start.

The adventures of Dom, Al, and their companions are far from over, and they will have to face far greater dangers before the end.

Roman place names and their modern equivalent:

Britannia—Britain

Dubris—Dover Fort

Camulodunum—Colchester, Roman Capital of Britannia

Cornoviorum—Roman Fort near Shrewsbury

Eburacum—York

Hibernia—Ireland

Hispania—Spain

Londinium—London

Lunt—Roman Fort near Coventry

Pannonia—Roman province along the Danube River, encompassing parts of modern-day Hungary, Austria, Croatia, Slovakia, Slovenia, Serbia, and Bosnia and Herzegovina.

Rutupiae—Richborough Fort (Kent)

Printed in Great Britain
by Amazon

44779948R00106